The Rebel (

ISBN: 9781957290409 (eBook)
Print: 9781957290416

This is a work of fiction. Any references to historical events, real
people, or real places are used fictitiously. Names, characters, and
places are products of the author's imagination. Inclusion of or
reference to any Christian elements or themes are used in a fictitious
manner and are not meant to be perceived or interpreted as an act of
disrespect against such a wonderful and beautiful belief system.

Cover designed by Valicity Elaine using prompted imaging via
Midjourney

The Rebel Christian Publishing LLC
350 Northern Blvd STE 324 - 1390
Albany, NY 12204-1000

Visit us: http://www.therebelchristian.com/
Email us: rebel@therebelchristian.com

Contents

Series Order

MAGOG

The Rise of Desolation

The One Who is Man and Beast

The Broken Seals

The Darkest Hour

Other Books by A Bean

The End of the World (Christian End Times series)

Singlehood (Christian Romance)

The Woof Pack (Christian Romantic Suspense trilogy)

The Living Water (Christian Contemporary Fiction)

The Scribe (Christian Historical Fantasy)

The Rise of Desolation

Book II in the Ordained Catastrophe Saga

By A. Bean

A Rebel Christian Publishing Book

AUTHOR'S NOTE

Zombies are not real. The Bible is very real, but zombies are not. In no way is my work an outline of the Book of Revelation. It is a work of fiction that depicts adventure, love, and fear in the fashion of entertainment. Please read at your own risk. If the thought of zombies during the Biblical apocalypse is too farfetched, please feel free to read my other end times series, The End of the World, that features no zombies whatsoever.

I also want to mention that this series is not to incriminate any man, person, being, country, or religion. It is a work of fiction; ideas I pulled together with the Holy Spirit's influence to produce a story for readers. Surely there are things to gain from this, but this depiction is just another go at end times fiction. I am not in any way saying that the events in the Book of Revelation will unfold the way I describe or happen following the timeline I created for this book.

Please refer to the Bible for accuracy, not my work.

As a Christian author, it is my duty to glorify God first, and present fiction in a respectful way second. Please remember that as you go forward.

Prologue

Abomination of Desolation

When I was twelve, someone prophesied to me. My pastor told me that I would be like Job from the Bible. I would lose everything but regain it with a double portion. But there was a sense of darkness to the prophecy. If I did not wait on God and tried to fix things myself, I would remain desolate.

Satan was after me. The pastor had explained that my faith would truly turn the world upside down if I stayed the course. But if corruption crept in, the darkness would be twice the strength of my faith, just to keep me from believing again.

I could never forget the haunting words of the pastor, the way his eyes narrowed as he warned me. That warning, as a kid, scared me. I thought because of the fear, I would never stray the path, I would remain faithful so I wouldn't remain desolate.

Everyone has always preached that you only walk *through* the valley. No one ever tells you that valleys are long and walking instead of running lengthens your time there. What happened to Job, losing everything as a test of patience and a

1

boast on God's behalf, was encouraging and exciting. It was a wonderful story on paper, but what about living it? What about embodying the very essence of pain? The people around you may clap and cheer for you, but they're not standing with you.

They're smiling because it's you and not them. They pat your back because they're relieved. Tainted and dark, that's the world we live in. There is no light, not even for the city on the hill.

When I turned sixteen, the prophecy manifested in my life. I came down with a sickness with no cure. Boils that itched and burned, pus that oozed onto the sheets, a funk that was nearly visible as it rose from my body. I was decaying from the inside out and there was nothing I could do.

I was in my junior year of high school, a handsome kid with a hot girlfriend. Lots of friends, a few enemies who didn't matter, and I was a football player. But, when I fell ill, my team didn't come to see me. My friends avoided me while my enemies laughed at me. And my girlfriend? She was terrified of me.

I thought I'd lost everything in high school, I didn't even finish the year out. I was too sick to go, so they held me back. A year later, I repeated my junior year and then my senior year. I was slowly getting better, and I was happy and determined to stay strong. To stay faithful. I knew this was all part of the *test*, it was all part of my redemption that would bring me a double portion. My smile hadn't faded, and my grit was still present… until things changed.

In a turn of events, I got completely better. I was doing so good that I decided to join the military. The sickness simply went away one day, and I got strong enough to join the Navy. It took a long time to join since they had to research my mysterious illness. But with my body completely healthy, I was able to pass under the radar.

With that, I was thinking that my misery was finally over, and that my life was about to get better. However, I was in for a spin after I became a Navy SEAL. It started with my younger sister. She fell ill suddenly, and never recovered. She had the same boils and pus that I had, but her sickness was the start of her rapid deterioration. A few years after that, my older brother fell ill on his wedding day. Just as he kissed his bride with beads of sweat rolling down his face, he passed out... and never woke up.

Over my twelve years in service, one by one, my family was picked off by some version of the sickness I'd had when I was sixteen. Bigger boils, more pus, a stronger stench, vomiting, hair loss, even tumors. My mother had a tumor so large it broke her hip and sat partially on her stomach. When they tried to remove it, the operation went awry, and she died right there on the table. But it didn't matter because my father was sick as well. Too sick to be conscious. He died a suffocating death three months later.

Somehow, I managed to keep my head on straight. I managed to fall in love, find a wife, and have twin boys. I still believed that God would fulfill His prophecy. Though I couldn't get my parents and loved ones back, I did have my own family to count on. Until I didn't.

III

The twins became ill while I was on a mission in Syria. My wife called me every day to give me updates. Their little bodies fought hard for six days straight, when I noticed my wife's voice sounded tired ... haggard. I thought she was just sad, but I didn't know she had fallen ill too. Within six hours of my sons' death, I received a call from the hospital that my wife had passed too. I had truly lost everything, but I clung to God even tighter.

The day after my wife passed, I was cleared to return home for the funeral when our hideout was discovered. The enemy had found us and was wreaking havoc on our small team. They chased us, shot at us all the way to the border where we'd called for backup. Our backup did come, but I'd been shot and didn't make it onto the helicopter. I became a prisoner of war, held in a Syrian internment camp where I was tortured and beaten every day. And every day, I stopped believing a little more.

After four years, no one came for me. I stayed in a dark hole, where creatures I couldn't even see crawled over me, bit me, scared me. The darkness was so thick, you never knew what time it was. And the silence was so piercing, you weren't even sure if you were thinking or speaking aloud.

I was pulled out of that hole twice a day into the dizzying sun. Each time I was pulled out, I was asked if I wanted to tell them a secret to avoid a beating. I'd held my poise, and never gave in. But there's only so much one can do before their mind slips away.

I'll never forget the first day I was pulled from the hole and *wasn't* beaten. I'd been murmuring in my hole about a ship.

When they could get any sense out of me, they pieced together that I was remembering the ship I dived off to swim to the Syrian shores.

From that day, I began telling secrets in exchange for no beatings and a little more food. When the information began to line up with things they'd already known, they pulled me from that hole completely, and placed me in a little shack. It was guarded twenty-four-seven; however, I had food, cleaner clothes, and I wasn't swamped in my own thoughts anymore. I was talking to someone every day as they picked my brain for information on the greatest country in the world.

Six years after I began spilling secrets, I started teaching Syrian forces how to fight. As a Navy SEAL of twelve years, I had so much training under my belt. The people and government of Syria began to call me a saint. Someone who came along to help them on their way to victory. I became the Patron Saint of Victory and was set in a temple to be worshipped. Their praises, their howls, and cries for me to kiss their children made my previous life seem like a dark memory that maybe never even happened.

The Syrian forces once called me to a council meeting. They'd received a serious offer. They could join the Chinese forces who were also paired up with Russia to invade the US. China would offer us food and protection in exchange for intel, soldiers, and training. Which meant, Syria was looking to me to be their sacrifice. It had been the Syrian dream to conquer America for themselves. They'd conquer the land of the free first, and with an army so large, they'd conquer the one territory their ancestors wished for long ago: Israel.

Sitting at that table, I knew I'd have to join the Chinese forces. I had no choice. The people were depending on me, and I wanted to prove myself as the Patron Saint of Victory.

I agreed and joined the Chinese forces with some of the best soldiers I'd trained. For the next decade, I spent that time proving to China that I was who the Syrians believed I was. I advised them on US affairs, told them about US ships. Had even told them how the mindset of the US military worked. And when China was able to capture a US ship, I had no problem explaining the functions of it to them. Day in and day out, we trained on the ship, each of their men learning the functions that I taught them.

It took a while, but once I gained the trust of the Chinese and Russian forces, they began taking my advice. I told them America's weak spot is her sympathy. If her heart is broken, she will be weak. So we planned an invasion, and when the famine hit, we knew time was of the essence.

Regarded as the Saint of the Red Dragon in China, and the Patron Saint of Victory in Syria, I began to value myself more and more. I was a god in my own right. I had made it to the top seat by my own hand. No one had helped me, God had forgotten me, and the US did not come for me. It was me alone who rose like a phoenix from the ashes of my past.

God did not keep His promise. Though I waited for Him. He never sent a single US soldier to find me. Instead, He took everything from me and forced me to betray my country.

Well, it's not my country anymore. And God is not my god

anymore.

I am my own god.

I am the one who will become everything God hates just to spite Him—just to have my revenge on Him. I will take this world from Him and claim it as mine, and I will make everyone hate the Christ.

1

Abigail

3 Weeks Ago

I stood in the entrance of the Reinhardt's mansion. Polished concrete floors stretched into the glory of the home. High ceilings that were held up by grey walls to match the floors. Mrs. Reinhardt had asked me to stay put at the front door. In all the time I've known her, I'd never once been to her home.

I met Zion through his mom. She introduced me to him when he was working the new members' event. Mrs. Reinhardt had been the teacher of the welcoming class and was putting on a big event to officiate us as members of the church. The church was so big, I never thought I'd meet the first lady. One day, I told Mrs. Reinhardt this after class and she took me for coffee. She told me all about how she wanted to be more personal and wouldn't have anyone else teach the new members' welcoming course but herself.

At the event, Mrs. Reinhardt and I were chatting over cake

when Zion came over. He was strikingly handsome. He caught you off guard. Church boys certainly didn't look like him. Peachy tan skin, with warm eyes and heavy lashes. His thick dark hair was pulled into a bun, and he had just a dash of facial hair. I thought my knees would give out at just the sight of him. His strong jaw, and perfect lips that curled into a smile when he greeted his mother. They hugged, exchanging words before Mrs. Reinhardt turned to me. His eyes left his mother and slid over to mine.

I almost fainted.

Zion's always been the type of guy who seems too young to be a man, but he has all the right attributes of one. He was mature and funny. Concerned and kind. He listened, and when you were angry, he actually apologized. And he was good at everything. Making you smile, making you happy, getting you out of a funk. Zion was so dependable that you never notice he's the pillar holding you up. It's effortless with him, and I think that's what made me fall in love with him.

"Abbey," Mrs. Reinhardt had returned, pulling me from my swirling memories. I could barely raise my eyes to meet hers, but when I did, I found no condemnation. She reached for my hand and told me to come along.

"So," she started as we walked the maze of the mansion. "Zion left you here and he's running with his tail tucked."

"Well, I'm not so sure. He was called into duty, but when he has a break, he'll be here to talk about everything."

"Alright, then why don't you get a head start."

We stopped in the dining room where an assortment of

fruits lay on the long glass table. She offered me a seat as she marched around the table to put fruit on a plate for me.

"Mrs. Reinhardt, I'm so sorry," I began. "What we did was wrong and—"

She dropped her serving spoon and her calm demeanor fell with it. Snorting, she placed a trembling hand to her mouth and whispered, "All this time, behind our backs…"

"Please, it was a mistake."

"Are you the only one?"

"Pregnant?"

She stared with wide eyes. That was the worst possible answer. Fumbling for words and shaking my head, I said, "No, what I meant was—"

Mrs. Reinhardt held up a hand and I snapped my mouth shut. I knew this would be hard, but I didn't think it would be this emotional. I was beginning to wish I'd gotten the abortion as I looked at a broken-hearted Rhoda. I'd betrayed her kindness and slept with her son behind her back. Now, I was here asking for help.

I groaned as I felt another contraction and hunched forward onto the table. They'd calmed down ever since Zion and I left our place. Now they were flaring up again and I could hardly take it. Inhaling, I tried to steady my breathing.

"Why didn't he just take you to the hospital?" Rhoda said as she wiped at her tears.

I raised my head and squinted. "Zion was called in for duty."

"I know. Routines or whatever, right?" Her eyes that held

3

tears of disappointment were now full of anxiety.

"No, Mrs. Reinhardt. Have you seen the news?"

"It's five in the morning. We weren't up before you arrived."

"Mrs. Reinhardt, Zion brought me here because there's been an invasion. We're under attack and most likely hospitals are already run over."

Her brows rushed at each other to meet at the center of her forehead, allowing wrinkles to fold her normally smooth brown skin. "What did you say?" she finally managed. "My son is out there fighting? America has been invaded? By whom!?"

"China."

She took a wobbly step back, gripping the chair for security.

I jumped to my feet, holding my aching belly as I rushed across the room to her. "Mrs. Reinhardt, you should sit down."

"Jillian! Jillian!" she wailed as I helped her sit. I could hear Mr. Reinhardt somewhere above us moving around. It took a few minutes before he came downstairs in a panic. His cream robe with *Reinhardt* embroidered across the breast pocket, flowed behind him as he came into the dining room in his silk pajamas.

"Rhoda," he blinked at me and then back at Rhoda. "What's going on?"

"America has been invaded," I said.

"Wha—"

"Zion's out there!" Rhoda wailed as she collapsed into Mr. Reinhardt's arms. "Our son is out there!"

Obviously, Pastor Reinhardt was just as shaken as his wife. But he held a strong face as he rubbed circles on Rhoda's back, whispering to her that everything would be ok. He said God would protect him. I think the pastor found relief in that until Rhoda hollered, "He's been sleeping with her! That's his baby! God won't protect him!"

Jillian slowly lifted his gaze to me. His eyes hit my belly first, lingering there a moment before they lifted to my face.

I decided this was a good moment to take a step back and give them some space.

I was dealing with it all too. Zion was my fiancée, he was about to be the father of our daughter. Yet, he'd chosen his duty before his family. Somehow the military had remolded his mind in just three short months to love this country more than the people in it. He said they needed him and looked crossed when I told him that *I* needed him. But I knew he'd never be okay just sitting by, so I agreed quietly and let my fiancée run into danger.

I wanted to pray, but I was too far from God for Him to hear me now. If God wouldn't protect him, then there was no point in praying anyway. Our sin was evident, it had grown for the past eight months right in my own womb. To ask God to excuse that sin seemed callous. Mostly because in all this time, I hadn't asked God for anything, and hadn't given Him anything. It seemed wrong to only speak to Him now because I was desperate. In my stubbornness, I retreated to the living room without muttering a word to God.

At some point, the crying stopped from Rhoda and Mr. and Mrs. Reinhardt left me to myself in the living room. With my contractions seemingly calmed, I raided their fridge through the night, finding all kinds of goodies that satisfied me until morning. I was going to have a conversation with them, but as I entered the dining room to find them seated at the table as if they were waiting for me … my water broke.

The moment my water broke, I called Zion, but he didn't answer. I didn't get another chance to try and call him because labor lasted for hours. I was pushing hard, gritting my teeth in pain, and passing out here and there.

The labor was intense, like our little Flower didn't want to budge. Despite all the things I hadn't said to the Reinhardts, they were there, helping me give birth. They'd helped me to the guest bathroom and into the tub. Pastor Reinhardt kept fresh towels coming and Mrs. Reinhardt coached me and kept herself ready for when the baby came.

I clutched the edge of the tub as I panted for air. I'd been pushing so long I didn't think I had it in me to push any further.

Beside me, Mrs. Reinhardt had been patting my hand, but she suddenly stopped and cocked her head to the side. There was a curious look on her face, eyebrows scrunched, lips pressed together. "Do you hear that?" she finally asked.

I took another short breath and tried to focus. "I don't hear anything."

Rhoda stood and looked around, brushing her curly afro hair away from her ears. "It sounds like trumpets..." she whispered. Then she stepped closer to the door. "Jillian? Are you playing music—" She was mid-sentence when she dropped to the floor.

I screamed as I sat in the bathtub. "Rhoda! Wake up! Rhoda! Pastor Reinhardt!"

No one answered. A jolt of pain made me shriek in horror and I tried to bear down, but I was too weak.

"Rhoda, get up!" I shouted, leaning out the tub. I reached as far as I could and shook her shoulder in a panic. "Please!"

There was more pain than I could bear, screaming through my body, making every muscle inside me tremble in horror. I sank back into the tub, wiping sweat from my forehead. I was naked from the waist down, blood streaking my knees and shins. No one ever told me giving birth would be so messy. No one ever told me I'd have to do this alone with an unconscious woman lying three feet away. But I had no choice except to keep going.

Gritting my teeth, I clutched the edge of the bathtub and forced myself to push once more. I hadn't realized how much I was depending on Rhoda's coaching until I had to do it myself.

Finally, as I pushed and hollered out, little Flower Reinhardt was born. Lifting her out the water, I cupped the wet and bloody baby in my arms. She wailed and hiccupped, crying into my chest as I tried to regain myself.

"Shh," I cooed at Flower. I'd chosen the name when I

found out I was pregnant. I'd decided if the baby was a girl, she'd be my little flower.

As I cooed at the baby, I heard a strange noise beside me. That's when I remembered that Rhoda had fainted; I leaned over the tub, expecting to find her coming around to consciousness. Instead, I found her writhing on the floor. She jerked and kicked. Flopping around like her body was out of air.

"Rhoda!? Rhoda!"

At the sound of my voice, her head twisted at an ungodly angle. The woman staring back at me was not Rhoda Reinhardt. She wasn't even human with her neck turned almost all the way around. She bellowed out a high-pitched noise, the pain that pierced my eardrums almost made me drop the baby as I tried to cover my ears.

When Rhoda stopped screeching, she began to flop and contort even more. Twisting in scary angles and hacking up blood.

"Oh my goodness!" I screamed as I climbed from the tub.

I tried to step around her when her hand reached for me. I hollered, clutching Flower closer to me before racing from the bathroom.

I was soaked, with no underwear, still bleeding, and carrying a newborn. As I ran across the tiled floor, my wet feet slipped and I screamed as I slammed into the wall. Rhoda was standing now, her body posed in an awkward angle, like she'd just learned how to stand.

There was no time to process what I was seeing. There was

no time to question the science-fiction nightmare playing out in front of me. I could only think of Flower screaming in my arms, so I snatched the bathroom door open and ran for the bedroom, slamming the door shut behind me when I made it inside.

I leaned against it heavily, panting and blinking around the room. I couldn't catch my breath. My heart was ramming in my chest, its rapid pace matched by the thumping footsteps I heard moving toward the bedroom.

Before I could move, something slammed into the door, crying out in response. I shouted as I fell to the floor, trying to protect a crying Flower. Another thud came, and then they repeatedly rammed the door without stopping. My eyes darted around the room, desperately searching for a way out.

I spotted my overnight bag lying on the bed. The door bumped into my backside with every thud from the hall. The screeching threatened to send me into a maddening spiral of chaotic fear, but Flower's wails kept me focused.

I sucked in a breath and turned to click the lock on the door. Then I ran across the room and snatched my bag from the bed. The hallway was filled with monsters. My only escape was the window beside my unmade bed.

Without even thinking about it, I threw my naked legs over the ledge and climbed out the window onto the roof. The room was on the third floor, so the roof was slanted, dropping off to a balcony on the second floor below—if I could make the landing. I struggled, clutching to the side of the house with one hand and trying to keep Flower safely tucked against me with the other. My bag dangled helplessly from my mouth, the strap clutched painfully between my gritted teeth.

Just as I got my footing right, the door burst open, and both Rhoda and Jillian fell inside. I didn't even know I was screaming until my ears popped and all the sound came rushing back. My own shrieks were the loudest in the room, even overwhelming Flower's baby shrieks. The strap of the duffle bag fell from my mouth as I screamed and slid along the roof of the house. It brought me back to my senses, but I couldn't reach for the bag without tilting over and nosediving off the ledge of the house. Instead, I took my chances and glanced back into the room.

I stared at Rhoda and Jillian. They weren't themselves anymore. They weren't alive anymore. Their limbs were twisted, their heads bleeding from every crevice—eyes, nose, mouth. Their skin had turned grey and saggy like … like they were decomposing.

Empty eyes stared back at me, scaring me more than the incoherent sounds that rolled from their loose jaws. I blinked back to reality as they fumbled over each other awkwardly, growling and grunting while fighting to get to their feet. They weren't people anymore. These two things looked more like monsters that'd taken over. Awkward in their human bodies, not used to their legs and arms and feet.

I shook my head, panting for breath. There was no time to figure this out.

I held tightly to the side of the house as I hunched over and crab-walked along the slanted roof toward my duffle bag.

I could hear Rhoda and Jillian rolling around in the room—then I heard footsteps, and a growl so close that I screamed and threw myself at the bag.

I missed, tumbling along the roof of the house as the Rhoda-monster clumsily climbed out the window. As I fell, I reached for the bag, *barely* grabbing hold of the strap—but momentum kept me going. I overshot the second-floor balcony, whacking the metal bars of the ledge with my leg as I fell from the third-floor roof all the way to the bushes below.

With a scream, I twisted my body, so I'd land on top of my bag, holding Flower close. Sharp twigs stabbed into my back, thorns scratched my arms, legs, and naked buttocks. But I didn't care. There were two wild monsters trying to get onto the roof and my infant in my arms. I could not stop here.

Up above, I could see Rhoda hanging halfway out the window, shrieking at me. The fear that shot through me as I stared at her made my body jump into action, leaving my mind behind.

The first thing I did when I up righted myself was check Flower for injuries. She was still crying in my arms, and covered in blood from being born less than ten minutes ago, but I think she was fine otherwise, just shaken up.

There was a cry that came from the house, and when I looked up, I saw Rhoda fall out the window with a thump, Jillian was trying to get out now as well.

With one last huff, I snatched up my duffle bag and raced for the streets. I had no idea where to go, but I had to run. When I looked back, Rhoda was tripping and sliding down the sloped roof while Jillian was falling out the window now.

I picked up the pace, running as fast as I could, ignoring all the pain of childbirth, and heading for the first house I found further down the street.

2

Abigail

I couldn't get into the house, but there was a pickup truck parked out front with the bed open. Thankfully, there was a hard cover on it, so I was able to hide inside. Panting hard, I dug through my overnight bag and pulled out the small blanket I'd packed for Flower to lay on. She was crying, hiccupping, and gasping for air as she turned pinker than the blood staining her skin.

"Shh," I cooed at her, but it was no use. Flower screamed as she riled on the blanket, naked and wet.

I quickly checked our surroundings, the creatures had chased me to the house, but one got stuck in a bush trying to get to me. The other creature chased me to the truck, but I wasn't sure where it was now. When I climbed inside and pulled the door shut, I heard the creature screeching for a few moments and it sounded like the footsteps wandered off.

I flipped the bag over as I dug frantically for a bottle. I'd packed a little of everything for the baby after I'd read in a magazine about a woman whose hospital ran out of diapers when she had her baby. It freaked me out, so I packed two diapers, some baby wipes, a bottle and pump, and some other items with my clothes and essentials.

I snatched up the pump first, tearing off my shirt and quickly attaching it so I could fill the bottle as much as I could while constantly looking around. Tears stung my eyes, I'd never breastfed before, but I also hadn't heard that it was painful before. Then again, I wasn't breastfeeding, I was pumping milk into a bottle as quickly as possible while hiding out in the bed of an abandoned pickup truck while two monsters hunted me down.

I blinked back my tears. If I cried, I wouldn't be able to see the creatures if they returned. I didn't know when those things would be back, or if someone would find me. I had to remain alert. I couldn't afford any tears right now.

"Please, God," I whispered as I removed the pump and tightened the cap on the bottle, "help me."

All my stubbornness and pride were gone. I needed help, *real* help, and God was the only One who could give it to me. So, right there on the bed of the truck, hunched over, covered in blood, and entirely naked, I begged God for help.

"Please…" my lower lip trembled as I tried with all my might to keep the tears at bay. "Please help me, Jesus. Please help my little girl."

Flower blubbered loudly, her face red and mottled with emotion. She was probably twice as scared as me. What a way to come into the world.

14

I lifted Flower from the blanket and held her against my breast; she began to suckle without any prodding. Despite everything, I smiled. At least she wouldn't be difficult to please. Mercifully, Flower didn't want very much milk, but it did quiet her down, and she fell asleep on the blanket finally. That gave me time to take care of myself.

As she slept, I looked down at my body. I'd just given birth, and then I'd been forced to run for my life in nothing but a night shirt with my own baby in my arms. I'd climbed out a window and thrown myself off the roof. My legs were stained in dried blood, dirt, and grass stuck to my sweaty skin, and there were scratches from thorns lining almost every part of my body.

"First things first," I whispered.

Carefully, I tugged the umbilical cord. I chewed my lip until the bitter taste of blood poured into my mouth as the placenta slipped free and spilled into the truck. Using one of the skirts I packed, I sat on it to keep the blood from reaching the baby and worked on the side of the umbilical cord attached to Flower. It was certainly done pulsating, all I needed to do was cut it. But, with no scissors, I tied the cord around itself a few times tightly closer to Flower's belly.

With a huff, I leaned back. I could feel myself shaking as I sat with my sleeping Flower. I'd have to dress her, and myself before I could get moving. But I had no idea when those things would come back. As quietly as I could, I shifted closer to the small window and peered out, the day was only beginning. The sun was barely in the sky as I looked around for the monsters.

I didn't want to think about just how insane my day had been.

Literal monsters, who were Zion's parents, were after me...

Hugging myself tightly, I squirmed as I thought of the unholy incident. The way the two of them griped and bent, twisted and screeched, and finally came after me. Fast and clumsy, those creatures were everything you could imagine in a nightmare. They're the type of things you see at night and when you wake up, you're too afraid to go back to sleep. You're not even afraid of the dark, you're afraid of getting tired—of being paralyzed with fear and caught by the monsters in your head. Except these weren't in your head, or even under your bed, the creepy feeling that something is watching you. These creatures were your family, friends, real people who suddenly didn't have a mind.

Covering my mouth, I gagged into it, salty saliva poured from my lips into my hand. *What would I even tell Zion? How do I get to him? What do I do?* I was about to crack, about to shrivel into fetal position and wail like a madwoman when Flower coughed. Her small baby noises pulled me from the sickening fear inside, and I knew she'd be my focus until I got to safety.

God sent me something to focus on to get me out of here, I thought. I didn't care what I told myself, I needed to believe something to keep my mind from breaking in fear.

Picking through the bag, I spared myself two baby wipes to get rid of the worst of the blood and dirt on my legs and hands. The fresh cuts stung but I grimaced through it. Then I grabbed some underwear and a big overnight pad I'd packed and put them on. I changed into the sweatpants and shirt I'd packed.

When I was finished, I stared down at the baggy pants as Flower wiggled on the blanket. All my movements were waking her up, but I was distracted for a moment as I recalled the day I was put out. I had no food, barely any clothes. Just a little money to catch a bus to Zion's place. I knew he'd let me stay, even if it was just a few days. He'd give me money and I'd be on my way. But then he told me to get an abortion—which I was not expecting—and we ended up keeping Flower. We ended up falling in love again.

"Zion," I whispered through a short breath. Tears were pricking my eyes as I thought about him. What he'd say when we met up. His apologies for leaving me… but what if I never found him again?

Hunching over, I cried into my hands. "What am I supposed to do!?"

Flower began crying too. I wanted to ignore her, to wallow in the fear a little longer, but I couldn't for her sake.

"Come here, little Flower," I whispered as I scooped her into my arms. "We'll find Daddy, I promise."

Flower continued to cry when I laid her back on the bloody blanket and began wiping her down with the baby wipes. The wiping seemed to calm her a little. She let me get her diaper on with ease, and then her clothes. Thankfully, I brought her the footy pajamas instead of the sunshine outfit Zion wanted her to wear home from the hospital. I'd told him that she'd need to be warm, and he finally agreed to the red footy PJs.

Pulling her hood over her head, I laid her beside the blanket as I rolled it back up to put it in the bag. I was down to one diaper, and one pad. No more clothes, a bag of pretzels, and a half bottle of pumped milk, along with the blanket. Somehow, Flower and I would need to survive off of this until we could find safety.

But I had another dilemma now; how long could I carry Flower? The thought hadn't crossed my mind until now, and now I was worried. She was only a baby but carrying a baby while possibly running from danger was a totally different thing. Quickly, I unpacked the bag, leaving the blanket on the bottom. I put Flower inside, and put the pretzels, diaper, and pad in the outside zipped pocket. I didn't need the pump and bottle, though I preferred them. Zion preferred us to buy formula, complaining that he was the son of one of the richest pastors in America.

"We can afford formula!" he'd always said, totally missing the point of why I didn't want formula. It had nothing to do with money—it was about all the stuff that goes into formula, powders, and baby food. But all that went over Zion's head.

I just thank God I never budged on that point!

Zipping the bag halfway, I peered down into it at Flower. Her round eyes were blinking sleepily at me as I pulled the big strap over my shoulder and clutched the two smaller straps in my hands. The only shoes I had were a pair of house shoes Zion forced me to pack since I didn't pack the sunshine outfit. He said the flat ones at the hospital probably wouldn't be comfortable.

I chuckled a bitter laugh at the sweet memory. I'd have to save the memories for later.

I crawled towards the door of the trunk and pulled on it... it didn't move. I pushed on it... and it still didn't move—because I was locked in.

Taking quick breaths, I ignored the pain in my lower body, and crawled around looking for another way out. There wasn't one. I was trapped.

"I'm an idiot!" I screamed as I hit the window. Flower was crying again, but so was I. We were trapped in here, and we'd die within hours from no oxygen, or a painful death in days from starvation.

"God, please," I whispered, "I need Your help. I'm stuck in here! Help me! Help me, God! I know I haven't been right and I'm so sorry," I began to weep, "but I'm begging You to help me. Please..."

In the silence, I took a deep breath to try to calm myself and think. Flower was still crying, but she'd be dead if I didn't find a way out. I stared out the window at the world around us. Shakily, I pressed a hand to the window, nearly succumbing to the fear of dying inside the bed of this truck.

"Please, God," I whispered again. "Jesus, help me." My tears began to blur the world outside when they suddenly stopped.

"This is a window," I whispered, "I can break it."

Glancing around the truck, I remembered this was just a truck cap. There was probably a way to get the whole thing off.

19

Pulling the bag strap from over my head, I moved for the rusting toolbox in the corner of the truck. My hands shook as I flipped the top open, gasping at the gun sitting on top.

Carefully, I set it aside, and grabbed the hammer I found. Whispering my gratitude to God, I took the hammer back as far as I could and slammed it into the window. The clanking made my entire hand burn, but I kept swinging anyway. Finally, the window cracked. Out of breath, and agitated at the screams of Flower, I kept beating the glass until it splintered and cracked. Then I shoved the spider webbed glass from the frame, and reached out the window to pull on the handle, freeing us.

"Thank you, Jesus!" I cried as I fell backwards on my butt. Exhaustion was easing in as I sat there trying to catch my breath. I was aching all over, but there was a new bout of adrenaline pumping through me, or rather, a reignited flame of fear that consumed me as the screeching cry of one of those creatures rang out.

I grabbed Flower and threw the strap over my head. Snatching up the hammer, I tucked it into that outside pocket and grabbed the gun on my way out of the truck. I didn't look back to see where the creatures were, I just ran in whatever direction was clear—clutching the bag against my chest so Flower wouldn't bounce so much.

When I got to the end of the street, I slowed down, glancing around in fear but my nerves calmed when I didn't find anything behind me. Swallowing thickly, I checked on Flower; she was looking back at me, tears in her eyes. The bouncing probably scared her, but she was fine other than that.

The walk was long, nothing but burning smoke, and darkness as I finally made it closer to the city. I was going to find the church, maybe someone could help me there, but that would be another few days away on foot. In an invasion with monsters all around, there was no way I would survive all the way there… but where else could I go? Maybe there was a shelter nearby, maybe I could find somewhere to hunker down just for a little while.

Leaning against a building, I tried to catch my breath. I was aching really badly now. I wasn't sure what was wrong, maybe it was just soreness from childbirth, or maybe I had a tear. But I couldn't think about that now. I needed to find shelter before a creature showed up.

I adjusted the bag, thankful that Flower was quiet now, then I began down the street again. We passed burned buildings and hissing fires, there was a wailing in the background that I wasn't sure belonged solely to medical vehicles. It sounded like voices being lifted in agony. Cries from the invasion of our city.

Rounding the corner, I spotted a soldier standing outside of a building. "Help!" I shouted to him. "Help me!"

He looked over and ducked as he raced across the street toward me. "Miss, are you alright?" he said as he grabbed my arm.

"Please, I need help. Somewhere to stay—somewhere to go."

"This is an evacuation shelter." He gestured toward the

21

building he'd been guarding. "I can bring you inside. Have you been exposed or have broken skin?"

I paused, blinking up at him. Slowly, I pulled the gun closer to my body to hide it. "Exposed?"

"Have you been in contact with a Wrong?"

"Those things? I-I-I've seen them, but I was inside and ran out of food," I began to lie as I understood the soldier's focused eyes. "I just need a place to stay, with my daughter." I shrugged my shoulder, and the soldier glanced over at the bag. When he saw Flower, he nodded and guided me across the street to the shelter.

"Wait here," he said as he opened the door and stepped inside.

Quickly, I stuffed the gun into my waistband, and lowered Flower to the ground. Lifting her out the bag, I tossed her bloody blanket into the nearby bushes, afraid the blood would scare everyone, and placed her back inside. I wasn't sure what I could've been exposed to, but apparently those creatures, the Wrongs, must be carrying some kind of virus.

The door creaked open, and the soldier stepped out. "Come on in. We've got room."

3

Victory

Three Weeks Ago

"Fatima, dear, I'm ready for my Arak." A young girl wearing a long white tunic with a matching cream-colored headwrap nodded as she stood from her rouge pillow. She set a short glass down before me and the strong smell reached my nostrils as she poured a frothy white liquid inside. It had a bitter smell of anise, or what most Americans recognized as black licorice. There was a sweetness beneath the dark flavor, but it wasn't as noticeable when I first drank it.

As I recall, a young woman, much like Fatima, served me and a group of Syrian soldiers the drink with one-third water to the two-thirds white drink. My first time trying it, the drink was so bitter I almost spat it out. But I had only just gotten on the Syrians' good side and didn't want to offend them. So, I tilted my head back and gulped the dark flavor back, shouting a cheer when I'd swallowed. It was more for me that I'd survived that horrible drink, than for them. But they didn't need to know that.

Fatima was plopping ice into my cup when the doors to my dining hall flung open.

"Who dares interrupt me while I feast with my wives?" I snapped.

"My lord," a man stepped forward, a black gloved hand over his chest, his head bowed.

"Speak," I said as my eyes raked over him.

Lifting his head, the burns on his face meant he could be none other than Bastion, my closest man. He was a Black American man who was a prisoner of war in China. I freed him just three years after I began working with China on behalf of the Syrian forces. Bass was a good man. He believed in the American dream, and was willing to die for it, until I told him that America had forgotten him. America had stopped caring about his dreams long ago, and when he realized I was telling the truth, he joined my forces.

The new American rebel was speaking now, explaining how there'd been a halt in our progression with the invasion.

"What do you mean we can't move forward?" I demanded.

"Sir, something else is out there. Our men were invading and then something hit them."

"What? Bastion, don't toy with me."

He gave me a short nod before quickly looking around the room at the harem of women. Only my twelve wives ate with me every day, and I visited my concubines when I had the time. Most men were subject to one—maybe two—wives, but since I was the Saint of Syria, I was given what I wanted. Women,

24

riches, you name it. They were all my possessions, all of Syria and everything thereof, and I would indulge myself when I felt it necessary.

"Sabiya," I called to my head wife. A brown woman stood with thick curls that flowed all around her. Sabiya's ancestors were originally African, but her family settled in Syria three generations ago to work off a debt they owed. She was a beauty beyond words. Warm hazelwood skin and wondrous blue eyes that stirred me like the sea held in them. She wore a golden ring in her nose that connected with a thick chain to her ear. There were all kinds of jewels on her body, and the swirled green skirt that was wrapped around her hips matched perfectly with her bejeweled green bralette trimmed in gold. She was the only one I allowed to wear such jewelry. Heavy bangles on her arms, dangling bracelets on her wrists, Sabiya was always treated as royalty.

My younger brides, Fatima, Iba, and Imoni were ordered to wear hijabs and tunics to hide their youthful beauty. When they are of age, they will be allowed to wear garments chosen by the older brides. Each of them wore skirts and dressed nicely, but I never let anyone dress more daring or outshine my precious Sabiya.

"Take the women to their quarters," I said—then I added, "I want Afra in my quarters tonight."

Sabiya inclined her head. "Yes, my lord."

"And, Sabiya," I called as she stopped walking. "Do not murmur a word of this to the rest of the girls if they come asking. Be sure this stays silent."

25

"Of course, Saint Victory."

"Go now." I waved her on, and she beckoned for the girls to stand and follow her out.

When the room was empty, I could still smell the sweet perfume of my wives in the air. It was the only thing that kept me calm.

"May I speak?" Bastion broke the silence.

"Don't be so uptight, everyone's gone, Bass," I said as I stood from my throne. My long black garments trailed the stairs as I stepped down them to enter the dining courts where Bass stood. "What is this thing you tell me of?"

"Monsters, Victory."

I squinted. "Monsters? You'll have to give me more than that."

He cleared his throat as he looked uncomfortable all of a sudden. "Wrongs. Things that have come back to life—some say."

"What?"

"It's like they've awakened somehow."

"And they're in America? Is it some kind of attack on our men?"

He shook his head as he stepped away, finally loosening up. Bastion took his job more seriously than I took mine.

"These things are attacking invaders *and* Americans."

"So no one has control of it?"

"No."

I sighed, feeling relieved. "Good. Have the Chinese said anything? Taken credit for it?"

"Not yet, sir. I came right here when I found out. There have been reports popping up everywhere just nothing from China. Uncontrollable beings that reawakened after death. Eating people alive. And when their victims die, they come back as those same things, multiplying their army."

"Hold on," I raised a hand, "you're saying those things are literally humans who have died and rose again?"

"Yes."

I rubbed the back of my neck. "How did this start?"

"Reports said that people just started dropping dead. Mid-sentence, mid stride, they just dropped dead. All around the world, but it mostly affected America. Some are calling it a virus, others are calling it—" he stopped.

"What?" I stepped closer.

With a big gulp, Bastion's eyes shifted to the floor. "The Rapture, sir."

I stiffened. I'd ordered my council to get rid of all religious material and create new material based on me, which they were still working on. Bastion was right to hesitate to tell me such putrid information.

Closing my eyes and taking a deep breath, I promised myself I wouldn't let it bother me. God would not win. I'd heard of the rapture before, never cared to pay attention to it though since I was so focused on my own prophecy. I was focused on being a modern-day Job, until God didn't prove Himself to me. He left me in the cold with nothing. All that I knew of the rapture was that God would save His people... how selfish. If He wouldn't save the world, then I would. I would save the ones left behind, keep them as my own and get rid of anyone who dared to still call themselves His. With the way things were going, I didn't think it would be difficult to claim the world as my own.

This happening was strange, but I doubted it was the fabled Rapture. I had grown up Christian. I'd read the texts myself and nothing had ever mentioned people dropping dead or their bodies coming back to life.

Well…

I squinted.

The Bible had mentioned that God's children would be taken in the twinkling of an eye. It said they would get new bodies—so I *suppose* they could leave their old useless bodies behind. But what about them rising again?

Though I hated it, I ran through Scriptures in my head. The Bible did say something odd about death and resurrection…

The dead in Christ will rise again.

What does that mean?

I shook my head to clear it. It didn't matter what it meant because my mission did not depend on the Bible. It depended solely on me. I would succeed. No matter what.

"If we get ahead of this," I said slowly, "we can steer things the way we need to. Get the rest of the board together, I want to have a meeting in three days."

"Yes, sir." Bastion took his leave and I found myself wandering back to my seat. Gripping the small cup of arak, I only stared as the ice melted into the drink. "You won't beat me, do You understand me? You will never beat me!" I shouted as I threw the glass across the room.

Slamming my fist into the armrest of my throne, I tried to calm myself. I'd need to be completely unbothered by the mention of the Rapture or anything religious when the board met together. The group of us had been meeting since we began preparing for these invasions. Taking a deep breath, I reminded myself to keep a level head like I always did. I needed to be able to make good decisions and come up with the best ideas. I wouldn't let anger get in the way of the progress we'd need to make quickly.

...❀...

"Gentlemen, thank you for meeting with me today," I said as I stood at the head of the shimmering black stone table. There were sixteen men before me. Bastion on my right, and General Yang Pen on my left. He was the leader of the Chinese army, and beside him was Jun Sun, the representative of the Chinese forces in our alliance. There were many of us at this table, nearly all of the eastern world was here.

The Russians, who were allied with China for the past two decades were here with three leaders they could spare since they had their own invasion to deal with. The twin princes of Egypt were here along with a few representatives of other African countries. Recently, Africa had "shrank," bringing many of their smaller countries together during the famine to have stronger forces. Most places died out, and the lands were

29

given to those who remained. Countries were now refugee camps, and their leader was the nearby country that was still standing.

The Middle East and all of Europe had faced the same problems and found the same solution as Africa. Europe, of course, united under the guidance of the King of England, who had been a long-time friend of the rulers of the Middle East. With the Taliban making its mark in Afghanistan years back, the threat traveled the rest of the Middle East and their alliance with Europe made them stronger. But it was their backseat alliance with China that kept them in power, uniting the countries under their brutal reign.

"What is this about?" Prince Tafeef snapped. His square jaw and rigid manner mimicked his twin brother, Prince Jabari.

"I know this was sudden, but I assure you, it's worth it."

"Are we here to talk about the monsters? Because I've got men dropping like flies in my army and we don't know what to do." Volkov, a greying Russian, said.

"Yes, that's what I called us here for. We need to do something."

"Our people are calling it a virus," Adnan of India said, "we got word from China to call it a virus."

"From China?" I looked over at Yang and Jun, but Jun spoke on their behalf.

"You have forgotten that you are a saint here in Syria, but you are but an ally in China."

"Funny," I tsked, "I remember China regarding me as the saint of the Red Dragon."

"Mind your tongue when you speak of our people," Jun hissed.

"I wouldn't have to if alliances meant anything to China. You're going around telling everyone but me your thoughts. When did things change?"

"I don't think now is the time to settle a feud," Bastion reminded me.

"No, you're right." I shook my head, trying to regain my calm demeanor. "I just didn't know who started the virus idea."

"It is the only explanation," Jun said confidently.

I nodded as Adnan began to speak on the reports of people coming back to life. It was all information I'd heard before, which gave me time to think over China's bold move. They were making decisions on their own, though they promised to include the board, or at least me. This didn't look good. I needed to get a handle on the situation and quickly before China did. It was a race now and that was the only reason China came to the meeting. They have their own agenda and need to know what I know for their own use.

Curses, I spewed them in my head at China. They had always been a strong force who had a goal they'd reach by any means necessary. However, invading the US was not the only goal of the Chinese forces. Being the world's sole superpower was the actual goal. The bald eagle had only stood in the way of the Red Dragon.

"Victory?" I glanced up to find Bastion had a raised brow. "What are your thoughts on the wrongs?"

"The wrongs." I glanced around the room. Jun Sun sat

primly in his Chinese regalia, but I knew he was holding a strong poker face behind his white beard. My thoughts were the only reason he'd arrived, and the only reason his life would be his when he returned to his land. I could use the Chinese desperation for my own benefit since they didn't know how much I knew about the situation, but I needed to act fast before they stopped caring about what I knew.

"We should go the virus route," I announced. "A sickness that just takes over rapidly because of stress. We can say Americans felt it first with the invasion and then—"

"Some say it's the Rapture," Prince Tafeef said.

I held my head high as I asked, "Eldest twin prince of Egypt, what do you think this strange occurrence could be? Is it truly a man in the sky, soul snatching?" I tossed my hands open with a laugh and said, "Come on, my prince, you know that sounds silly. And when people can't explain something, they'll grab things from thin air."

"Much like we are now," Henry Caille, the Duke of Malta seethed. Pushing dusty blonde hair from his face, he said, "I don't like lying."

"Then you don't belong here," Volkov said frostily. "We cannot afford to insight people to believe in something other than us."

Henry looked away, like he agreed but didn't want to say it.

"Belief," I waved a hand, "it is a powerful tool. Getting our world to believe something in this desperate time would mean their loyalty."

"How can we get loyalty when China's invading the US and Russia's dying in Israel!" Henry yelled. "We're doing the total opposite!"

"Please," General Pen snapped, "China is paving the way for the world to be as one. The US is a hurdle none of you could conquer."

"And you couldn't do it alone," Henry said darkly. "You quickly forget that this pavement was not laid by just China. Russian bodies and Indian bodies are being slaughtered. European resources and African resources are being drained to fill the barns of the Middle East who's feeding your soldiers!"

"That's enough!" My voice cracked through the room like a whip around the entire table. Sixteen grimaces, sixteen opinions. I took a breath. "We won't get anywhere like this. We are allies, not foes. We need to remember that." My eyes darted to Jun Sun.

He grunted, turning away to stand. "We are leaving," he announced.

"Fine." I raised a hand at Volkov who had lurched forward to express his distaste, and said, "Before you go, please make note that since we could not figure something out here, I will do it on my own."

Jun looked me over and sucked his teeth before the general stood with him and bowed. The two men left, followed by a few more men from India and Arabia. Henry took his troop of men, and the Princes of Egypt led the African forces back home. Volkov remained, tired and drained. His country was losing by the second in Israel and a retreat was being discussed back in Russia as we spoke.

"How do we trust them?" he said in the empty room.

I glanced at Bastion who nodded and took his leave. When the porcelain white doors closed behind him, I took a seat beside the Wolf of Russia. I'd heard of his determination in Russian conflicts in the past. He earned the title, 'The Wolf of Russia,' not just because his name meant wolf.

"You trust what you know. And when you don't know something, you trust what you can make of it. Never trust in the unknown or whom you can't see behind closed doors."

"Are you suggesting that I can't trust you?" He raised his greying head and I shrugged.

"Trust is a funny thing, Wolf. But confidence is different." I placed my hand on his shoulder, using this gaping opportunity to turn Russian forces away from China and into the palm of my hand. With the two forces split, I could be sitting on a pot of gold with half of the eastern world at my leisure through Russia.

"Volkov, I'm not asking you to trust me. I'm asking you to have confidence that I will make this right."

"And if you do? Then what?"

"Then maybe I was wrong about not trusting the one's you can't see. Only the ones whose odor is foul enough to smell across the sea. A strong nose like the wolf's would be sensitive enough to do that, wouldn't it?"

His grey eyes studied mine for a moment before he extended a hand. I took his and shook it firmly.

34

"Give me this chance to change confidence into trust, and trust into friendship. And friendship," I paused as I pulled his hand towards me, "into brotherhood."

4

Claudius
Present Day

"Cloud! I made cinnamon rolls!" Lyla stormed into the living room where I'd been staying for the last three weeks.

The girls let me sleep on the couch so that my leg could heal. Kingsley even went through the trouble of looting some clothes for me when she and Chemistry went out. This side of town hadn't seen as much wreckage as the rest of Springfield, so there were still some stores nearby with supplies to loot and electricity was spotty enough to keep things running.

We were fortunate to have running water—which was due to the well I'd heard the girls mention to each other—and the house had a wood burning stove to keep everyone warm. That's where all the meals were cooked. And anything that needed to be baked was wrapped in foil and sat on top.

Though I lived in this house, the girls (at Chemistry's command) made it painfully obvious I was not part of the family. Chemistry barely spoke to me. Kingsley spoke when Chemistry wouldn't, but I didn't sense any animosity the way Chemistry felt towards me. And Acoye was just shy. She told me goodnight and good morning every day but limited her conversations with me to keep her sisters from scolding her. However, no one stopped Lyla. It was like no one wanted to tell her no, so they let her spend time with me, all day if she wanted. I didn't mind since Lyla kept my mind from missing Keoni.

I thought about her every day and every night. Keoni was my reason for technically betraying my country and becoming an enemy of America. I don't regret my choice, but I don't know if I can confidently say I'm never bothered by it.

I think if Keoni and I hadn't gotten separated, I'd feel less guilty about the invasion. Though it still would've happened, we could've been better prepared. I chose to keep my mouth shut, but I also chose to save Keoni. I just hoped she was actually saved.

"Lyla, my little pumpkin, I'm so proud of you!" I exclaimed as she stood in front of me with a steaming plate of cinnamon rolls. The ridiculously sweet pastry had always been one of Keoni's favorites. A knot formed in my throat as I stared at the plate.

"You don't want one?" Lyla asked woefully. Her big eyes were turned down as she frowned.

"Of course! I was just thinking that my fiancée loved these."

"Fiancée? What's that?"

"Uh, actually, these look good. I better get one while it's hot."

"Yes!"

I took one and nodded at the little girl as she twirled off with the plate. I couldn't break her heart and end my only lifeline by telling her I was almost hitched three weeks ago. Lyla has fallen in love with me, and she's told her sisters that she's going to marry me when she gets older. Tough luck.

"Hey," Chemistry called as she stepped into the doorway.

"Hi."

"We need to talk."

I waved my arms around sarcastically, indicating there was nothing stopping her. She rolled her eyes and grabbed a folding chair, stared at the roll in my hand as she sat. "Aren't you going to eat it?"

"I don't know. Brings back memories."

"Bad ones?"

I raised a brow. "What did you want to talk about?"

"We're going looting again. Our supplies are low thanks to a certain someone."

Resisting the urge to roll my eyes took strength I didn't know I could muster in such short notice. "So, go loot."

"We're taking Acoye this time. We need a lookout."

I shrugged. She sighed.

"That means you're on Lyla duty."

"Aren't I always?"

"Gotta earn your keep some kind of way."

"Whatever. I'll watch her."

"It's not that simple." She lifted three bottles of prescription drugs. "Lyla is sick—very sick. She was born with damaged lungs. She used to wear a breathing machine but she's better now. But she still suffers greatly from basically chronic asthma."

I stumbled for words as she went on.

"She takes pills to help with all the symptoms, but truthfully, there's nothing we can do except keep her comfortable."

"I see. I'm sorry."

For the first time since I arrived, Chemistry wasn't piercing me with grimacing eyes. She shyly looked away at the pills in her hands.

"This world is cruel," she muttered. "I have no idea if she'll make it in times like this." She shook her head like reality was beating down the door she wouldn't answer. "If we ever had to run, what would happen?"

"I'd carry her," I replied.

She raised her head, like she hadn't quite heard what I'd said.

"Lyla is important to me," I said honestly. "She's a child, but she's shown me kindness I really don't deserve. And she's the only reason I'm still here. She stood up for me." I shrugged. "I'd do everything I could to save her."

Chemistry sat quietly for a moment. Though I meant every word, I had strung a delicate melody of words together to hopefully touch Chem's heart. It seemed to be working as her puzzled gaze met mine.

"You would protect Lyla?"

"Of course I would. She's a child, a sick one. There's no reason not to protect her. However, Lyla and I have come to know each other well these last few weeks."

"I see," she said.

"You know, I can protect all of you."

"Your leg's broken." Her attitude had suddenly returned, but I was determined to soften Chemistry. She was the eldest sister, and she set the tone for my treatment here. If I was able to tap into her sensitive side, then things would be a little better for me here.

"That's true. However, I can still wield a gun, and a knife. I'm a general, I've been through some thick training as a young soldier."

"So, you mean you'd train us?"

"The sooner you guys can get me some crutches, the sooner I can help you all protect yourselves better during this invasion. We can fortify the house, even make it an impenetrable fortress." I was lying about the house, but I could at least train the girls. All of them were more than capable of wielding a weapon with some practice.

She thought for a moment, sweeping long dreadlocks over her shoulders to reveal her beauty. Chemistry reminded me a lot of Keoni. Her strength and determination, while still having a heart made her a Keoni replica. My lieutenant was the best soldier I'd ever met. I could fight by Keoni's side or fight for her, and I felt like Chemistry had the potential to be just like her. She just needed a little refining, but she'd make a great soldier.

Chemistry had a strong physique already. Strong legs, a tight core, and muscular arms, but she had a soft face that was womanly and girly at the same time. She was nice to look at, and her sisters loved her, and I knew why. Though Chemistry was not fond of me, her smile was contagious, and her gentle demeanor with her sisters was something to relish. She definitely was a mom, but she was certainly an older sister. Responsible, dependable, a mediator; she was good to her sisters, despite how tiring it may have been for her.

There were nights when I found Chemistry standing watch for the house and never getting a wink of sleep. The girls had no idea their sister kept watch over them, but since I was staying in the living room, I saw her every few nights coming to stand guard. Initially, I thought it was the invasion that had Chemistry spooked. But Lyla and Chem had mentioned once that there were monsters out there. I'd even heard Coco sneaking into Kingsley's room because she was afraid of the monsters outside. And Kingsley and Chemistry began to share secret conversations more after a grocery haul.

I was curious about the monsters. I hadn't had any updates about the status of the world outside since I came here. No one watches the news, no one goes out unless they have to, and they certainly don't tell me about their findings. But now, with Chemistry seemingly interested in my offer to train them, I might be able to find out more about these monsters.

"Wouldn't it be good to worry a little less about your sisters if they know how to protect themselves? If every time

41

you went on a supply run, you knew the house was protected and Lyla too?"

She shifted in her chair, and I could tell the offer was getting to her.

"Come on, Chemistry. Let's be realistic. I've heard you all talking about monsters out there. You'll need a fortified house, *and* everyone will need to know how to defend themselves if there are monsters out there, right?"

"*If?*" She scowled. "*If* there are monsters? You have no idea what's out there."

I tried to remain neutral. "I've been in here. Last thing I knew there was an invasion."

"Yeah, well you made it just in time."

"What?"

"You ever wonder why we never show the news or play the television? Because if Coco sees those things one more time, she'll freak out. It was hard enough getting her not to scare Lyla. We had to hold her down in the back of the car until she stopped screaming before we came inside."

I was lost for words, just staring at her. Monsters? There was no way there were monsters running around out there. Dead bodies lying around? Sure. Badly burned or bruised bodies, definitely. But monsters? There was no way.

"And poor Lyla," Chemistry started again, "she'd have a fit and we wouldn't be able to calm her down for weeks."

"What do you mean by monsters?"

Chemistry looked like she would vomit as she doubled over. It was like her own memories were churning a sickness in her belly as she stared blankly at the floor. I was beginning to feel fearful even though I didn't know if I could believe her. But why would she lie? And her reaction, what was that for if there weren't actually any monsters?

"They're like creatures you only see in movies. Not even the best CGI or makeup could create the horror that's out there." She stopped, like one more word would break her. Taking a deep breath, she began again. "They're called the 'Awakened' on the radio, but most folk call them the 'Wrongs.'"

"The Awakened? What's that mean?"

She shivered and took her time formulating her words. It was like she didn't want to say it. "Some reports have said that people are coming back to life."

"You're kidding me, right?" I laughed. "They have a word for that, you know? It starts with a 'Z'—it's in way too many sci-fi shows and books these days." I laughed again, but Chem couldn't lift her eyes from the floor, and I realized she'd seen one.

"You're not kidding. You've seen one of these things?"

Chemistry nodded. She looked as delicate as a flower as she trembled in her chair. All this time, she'd been fighting her own memories, trying to stay alert, trying to keep watch, while also grateful for the lack of sleep. Staying awake meant she didn't have to relive her nightmares.

"They're horrifying. Decaying skin, broken bones but they keep moving. The only thing that stops them is a bullet to the head."

"And what do they do?"

"They chase you, and if you're caught," she swallowed loudly, "they eat you."

Jerking back into the couch, I gripped the blankets. Man eating monsters running around with decaying flesh and broken bones?

"But that's not the worst part," she interrupted my thoughts. Her eyes were connected to mine now with a fierce yet fearful gaze. "They bite you, and then you turn into a Wrong. You are awakened."

"Chemistry—" I cut myself off when I noticed Kingsley standing in the doorway passing glances between us. I'm not sure what kind of expressions we were making, but I'm sure the tense silence between us alone forced the question out of her.

"What's going on?"

"Nothing," Chemistry said shakily.

"We're talking about the Wrongs," I said. I wanted her reaction, to see if Chemistry was lying. It was just so hard to believe, but when Kingsley dropped the plate in her hand, I knew it was real. She began to tremble in the doorway, wrapping her arms around herself in a tight hug to stop the shaking.

"What is wrong with you?" Chem said hotly.

"I needed to know if it was real."

"You think I'd lie about that!? People are dying, Claudius! We're scared to death while you sit propped on the couch thinking we're lying!"

"No," I waved my hand, "it's just hard to believe! I'm here, inside all day. Don't you think it would be hard to believe if you've never seen them?"

"I do," Kingsley agonized. "I... I didn't believe it at first either when Chemistry came running back into the store when she couldn't find Coco. She's always the getaway driver since it's safer for her to be in the car than rushing through the crowds of people. But when we finally found the car, Coco was hiding in the backseats weeping like a child. We couldn't get any sense out of her."

"Coco saw one first?"

"Yes," she answered as Chemistry turned away from me. I wasn't sure if she was still angry or she just hated talking about the wrongs. "But it didn't take long for us to see them either. They rushed into the crowd, screeching and flailing. Jumping onto people and biting them. We drove off immediately, but the broadcasters on the radio were saying that the wrongs had the ability to change whoever they bit."

"How did this happen?" I sighed worriedly. There was a knot in my belly that was sickening as I wondered about Keoni. I wanted to jump to my feet and race to find her, but I didn't even have a place to start. I'd told Keoni to go to the cabin and wait for me. If I didn't show up in three days, I told her to head to Washington. But what now? What if she couldn't get there? What if she'd been bitten?

"They say that people just dropped dead, and then they came back in an aggressive manner to be the creatures they called the Awakened," Kingsley explained.

"People dropped dead? What does that mean? What does any of this mean?"

"Keep your voice down," Chemistry snapped. "I don't want the other two hearing us."

I nodded as I took a calming breath. Kingsley was still holding herself as she looked at me. Her eyes were easy on me, not forceful like her older sister's.

"People, out of the blue, just began to fall dead. But it wasn't just any people."

"Who were they?" I asked, thankful for more useful information.

"They were pastors, church goers. People who identified with the Christian faith. But not every one of them dropped dead. Only some of them," Kingsley said.

Chemistry looked uncomfortable as she added, "They're calling it the Biblical Rapture."

My brows lowered. I'd heard of that before. When I was a child, my mom was a devout Catholic, and my father a Christian. He always said that we needed to stay ready for the return of Jesus, the Messiah of Christianity. Unfortunately, my parents passed long ago, when I was still a wayward kid, and I never stopped being wayward. But those biblical stories were just things our parents told us to keep us in line. There was no Rapture, no Jesus. Just the world and all its nature… right?

"The Rapture," I muttered.

"You've heard of it?" Chemistry asked.

"Yeah, but I don't know if this is it."

"Tell us what you know," she urged.

46

"Well, just that the Messiah of Christianity would return. He'd take the people who followed all His commands. There was something about, two in a field, and one would go missing or disappear. I don't remember anymore."

"I studied religions, Christianity included," Chemistry said. "We only spoke of the Rapture briefly though, so I'm not familiar with it."

We all stayed quiet as thoughts of a possible 'rapture' could be happening, or already happened.

"What else could explain this phenomenon, then?" Kingsley asked.

"I don't know. But I'm certain these creatures weren't mentioned in the Bible," I answered.

"Maybe not, but that doesn't mean it's not happening," Chemistry said gruffly.

The silence stretched on a little longer as we sat there. Was it possible that my parents had been right? Was the Bible actually true? Had the Rapture happened, and those who were called away came back to life? Soulless beings running around eating other people. Even if all of this was true, why are these things eating people? And why are they coming back to life?

5

Claudius

"Hey," Kingsley said as she entered the living room. I was mid-bite when I tried to manage a greeting. She laughed lightly as she took a seat on a folding chair across from me.

"I came to check on you, since Coco took Lyla to bed, and Chemistry is cleaning up."

"Check on me?"

She shrugged, pushing her long bangs out of her face. "You seemed a little shaken up after we told you about the wrongs. I just thought I'd say something on my way to bed."

That's when I noticed her apparel for the first time. A loosely tied lavender robe hung over her thick frame. Kingsley was the color of caramel with a little extra pudge on her belly and in all the right places. With her robe so badly tied, I got a glimpse of her full chest, and heavy thighs, which I'm certain she wanted me to see.

King was mostly quiet, always following behind Chemistry to get things done. However, I hadn't noticed her beyond that, or any of the girls really. Except Chemistry because she reminded me so much of my fiancée.

King adjusted in the chair, with the small lantern I used when everyone was asleep sitting behind her. It gave off a small orange glow since it was only battery operated, but that was enough to give her an ambient backlight that accentuated her curvy figure. Though I'd always referred to these four sisters as girls, Kingsley and Chemistry certainly were not. And if I'd had any uncertainties, Kingsley was here to prove her womanhood.

"Well," I finally said after letting my eyes trace over her frame, "I appreciate you stopping by."

She gave me a stiff smile, like she didn't like that I was cutting our time short. I was engaged. I had, in part, caused this entire invasion over the love of my life. Not to mention… we were being invaded and there were monsters running around. Who had time for new developments in the love department? I needed to hurry up and get better so that I could go find Keoni, that was all I was focused on.

"We haven't talked much before now," Kingsley said, extending her stay. "Tell me a little about yourself, general."

My rank rolled off her tongue in a purr. Kingsley was a beautiful woman, and if I didn't already have plans to get hitched, and the world wasn't in chaos, I might've considered Kingsley as a woman I was interested in.

"What do you want to know?" I asked.

"I don't know, tell me anything."

"Well, you already know I grew up in a Christian and

Catholic home. You know I'm a Major General." I shrugged. "Not much else to know."

She nodded. "Well, general, there's not much to my story either. Chem and I share the same mother, but Lyla and Coco have different moms. We all share the same father though."

"Lyla mentioned something like that once."

"She's always blabbing about everything," she chuckled.

I continued to munch on my sandwich as Kingsley's eyes dropped to the floor. She was suddenly looking discouraged and worried.

"King," I said carefully, "is something wrong?"

"We're out of water."

I stopped chewing and stared at her. The house had been functioning perfectly fine for the past three weeks since the invasion started. I'd overheard Chemistry telling Coco not to worry when the water ran cold a few times. She said something about well water, and I figured we were fine. Even if the water got cold because the electricity went out, there was a wood burning stove in the house, we could just heat everything on there, and use candles at night. But now I'm wondering if there was ever even a well. And if there was a well, how could it be drained already? Wells last families a lifetime. How could it be dried up or out of water?

"What are you talking about?"

"We've been using our water supply to keep the toilets working, to cook, to bathe, to clean. But we don't have any more water."

"Isn't there a well here? There's plenty of water."

"The power stopped working today. It's been spotty, and we've been able to survive, but with it completely off now, our water supply is gone. We'll use the well reservoir before the week is out, and with no electricity, the pumps won't bring the water to us."

"We need to leave, right now." I pulled the blankets back, and carefully moved my leg to the floor.

"What? Why do we need to leave?"

"Because the power's out."

"I know, but—"

Snapping my vision to her, King looked thoroughly confused. Taking a breath, I tried to explain calmly. "If the power is out, that means something, or someone *caused* the power to go out. Like when trees go down and pull power lines, this is the same thing. Something has moved in and disrupted the power grid. That can be anything from those monsters to the next phase of the invasion." I shook my head, honestly preferring the monsters over another invasion phase. "But all that matters is the threat has reached us, and if we don't move now, then we'll be too late."

"How can you be so sure?"

"Because we've been fine all this time. Now we're not. We need to move."

King sat still on the chair, like she thought this home would seriously be their safe haven forever.

"Chemistry!" I shouted as I reached for my makeshift crutches. I'd put together a second crutch while I sat on the couch for three weeks. "Chemistry!" I shouted again.

Her shoes echoed through the house quickly as she stomped into the front room from the darkness with anger all over her face. "What is your—"

"We need to move. Get a bag, put food and canned goods inside. Pack up water, and medicine, bandages, clothes, blankets, and get the other two ready."

"What are you talking about?"

I struggled, gripping the makeshift crutches as I stood from the couch. I was used to using them since I would visit the bathroom frequently but getting off the couch was always hard.

"Kingsley told me that the power's out. Means something's going on and we need to move before we find out whatever it is."

Chemistry looked cross as she glared at Kingsley who wouldn't raise her head. "It's literally the middle of the night, we can't leave now."

"Either we leave now," I said harshly, "or we stay long enough to find out what caused the power outage."

With closed eyes and a deep breath, Chemistry finally nodded. "Alright," she said, looking me over, "but we're not slowing down for you."

"You don't need to. I'll be fine."

"King, go wake Coco up and start packing up."

Slowly, King stood, and I'm certain Chemistry noticed her lacy attire from the raised brow she had, but she chose to say nothing. When Kingsley had disappeared into the darkness of the house, Chemistry folded her arms and said, "We had a deal."

"And I intend to keep it. But I can't if I'm dead."

"So, this is about you?"

"No, it's about Lyla."

Her tightlipped expression softened, and she dropped her arms as I explained, "If we leave now, we can walk at a pace that won't cause Lyla any trouble. But if we stay and wait for daylight, we're now a day closer to another attack or whatever is coming."

"I... I didn't know you cared that much."

"Believe it or not, I care about all four of you."

A heartbeat of silenced pass before the shock on her face melted into a defeated look. Lips pressed into a line, brows almost furrowed, Chemistry was lost for words at my sudden admission. It wasn't meant to be anything more than it was, but after spending three weeks here, I can admit that these girls were growing on me, despite the distance we all had.

"Thank you, Claudius."

"Don't thank me until we're out of here and have found another safe place to hunker down."

She nodded before turning to leave.

The car wasn't an option. It was conveniently sporting a flat tire. King explained that on the last trip with Chemistry, they drove over some glass and burst a tire. Their plan for the next supply run was to steal a new car, or a tire, whichever was easier, however, plans were now changed. We didn't have time to find a car or repair this one. We needed to move.

When we were ready, I took the backpack of canned goods and water bottles, and the shotgun, while Chemistry carried Lyla on her back, and King and Coco partnered up. We knew the darkness would scare Lyla, so she kept her hood up and promised to keep her eyes closed. But it didn't matter once we stepped outside. With no streetlights, and no traffic, just my little lantern, you couldn't tell if your eyes were opened or closed.

I could feel my eyes peeling back as I limped on my crutches through the night. We'd lost the element of surprise since my hobbling echoed through the quiet streets. Unfortunately, there just wasn't much I could do about the amount of noise I was making. We needed to get to safety fast, because the city smelled like smoke, and that could only mean that the second phase of the invasion had begun. We'd be found pretty quickly since we're such a large group, moving clumsily and slowly. I was worried, but I tried not to think about it and just stayed focused on moving.

Invasions are never just a matter of running in and taking over as the media and movies portray them. There are phases, there's planning, there's more death than anyone talks about. Invasions were horrific, I knew because I'd planned and participated in several invasions of small villages or remote cities when I was deployed.

We always had the scare phase, which was the initial invasion. The point of taking over a place is not to kill the inhabitants, but to establish your presence as the new authority. Then you moved into the second phase where you seize all the spoil you can from the places left empty and barren. And finally, of course, with control of so much of the city that'd been left behind by the occupants, you now have enough ground in that territory to claim it. That's how invasions are supposed to go, however, with people who are not here for dominance but for blood, none of the rules of an invasion matter.

The most important thing to remember when taking over a place is your motive. Why are you going to uproot people from their homes? Why are you going to take over a place where bodies lie asleep in their graves, dreaming of their past? Why are you going to cause casualties?

When your answers to these questions are rooted in something other than dominance and/or vengeance, then you can begin planning. While I can't say an invasion is good or bad, since I've only considered them missions—and with a mission it's us or the enemy—I do believe that an invasion rooted in a motive that has nothing to do with vengeance is an easier pill to swallow.

Unfortunately for the US, no one has come here to take back what we stole from them. No one has flooded our country because we wronged them. This invasion is China's long awaited final act. If they could eliminate—not beat—the strongest country in the world, then they would reign supreme, showcasing their abilities to the rest of the world.

With a country as massive as China doubling in power,

everyone else would have no chance but to submit to them. Who could win against China backed with the power of the US? No one. But all hope is not lost yet, at least I don't believe so. Though the smoke burned my eyes as we walked, and the silence threatened to make me scream just to hear something other than my hobbling, China was only as strong as the US was weak. If we held our forces, called our men back from Taiwan and whoever was left as an ally to fight with us, this battle could be won.

No matter what, I refused to believe America would not win.

My patriotism was all I could hold on to. I was embarrassed to even believe America would win after allowing Springfield to go up in flames.

I had no choice, I criticized. *I love Keoni, and I couldn't let her get killed.*

Thinking of my fiancée always made my heart stir. Now, I was grateful for that surge of energy she brought me. Thoughts of Keoni always kept me focused on the couch, plotting and planning an escape to find her when I was better. Now though, the thoughts would keep me motivated. Keep me from lagging behind when the pain was too much. Her smiling face would even keep me from dying. I had to stay alive to see her again, even if it was just to tell her the truth about the invasion instead of letting her live with the explanation I'd left in a letter for her.

As we continued to move in search of a new hideout, my leg blared with pain. It ached every time I moved, but I had to keep going. With the mounting stress of seeing one of those creatures, the silent burning of the city, and the slow group I was traveling with, my leg was the least of my concerns. I could grin and bear it for as long as I needed if it meant keeping us alive.

I slowed my pace when I spotted a light in the distance. It was coming from a house, a single window with a light shining in the darkness.

"What is it?" I recognized the voice as Kingsley's as she came and stood beside me. Holding up my dim lantern, she stepped into the light, squinting like it was the brightest light ever. In this darkness, it probably was.

"You see that? Straight ahead." I pointed.

"A light. Someone's home."

"Could be an enemy too."

"What do we do?" she asked as the others approached.

Turning with my crutch, I held the light up as Chemistry and Coco gathered. Chemistry had a flashlight too in case we got too far ahead and she couldn't follow the light of my lantern. Letting Lyla down for a moment, I saw her rubbing her shoulders out and I knew she was getting tired.

"What's going on?" Chem asked as she exhaled heavily.

"There's a house up there, but we don't know if they're friendly. And we can't go much further like this. You're tired," I said to Chemistry.

It was hard to make out her features beneath the little light, but I knew from the hiss in her voice that she was frowning. "I'm not tired."

"It doesn't matter. King, can you carry Lyla until we get to the house?"

"Yeah," she said but Chemistry cut her off.

"*King?* Since when did you two get so close?"

"We don't have time for this," I threw a hand open dramatically. "*Kingsley*," I said, "can you carry Lyla?" I held the lantern closer to Chemistry who was indeed sporting a frown and I snapped, "Happy now?"

"Guys," Kingsley called, "this is not the time for this."

"We're all just tired," Coco said quietly. She was standing close to Chemistry, so I could see the young sister with a frightened look in her eyes.

"Come on, we shouldn't stand here for too much longer. Let's move."

Kingsley took Lyla, but Chemistry still held the rear as Coco followed right behind me now. It was a journey to the house, further than I anticipated, but we didn't break again, which made the walk faster.

Gathering close to the house, I pulled the shotgun from over my shoulders and passed it to Coco. She traded with me, exchanging the pump for a semi-automatic handgun. I still needed to cling to my crutch, so a pistol worked better. I'd only carried the pump because it was heavier than the two pistols we had. In total there were three guns and a hunting knife.

Coco had the shotgun since she was smaller and probably couldn't win in hand-to-hand combat. I now had a pistol, and whoever had Lyla got the other pistol. Since Kingsley was carrying her, she had it, but I wanted her to keep it. Chemistry seemed tough enough on her own without a weapon, so she held on to the hunting knife. Whenever my leg got better, I'd keep the hunting knife so the girls would have more protection.

"Alright, when we get to the top of the stairs, Coco, you blow the handle off, and I step inside and fire. Coco follows behind me, and then Chemistry. Kingsley, you're the last one to come inside with Lyla, but try to keep her quiet, alright?"

"I'm scared," Lyla whined as she clasped her hands tightly around Kingsley.

"It'll be fine." I tried to comfort her, but my voice was coming out rigid. We didn't have time for fear or for reluctancy, we had to move.

"I don't want Coco going in next," Chemistry opposed, "she's too young."

"She's got a shotgun," I shrugged, "she'll be fine."

"I should be going in with you," she demanded.

"We need a line of defense to protect Lyla. Kingsley has to carry her *and* try to shoot; it'll be easier if you're there."

She had a rebuttal ready, but Acoye spoke up and said, "I'm fine, Chemi, I can do this."

All of us gathered around the light looked over at Coco. She was the quietest out of the four of them, and her small frame honestly worried me. But, for now, we just needed to get inside.

"She said she's fine." I looked over at Chemistry who still looked worried. She finally gave in with a reluctant nod. "Stay close," I said. "I'm turning out the lantern, so they won't see us coming. But it's a straight shot up the stairs and to the

59

door." As I raised the lantern to turn it off, I saw the sisters gripping hands. With my heart pumping in anxiety, I clicked out the lantern, and turned for the door.

I hobbled until I slowed and began feeling for the stairs with my crutch. I inched closer until I found the stairs, tucking my crutches under my arm, I hopped up the stairs. When I felt the top, I stood by the door and waited until I felt Coco's small hands patting me as she felt for me in the darkness. I waited until she patted my shoulder, signaling that everyone was there and ready.

"When you're ready," I whispered to her.

Clutching my sleeve with her free hand, she moved around me to stand in front. I felt along the door, running into her hand, and guided it down to the knob. "It's a blind shot," I whispered, "but you can do it."

She stayed silent an extra moment, and I could hear her hand touching the knob.

"Stand back."

Obeying her order, I hobbled back.

One pump and the gun fired.

She missed.

She fired again and missed. But there were two holes in the door now, and no one had come to the door yet.

"Hold on," I patted her shoulder. Passing her my pistol, I unclamped the lantern from my hip and clicked it on.

"What are you doing?" Chemistry snapped.

"No one's answered, and it's dark inside," I held up the light to the two holes in the door. There was no light piercing through.

"Have we been caught?"

"I don't think so," I said as I glanced around. "Take another shot, Coco. I'll keep the lantern on this time."

She obliged and passed me back the pistol before raising the gun and shooting off the doorknob. Clipping the lantern back to my hip, I passed my second crutch to Chemistry. Going in on two crutches with a pistol would be too difficult.

Carefully, I pushed past the door and hopped inside, aiming my gun. It looked like there'd been some kind of struggle. A table was knocked over and so were all the chairs. And it reeked of the old food sitting on the floors. I kept moving through the house, spotting a lantern in a window. It must've been the light we'd seen that brought us here. Around the corner was a flight of stairs. There was a stench coming from up there, it was strong like whatever died up there had been dead for a while.

"What's that smell?" Coco whispered behind me.

"A person or an animal is dead up there."

"We shouldn't go up there," Chemistry said.

"Why? We need to clear the whole place?" I fired back.

"If it's safe down here, then let's just stay down here. I don't want to go up there and find dead bodies."

"Well, I don't want there to be someone upstairs who finds us and kills us through the night."

"Then we'll do posts," she offered, and I knew that was her final offer.

With a worried sigh, I agreed. "I'll do the first shift."

61

6

Keoni

"A silence exchange?" I asked as I sat on the floor of the gymnasium. We'd been in this school for three weeks, camping out in the gymnasium, eating food from the cafeteria fridge. We went down to smaller rations last week when the power went out. Now, we're down to canned vegetables, and a few bottles of water. We've decided to leave soon, and take whatever leftover supplies we have with us.

"Yeah," Zion said. He was sitting next to me, head against the wall, a grim expression on his face. Last night, when our small team of four soldiers decided we'd leave tomorrow, Zion asked if he could speak with me privately. He said he'd been wanting to talk about something since we'd gotten here, and he didn't want to leave without first having a word. Little did I know it had to do with Jensen.

I sat quietly, wondering what the phrase, 'a silence exchange' meant. Someone had murdered Jensen and left him in my bed with that phrase carved into the wall above him. But why? They'd slashed his jaw and taped his mouth closed, claiming they were exchanging his death for my silence.

What did I know that needed to be kept quiet? What did Jensen have to do with this? I sighed as I came up short with ideas. The only thing, or person, I could tie any of this to was Ollie. The day before the explosion at headquarters, he was acting strangely. And then he was accused of helping the Red Dragons, a terrorist group that had been more myth than truth. But it didn't make sense. Someone killed Jensen as a silence exchange. Someone knew about Jensen and me, but who? And why would they kill him?

The letter sitting in my back pocket was burning now. I hadn't looked at it since Ollie gave it to me, didn't really have the time at first. Pulling it out now, I stared at the folded piece of paper in my hand. I remembered the fear in his eyes, but he'd also worn a knowing look that almost overshadowed the fear, like he knew something about the interrogation.

Since I'd woken up in that hospital after the explosion and the invasion began, I've come to my senses. I spent months idolizing a relationship with an old fling while the world fell apart around me. Now there was blood on my hands, Jensen's blood. He may have been my ex-boyfriend, but his life was not due to me. And yet because I'd chosen to blindly love Ollie, my hands were smeared with the blood of Jensen. But Claudius was the one smearing the blood on them.

I don't hate him in the slightest, but I remember these haunting feelings, ones I'd suppressed when I was reunited with Ollie. We spent a year apart because our relationship was dangerous. We were almost found out, almost lost our jobs, and had let important matters go under the radar because we weren't focused.

When I almost lost my job, I began to harbor a deep sense of regret regarding Claudius. I nearly hated that I loved him beyond passion. So I left. I ran away. I got far enough away to breathe on my own. But the first chance I got to let his love become my oxygen again, I found myself putting an O2 mask on.

Now, after reality set in and Jensen was gone because I'd pushed him away, those dark feelings of regret and distaste for Ollie had worked their way into my mind again. But I couldn't ignore the fact that the darkness was mostly misdirected hatred at my fiancée instead of myself.

America had been invaded. There were monsters running around. Things that kept me up at night for the first week. Every time I closed my eyes, I saw Poyer bending and breaking into one of those creatures. A wrong.

I'd heard the radio calling the creatures wrongs. Something about the dead's second life, or rather, the great awakening. I didn't have time to focus on Ollie anymore. I had three soldiers and a country depending on me to stop letting love and emotions rule my life. But that was all easier said than done.

Holding the letter in my hand, I wanted everything I'd thought until now about Ollie to stick. But my heart fluttered between anger and desperation. I loved Claudius more than I should. I didn't know how to find a healthy balance between loving him and everything else. So, I always chose to lock him

65

out of my life. But now, with the distance, the uncertainties, I was second guessing myself.

"What's that?" Zion asked beside me, pulling me from my worrying.

"It's a letter that I think will explain things."

"Who is the letter from?"

I paused. "My fiancée."

"What would he know?"

I paused again, hating the words I spoke, "I don't know. And that's what scares me the most."

"What are you going to do?" Zion was sitting forward now, eyes lifting from the paper in my hand to meet my gaze. Tan skin and short chocolate waves that were almost curls sat awkwardly on Zion. His hair was a little too short while equally a little too long as it began to grow over his ears.

"I'm not sure yet."

"You should read it." He carefully strung the anxious words together with his cool demeanor. However, his wide eyes told another story.

Sighing, I leaned my head against the wall and stared ahead for a moment. "This letter could contain incriminating information."

"Why do you say that?"

"The day before my fiancée gave me this letter something strange happened. He asked me a hypothetical question."

Zion nodded in my peripheral.

"He asked me…" I paused to recall Ollie's words. "If you had to save the world or the person you loved the most, what would you do? And he told me that everything he was doing was to save me. The next day, a woman entered headquarters and accused him of having knowledge about the war China would bring to America. When he refuted her, the whole place blew up."

"I remember seeing the smoke from my house," he added. "But he's passed away now. So, even if it's criminal information, no one can charge him with anything."

"No." I bit my lip, forcing my eyes to lock with his. "The man you found in my bed was my ex-boyfriend. We broke up when I got engaged to someone else."

Zion tried to hold in his surprise, but his tightlipped smile only made it more noticeable.

I shook my head, brushing off the finer details as I continued, "My fiancée gave me this letter before he was accused of knowing about this invasion. What if he knew? What if he chose to do nothing for America?"

The air around us became rigid and stale. I could feel Zion's uncertainty pouring from every single pore and hair follicle on his body. There were no words to be said as the weighty moment stirred. I'd told Ollie that I would save him too, but now, I'm afraid that maybe that was the wrong thing to say. What if I'm the reason the country is falling apart?

Taking a breath, I began to unfold the letter as Zion called, "Hold on. We need to decide what to do with the information in that letter."

"I'm not incriminating my fiancée," I said sourly.

"That letter is technically evidence—"

67

"Evidence of what? He could be telling me how much he loved me." I shifted to see him cowering now at my tone and I sighed. "Let me read it first."

"And if there's information in there that can help us fight back—then what?"

"Then we find someone to tell. But I won't let them know who I got the information from."

He moved after a moment of silence, cramming a hand into his pocket. Zion pulled out a few name patches.

"I killed my comrade by accident." He lifted the name patches with a shaky hand, and I recognized the name on top as Gabriel Reyes. He and Zion were close at bootcamp. "I took these nametags to make sure no one tried to pretend to be one of them, but, if there's vital information, I'm willing to give you a nametag to save your fiancée."

"What? No." I pushed his hand away. "We never blame our comrades."

"We have to," he urged. "No one will believe you simply heard that info down the grapevine. Everyone will assume you were part of the operation too if you don't tell the truth."

"This information wouldn't even be available to privates. And I can't do that, not to them, and not to you either, Zion."

He was trembling as he sniffled. Possibly incriminating Ollie was one thing, but falsely accusing our fallen comrades was another thing entirely. I was interested in knowing how he accidentally killed his comrade, but with Chinese soldiers running around in our uniforms, I was certain he wasn't the only one who made that mistake.

"Let me just read it first, okay?"

"Okay," he said.

With sweaty hands and a rapidly beating heart, I slowly unfolded the letter and began to read.

Keoni,

This letter isn't a confession. You already know that I love you. You know that I'd do anything to be with you, and these last few months have been the best in my entire life. Reuniting with you brought me a happiness I wanted to box up and save forever. I could forsake all the joys of life if it meant spending one day in love with you. I've treasured you for so long now, but to save you, I had to let you go.

What I'm about to tell you may scare you or anger you, but trust me, the decision wasn't taken lightly, though it was easy. What you do with this letter is up to you. You can turn it in as evidence or hold on to it for a keepsake. I won't hold anything against you no matter what you decide. Though, if you're reading this by now, you probably already know the situation and I'm in custody or I'm dead.

Last night, you told me that you fell in love with me a while ago. It sealed our fate. Though, I'd chosen to save you the moment Vice Admiral Ping Zhao told me America would be invaded. When he stormed from that meeting and I chased after him, he told me about the terrorist group, The Red Dragons.

We were led to believe it was just an old Chinese legend. No one knew it was real because there was only one report of followers of the Red Dragon attacking officials in Hong Kong. That was over fifty years ago, and it just seemed like a bunch of cult people angry over taxes. Nothing major.

They're in our land, in our jobs, in our uniforms. And what's worse, they have allies. The Red Dragons have gone undetected for so long because they've been watching everyone all along. Admiral Zhao knew about us. He knew how important you are to me and played on that.

He asked me to do the most despicable thing as a soldier: let him walk *free though I knew he was a traitor… and I did.*

I betrayed our beautiful country, our comrades—innocent people—just to save you. If I'd spoken a single word, your life would have been taken. In exchange for my silence, your life and my life would be spared.

I didn't tell you the truth to protect you, Keoni. Zhao said there are measures in place to keep me from acting out. Which I took it as there are people in place to harm you or kill you in exchange for my silence. My silence was your insurance. Your life was spared.

I was afraid you'd want to go to the authorities if I told you. I was afraid that measures would be taken against you to make sure you stayed silent too. So, I didn't tell you the truth.

I'm sorry, Keoni.

Hopefully, you'll forgive me, but I understand if you can't. That doesn't change my feelings for you, and it never will.

My only request is that you get to safety.

Washington, the White House, that's safety. No matter how long it takes. As long as the invasion rages, that means our capital hasn't been taken over. And that means you still have a chance to make it there and get real help. Tell them about The Red Dragons, tell everyone that this invasion has been planned for years. Just make it, Keoni. Survive. If for no other reason, survive because we always come back to each other.

I love you so much, Keoni Banks. My future wife, Mrs. Keoni Saint-Olliare.

We'll still make it happen, one way or another, unless I'm dead. Sorry, that was a little morbid.

I've mapped out a way for you to get to Washington from Missouri. Get to Charleston first, and from there get to the Cairo Ohio River Bridge and follow the Ohio River to West Virginia.

71

Find Fort Boreman Park to find Highway Fifty. It'll take you to Winchester, where you can pass the Shenandoah River. That river will guide you as far as the Potomac River, which will bring you to Theodore Roosevelt Island. After that it gets easy, find the Lock Keeper's House. It's on Constitution Avenue, which is right across the street from the White House. You've got top secret clearance, Kiki, don't forget that.

Don't save anyone. Don't risk your life. Get to Washington and hopefully, I'll meet you there.

With love,
Ollie.

I didn't cry. I just blinked as the information clicked into place. As I tried to wrap my brain around Jensen's death being a gift from these guys. The Red Dragons had watched me long enough to know that I'd been bouncing between Jensen and Ollie, with a preference for Ollie. They killed Jensen as an exchange for my silence. Freedom from that relationship. His death was my insurance. Or maybe they killed him as a warning.

A warning that they knew everything about me, and everything about Ollie. A preemptive measure taken against me to ensure my silence. And all this was done because Ollie had been pegged.

Zhao backed him into a corner, dangling my life above him as if it was something to play with. Claudius had done what he could to save me, and after reading his letter and finding out the truth, the dark feelings towards my future husband softened a little.

"Lieutenant?"

I looked up from the note to find Zion just sitting there. He was waiting to know more, but I couldn't speak yet. I was still clutching the paper.

Taking a breath, I pried my fingers from it, and passed it to him. His eyes darted across the paper quickly. He gasped and leaned closer to read with heavy brows and focused eyes.

"He... He knew there would be an invasion?" Zion lowered the paper. "My fiancée is out there! This is your fault!" In a moment's flicker, Zion was on his feet and heading for the door.

"Wait a second!" I hollered as I scrambled to my feet. "Zion, please wait!" He continued walking and I shouted, "You would've saved her too! You told me you sent her to your parents' house to keep her safe! You would've saved Abigail and your future daughter."

He stood there facing the door with the letter clutched in his hands. Looking over his shoulder, he said calmly, "No, I would've saved my country."

Then he opened the door and left.

7

Roll Up And Seal The Word Of The Scroll
Zion

I stood outside the gymnasium, and I could hear the Lieutenant Colonel sniffling on the other side of the door. She was in a tight spot. Her ex-boyfriend had been killed because of her ongoing relationship with the man who knew about the invasion.

Major General Claudius Saint-Olliare, Banks had mentioned him once or twice since we'd been here. I didn't know that was her fiancée though. She always seemed so professional when she talked about him. Calling him her superior, wanting to meet up with him for orders. But I guess that was all a lie. She didn't want to meet up with him for orders, she wanted to meet up with him because he was her lover.

Abigail was out there, somewhere, all because Claudius had chosen to save the colonel. Could I really blame him though? If I'd stayed behind with Abigail, I could be there with her right now, protecting her. But when I had the chance to stay by her side, I didn't take it. I wanted to be out there, fighting beside Gabby like we promised we would. I found my loyalty was to the United States Army, and not in the arms of my fiancée.

How could things have turned out like this? Me choosing the military instead of Abigail… but I guess there's a flipside to every coin.

You choose to save the one you love, and America falls. You choose America and leave your loved one to survive on their own. I've lived one half of that coin, Keoni the other half, and neither side is pretty.

Letting innocent people die, for one life, was it fair? But if you countered that, and asked if the life of your loved one was a fair offer in return for people who'd never even say thank you, what would you say? What would America say? Would she even protect my fiancée? Would America go out of her way to make sure that my loved one was saved? No… no one would, except for me, and I cheated Abigail of that. Yet, I feel so betrayed by the general that he and Keoni, who were examples to us privates of forsaking the life and love we knew, for the life of an American soldier, had broken that code of conduct. He chose her and not us…

I was so confused. I was so angry. But I understood. Regretful and ashamed, but still there was a secret part of me that was glad I chose the mission… I was lost now, broken even.

We've spent three weeks in a school that's running out of

food. We couldn't go out because there were a few of those wrongs outside of the main entrance and exit. We could've used the side doors or windows but had decided to wait it out to see if they'd leave. But it seemed like their numbers just grew the longer we waited. And all along, I was worried sick about Abigail. She could be anywhere by now.

What if one of those things had attacked her and our daughter? Then what? I didn't know if Abbey was dead or alive, but I would keep the hope in my heart and my faith in God that she was alive. I was worried about my parents too, but they had each other. I dumped Abbey on them when they knew nothing about her, and now the world was falling apart.

What have I done?

I swallowed the thought quickly; afraid I'd choke on it and weep until sunset if I dwelled on that any longer. All I could do now was try to find them, but I was in a dilemma. My team here needed me, and I needed them. Leaving to go off alone wasn't something I wanted to do. Now, I wish more than anything that I'd stayed behind with Abbey.

Never in a million decades would I have thought that creatures would be hunting humans while China hunted the US.

Sighing as I pushed off the door, I crammed Banks' letter into my pocket and headed for the cafeteria where Sam and Winston probably were. On my way there, I stopped in the chemistry room. The high school was pretty nice and was relatively intact. When we locked ourselves inside three weeks ago, there wasn't much out of order. It looked like everyone left in a rush, but there was no blood or dead bodies anywhere, thankfully.

Clicking on a burner, I watched the flame flicker to life before pulling Banks' letter out. I tore out the part of the letter that gave us directions to Washington and held the rest over the burner. No one needed to know the truth. No one needed to know that a man made a terrible mistake while it doubled as the right choice.

Choosing between saving a loved one and the world was probably scary. But every day, I struggle with wishing I'd chosen Abbey when I'd had the chance. I understood a little why Claudius had made this choice. Why he'd chosen to save the woman he loved and not the nation. It was a mistake, but it was the right thing to do in my opinion. But, that American pride, the heroic feeling of being here, fighting to protect everyone, it was birthed in me at bootcamp, swelling to the surface now. It means something to me, to do the right thing. To protect this country. I'd done wrong for so long, I felt like I needed to do this. Though, now was hardly the time for a spiritual journey.

"God tells us the future so we can change it. And sometimes, He tells us the future just to warn us."

I grunted at the words my mother had once spoken to me. Choices and decisions created our future. And when we get a glimpse into the future, we have the chance to make decisions to get us to that end goal. Or to avoid the darkness.

A sigh drew from my lips as I clicked off the burner. The paper had folded and crumpled, turning black before it crippled into grey dust.

"God," I whispered, "what do we do? I'm so lost, and scared. I've been so wrong towards You, Father, and I'm sorry. I'm sorry that it took a catastrophe to get me here, but I am begging for Your forgiveness. In Jesus' Name, I ask for forgiveness, for guidance, for help. Please," I lowered my head to the desk, "I need You."

I am with you, Zion.

My head snapped up so fast, I grabbed my neck from the aching crack it made.

"God?" I whispered as I looked around. "There's no way You just answered."

When you call upon My name with sincerity, and a true heart of repentance, I will hear you, and I will answer you.

"Repentance?"

Because you have acknowledged your sin, I can forgive you. Because you have apologized, I have opened my ears to you. Because you have called upon Me, I will remember your plea, and remember that you decided to trust Me.

There were no words coming from me. I could feel the tears gushing, but I could feel my heart throbbing like God was speaking right into it. I thought the poor thing would give out and I'd go meet my Maker right then. But there was a coolness that poured into my spirit, rushing down my spine to infiltrate my entire being, and I felt myself calming down.

"Thank You, God," I finally managed.

My son, you must move now before night falls.

Before night falls? I looked over at the clock in the classroom, it was almost five in the evening.

"Why before nightfall?"

Darkness makes weakness stronger, but the stillness makes silence a killer.

"What? God, I don't understand!"

"Zion?" I looked over my shoulder, tears still in my eyes. Lt. Banks stood in the doorway, brows knit together. "What's wrong?" she asked gently as she stepped inside.

"We've got to move before nightfall."

"Why?"

"Because..." I stopped. I didn't know how to tell her the truth... or rather *who* the truth had come from.

A lot of people believe in God, sure. But not that many *knew* Him, or even believed that God ever did anything more than just create the universe. They think He's done, that was it, and there's nothing more to Him.

"You can tell me," she said softly. "I heard you."

My eyes widened. "You heard me what?"

"Talking in here." She looked around, her hair loose from the bun she'd been keeping it in. "No one's in here. So, you must've been talking to God, right?"

"I know it sounds crazy," I started, "but I swear He responded."

"I just want to get out of here alive. I don't care who told you, or how you found out."

Swallowing, I realized Banks didn't believe me, but she was

80

desperate. Not to mention her fiancée was the reason we were all in this mess anyways.

"You have to believe me," I started, but stopped. *No, she doesn't,* I told myself. *She just needs to trust me... that's what God wants.* Riddles weren't to deter us, but to make us trust Him further, seek Him harder for understanding.

I almost laughed at this realization, but remembered Colonel Banks was nervously standing in front of me. Her strong lean frame looked weaker as she stood there, less like a soldier and more like a normal girl.

"Colonel, I can get us out of here, but you've got to trust me."

A tear rolled down her cheek as she nodded. "Ok. But what about the others?"

"They'll need some convincing, so you'll have to help me."

"What should I tell them?"

"I don't know." I shrugged. "Make up something. All I know is the riddle God gave me."

"A riddle?" She frowned.

"Yeah..." I took a breath and began to recite it. "Darkness makes weakness stronger, but the stillness makes silence a killer."

She folded her arms as she stared at the floor. She wasn't wearing her uniform jacket, and her shirt clung to her strong arms. "Darkness makes weakness stronger, but the stillness makes silence a killer. Silence..." She looked up. "The night is usually quiet, but stillness *makes* silence a killer. Wouldn't that mean we should move at night?"

I shook my head as I leaned against the table. "No, not us. He's not talking about us if we need to move before nightfall."

"The wrongs? You think God is telling you that in the dark the wrongs get stronger?" The smirk on her face died slowly as an idea blossomed in her mind.

"What is it?"

"When we first got here, I couldn't sleep. I stayed up all night, and I noticed there wasn't a sound, not even a growl or screech until the first sunlight. What if these things fall dormant at night, but sound wakes them?"

I snapped my jaw shut. "The night makes them stronger than normal, but their stillness… Dormancy." I pointed at her, and she nodded. "That makes silence deadly. Because one wrong step, a twig snapped, leaves rustled, they awaken."

"Then we need to leave now," she said sternly.

Banks was turning on her heels when I reached for her arm. "Wait," I called. She snapped around, confusion flicking over her face. "I found something, directions to Washington. I think going there with a pitstop to my parents' house would be our best bet as soldiers." I dug through my pocket and offered her the small slip of paper. She stared at it as I passed it to her, releasing her arm from my grip.

Her brown eyes studied the small paper, and there was a swirl of emotions she gated back with a firm nod. When her eyes rose to mine, Keoni Banks was gone, and only the Lieutenant Colonel remained.

"Good going, private." Her hand patted my arm, and she smiled tightly like she used to in bootcamp. Passing me back the slip of paper, she said, "We can use this to get to safety. And we can make that stop as long as we get moving now. I'll gather the others. Meet back here in fifteen minutes with your things and another copy of those directions."

"Keoni—"

She raised her hand to salute me and turned to leave the room. I think this hurt her more than anything. She wasn't angry, just broken that not only would I hold nothing against her or the general, but I was willing to treat it like it never happened, for my own good. I was protecting her and the general, and though it may hurt now, I knew the Lieutenant Colonel would appreciate my efforts later.

After rewriting the general's instructions two more times, I left the chemistry room and headed down to the gym to grab my things. Down the hall, I was trying to keep my mind focused when I was totally distracted as I passed by a classroom with the door left open. Inside, Sam was sitting on a desk, head back, and an interesting grimace on her face. But it was Winston's loud grunts and bare shoulders that sent me stumbling away from the door... too loudly.

Sam snapped her vision from her stupor and howled, "Reinhardt, you disgusting pig! Why are you spying on us?"

"I'm not! I swear!" I screamed as I tripped backwards again, then Winston burst open the door. He was holding his shirt to his lower body before snatching me up from the floor.

"What is wrong with you, Reinhardt?"

"I was just going to the gym!"

"Why'd you come this way? Most of the lights are off! Why take the dark empty hall?"

I nervously glanced around. I hadn't even noticed the lights were off. I was just rushing to make time and took the shortest route. I wanted to tell Winston this, but he was already blabbing again about me spying on him and Sam.

"I get it now." He shoved me to the floor. I rubbed my back as I got to my feet. The older man with a tense glare eyed me darkly as he said, "You like Sam too. So you're spying on us. How many times have you watched us, huh?"

Reflexively, I frowned at the statement and took a step back. It was no offense to either of them, Sam was a nice girl with freckles and a button nose, but Winston was older and scraggly. There was no amount of desperation in the world that should tempt anyone into willingly sleeping with Winston.

Looking him over, I asked, "How many times have you guys been together? The world is falling apart and you're having sex? How do you even have the energy?" I was too hungry to work up the energy for anything like that. I needed all I had for an attack or to run, like now.

"So you *do* like her," Winston cackled.

"No! I have a fiancée!"

He looked back at Sam who'd finally pulled her shirt on. Bouncing his shoulders in laughter, Winston returned his gaze to me. "So? I'm married." He shrugged. "What my wife Mary-Anne doesn't know won't kill her. Besides, Mary's safe. I sent her to one of those shelters before hitting up the armory. My mind is at peace."

"You coward." I shoved him to the floor.

He grunted as we struggled, shouting, "What is wrong with you, Reinhardt?"

"Get off of him!" Sam was yelling over my shoulder. But I was angry and jealous. Jealous that Mary-Anne was safe, and Abbey wasn't. I was angry that I was such an idiot and didn't realize there was a way to save the nation *and* the one you loved.

"Hey! Hey!" I felt strong hands pulling my shoulder, a firm grip I couldn't fight against.

I let Winston go, and backed off of him, panting heavily as I stared down at him.

"What is going on?" Lt. Col Banks demanded.

"He just attacked me!" Winston shot to his feet, jutting a hand at me as he spoke. But I wasn't sure the lieutenant was listening anymore as her raised brow and focused gaze took in Winston's mostly naked body, except the shirt he was holding against his lower half.

"Where are your clothes?" She looked over his shoulder to find Sam dressing silently and stiffly. When she understood the situation, Banks brought her vision back to me. "Why did you attack him?"

"Because he said he had a wife that was safe, and he didn't care that he was cheating on her."

"It's another man's business," Winston snapped. "Learn to mind your own."

Banks shook her head. "We're leaving in five minutes. Whoever isn't ready, isn't coming."

She turned to leave but Winston nagged behind her, "Who died and made you king? Why are we even leaving with no explanation? And since you're the king, you're going to let this kid just attack me?"

Banks stood still, looking ahead a moment as the words stood between her and Winston. With a swift movement, Keoni turned back around to face Winston. "Be ready in five minutes." Her words were cold, her gaze like fire. Winston only cleared his throat and went back into the room before slamming the door. The Colonel's boots clicked as she headed back down the hall.

I called after her, "Wait! Lieutenant!"

"What?" She whirled around. "What do you want?"

"I… I'm sorry about that."

"Please, just be ready in five minutes. Until then, give me my space."

"Yes, lieutenant."

Again, she left for the gym, and I followed in silence.

8

Chemistry

"We've been in this house for three days, and we still haven't checked the entire place," Claudius complained as he sipped some water.

"Why wake a sleeping giant?" I said, passing Coco the rest of my sandwich.

"Because giants don't sleep forever," he hissed. Claudius was seemingly paranoid. Afraid that the worst was going to happen. I wasn't sure why since we'd made it this far without incident.

In fact, we'd be better off without Claudius with his broken leg. But I needed him to help take care of Lyla ... and for that prize. They're offering a hundred thousand dollars or endless rations for a year for a family of four, which is just what we need. We'd be able to find a place, settle in it and be set for at least a year. That'd make life way easier than it has ever been for us.

I started taking care of my sisters right after college when our father killed Lyla's mother. He was abusive, and the beatings one night went too far. My sisters were left with no one but me, and I've been working hard to take care of them ever since. The family courts tried to send my sisters to their mothers, well, only Coco. Kingsley was already twenty-one and didn't need a guardian.

Lyla automatically went to me since I was old enough and Ly's grandmother didn't want her. Little Coco, she was only twelve back then, and needed a guardian. Her mother fought me hard, but it boiled down to the fact that she'd never shown any concern until then. She'd never wanted Coco when she stayed with us and our father and Ly's mom. Now that a check would be issued for the girl, Acoye's mother found her way to court. Thankfully, I won full custody of my sister.

The last five years have been rough. I've given my sisters everything. But I have no complaints. I just wish I could've given them more. Kingsley helped a lot, and Coco has always helped with Lyla. She practically raised the girl because King and I fell short in the maternity section. It was so natural for little Acoye, she was so mature with Lyla. Now, I was staring down at my seventeen-year-old sister, watching as she continued to try her hardest to care for Lyla, though I was certain Acoye was the most afraid.

When we left her in the car and she saw a wrong for the first time, King and I couldn't even get her to move. We had to physically shove her from the driver's seat before we could get away. And when she finally unfroze, she had a screaming fit. Fighting and flailing, begging for God to rescue her. I had no idea when she'd learned to pray, but she prayed a mouthful that day. Praying that if God was real and Jesus loved her, then He would save her.

King snapped her out of the religious daze, and we were able to calm her down. She's been different since then. More cautious, a lot quieter, very submissive. It's like Coco has shut down. She told me before we left three days ago that she just wanted to be safe. She was tired of being afraid.

I've been worried about her, though she hid her fear very well. Behind her golden smile, Acoye is nothing but a fearful girl... but she's no different from the rest of us. It's sad, fear will become normal, expected even. And one day, we won't remember the days when we weren't living in fear. Not with monsters, and an invasion.

Lyla was lying on the floor beside Coco, snoring away. As the air grew colder, her breathing became more labored. Mucus built up in her lungs, making it difficult to breathe and move freely. It was worse in the summer months, the fresh pollen choking her. The mucus buildup would get so bad that even the pills didn't help break it down. Staying indoors and sleeping with a mask helped, however, she didn't have an oxygen mask now. All she could do was try to fight on her own.

I hated watching Lyla like this. I felt like a failure. After all this time, I thought she'd gotten better. But she hadn't.

Claudius adjusted on the other side of her, grunting as he moved his broken leg. I was pretending not to notice how uncomfortable he'd been since we got here. I think the walking may have injured him further. But the man's too prideful to say anything.

"You need to get help," I said, keeping my focus on Lyla.

"I don't need help. I need security. Safety."

"You lost that the moment you betrayed our country."

"What?" Kingsley said as she stepped into the living room area. We decided to stay together, everyone taking shifts to watch the house except Coco and Lyla of course.

"It's a lie," Claudius said, passing his gaze to King. "I didn't betray the country."

"Then what is Chem talking about?"

Kingsley had taken a liking to Claudius. Chatting with him like they were buds. But I didn't trust him. I didn't trust anyone, and I didn't want my sisters trusting anyone and everyone either. However, King wasn't the type you could tell that to. Everything had to be proven to her. She was a sucker, that's for sure. Didn't believe things unless she saw them with her own eyes. During times like this, an attitude like King's could either be good or bad.

"I saw on the news. There's a reward for turning Major General Claudius Saint-Olliare in. You get money or rations."

King's eyes were wide as she stared at me in bewilderment. "Why haven't we turned him in, then?"

"We weren't supposed to leave the house right away. I was hoping we'd use him as leverage and be able to squeeze a little more out of the government. Maybe a safehouse along with the rations or—"

"You're a fool if you think the US would make a deal with you," Claudius interrupted.

"Excuse me?"

"During an invasion, you really think the US is going to be giving out rewards or cash? *Money?*" he said it again like I should get it, but thankfully, Kingsley looked as confused as I felt, and Claudius explained further. "Our money is going towards the invasion and fighting those monsters. Over fifty percent of all US rations will be allocated to the US military, and you think they're going to give you extra rations? You think they're going to do anything if you turn me in?"

"So, you used us?" Kingsley asked softly. Her thick hands were clasped together as she looked brokenheartedly at Claudius.

He sighed. "I was just trying to protect myself, Kingsley. I'm sorry."

She covered her mouth, backing away and storming off. I heard a door slam and I called, "King!"

"I'll go after her," Coco said. She stood and glanced back at Claudius. "I don't know if you're telling the truth that you're innocent. But even if you are a bad man, I forgive you because Lyla loves you. Be good for her."

The words hung in the air between us as Coco left. Claudius fidgeted beside Lyla, scratching at the makeshift brace. We sat in silence for a while. Time seemed to stretch on, like the minutes didn't want to pass. I felt a little guilty since Claudius looked pained.

Finally, I murmured, "They needed to know."

He didn't respond.

"Claudius—"

"What do you want me to say? You got what you wanted, right? Make me out to be the bad guy so your sisters will hate me. Well, good job. You did it." His green eyes were sorrowful, and the regret he masked behind his blank expression almost surfaced.

"I'm just trying to protect them."

"Yeah, well," he moved to get to his feet. "Do it on your own now. I'm leaving."

"What? You can't leave!" I jumped to my feet to stop him as he hobbled away. "You're in no condition to leave and… and…"

"And what?" He shrugged as he turned slowly. "Say it. I won't make it out there on my own. You don't want a dangerous man like me out there, hurting others or doing whatever traitors do?"

"N-N-No." I felt my cheeks burn with disparity as I mumbled, "We need you. Traveling alone right now and without enough people to help is hard. Everything would fall on King and me again, and right now, we're too tired and weak to do it all."

"Well, looking after one person is a heck of a lot easier than looking after three people and a child. I think I'm good." He turned to leave when the door hurled open, and a fearful Kingsley came inside.

"What's wrong?" I said immediately.

Her eyes filled with fat tears and my heart constricted in my chest.

"What's wrong!" I nearly yelled, startling her.

She gulped. "We were arguing, and then we were pushing and shoving, and…"

"And what?!" I snapped.

"Where's Acoye?" Claudius asked quickly.

"I don't know," she whispered.

"What do you mean?" I shouted.

"Kingsley, hey," Claudius limped and stood right in front of her. Grabbing her hands, he spoke gently to her. "King, I need you to tell me exactly what happened."

"Coco was trying to convince me that you weren't bad, and I told her I didn't want to hear it. We started arguing and I pushed her. And then," she swallowed thickly, her words shaky, my heart throbbing. "She shoved me back, and I tripped over a rock, and I think I hit my head. Next thing I knew, she was gone."

Claudius looked back at me. "King's hands are cold and stiff. Which means Coco's been gone at least three to five minutes. It sounds like King passed out, but that might've spooked Coco and she ran away. If we leave right now, we can catch up to her."

"Ok." I nodded as I turned to grab my bag.

King said, "My head, it's bleeding I think." She prodded gently, tucking a hand into her short curls. When she pulled her hand back, there was blood on her fingers.

"Oh my goodness!" I hollered as I rushed over to her.

"Sit her down, give her some water. I'll get bandages," Claudius called as he hobbled around the room. The clunking of his makeshift crutch woke Lyla. The little brown girl sat up and went into a coughing fit.

"Easy, Ly," I said as I knelt beside her and rubbed circles on her back. I was ready to rip my dreadlocks out and throw them out the window. Kingsley's head was bleeding, Lyla was having a coughing fit, Claudius was injured but wouldn't tell anyone, and Coco was gone. In all of ten minutes my life had fallen apart.

Why couldn't I protect them? What am I supposed to do?

I gritted my teeth. We'd lost Coco and I couldn't even go find her because Lyla was coughing, and Kingsley was bleeding out—from the head!

"I've got the bandages," Claudius said as he sat behind Kingsley. I watched her wince and shrug a few times as Claudius cleaned the back of her head.

Lyla eventually calmed down. But when she noticed Coco was missing, I was afraid she'd fall into another fit.

"Where's Coco?" she asked.

"Well," my eyes drifted to Kingsley who was sitting with tears all over her cheeks. I was lost for words, unsure of what to tell my kid sister.

"Coco went to fight the monsters without us," Claudius spoke up in the silence.

"Why'd she go without us?"

Claudius moved from behind Kingsley with a few dirty napkins and said, "Kingsley tripped, and we stayed behind to clean her up. We didn't want to wake you either. But now that you're awake, we can go catch up."

Lyla clapped her hands cheerfully. Claudius gave her a

dashing smile and my little sister seemed to smile even harder. There was no telling how far Coco had gotten, but the only thing we knew for certain was that she'd run away... and we would find her.

9

Abigail

"Did you get the shirts like I asked?"

"Yes," Everette said as he pulled the bundle of shirts from beneath his own.

"Perfect." I passed him the granola bar I'd promised him for getting me the shirts.

"When are we getting out of here?"

"*We?*"

The boy squinted at me as he hungrily ate the granola bar. I arrived at this shelter three weeks ago just after having Flower, and the rations have only gotten smaller. It's no surprise Eve's so hungry.

When he arrived a week after me, he was battered and bruised. They only took him in because they found him on the street. Anyone with broken skin, or bleeding, or even a scrape wasn't welcomed. They were afraid you may have contracted the virus that was causing people to drop dead out of nowhere and come back to life. I'm positive Flower and prayer was the only reason I got in. But Everette… he was nearly lifeless on the side of the street. They took him in and locked him in a back room of the shelter afraid he would eventually turn. But he got better, and I befriended the hungry teenager.

He was stealing the milk I'd pumped for Flower through the night. It kept going missing from our small room. Eventually, I caught him one night sitting outside the door chugging the baby milk. In return for keeping his thievery a secret, he'd be put to use. Though it was wrong, and I didn't like it, looting was the only way right now.

I needed things since I hadn't told anyone I was bleeding when I initially arrived. After a week of using toilet paper and my only other pad, I told a woman in charge that my period started. She got me tampons, but I told her I wanted pads, and she was able to get me some. With my bleeding getting lighter now, and Everette here to steal pads and diapers for me, I wasn't too worried.

The only thing, or rather *person*, that was missing was Zion. Over the last three weeks, I'd gotten stronger, and wasn't brought to tears by the simple thought of Zion. But I was still hurting. I was still distraught after having to run for my life and find safety. Though I'd gotten used to the safety of this place, I knew I couldn't stay forever. Not if I wanted to find my fiancée to figure things out together.

"You've got to take me with you. I can't stay here," Eve said.

"I don't know, kid." I worked on tying the shirts together to make a baby sack. I'd tie Flower to me when I got out of here to make things easier. Having Everette with me would probably help too. If nothing else, he'd be good company and would be able to loot things without a baby strapped to him. But could I truly endanger this kid? He was safer here instead of out there where the monsters were. I was only leaving to find Zion, but Eve had no reason to leave.

"Please? I know you want to find your fiancée. I can help you."

"You don't have anyone you want to find?"

He paused, eyes drifting to the floor. Everette and I talked a lot. He'd told me about his parents getting a divorce, but they still managed to be a happy family. His little sister who loved when he played the piano, and their dog, Felix, who was a mutt of some kind. But never once had he muttered a word about the condition he'd been found in. Never muttered a word about anything involving the invasion.

Noticing his silence, I clapped and said loudly, "There's no reason for you to leave, so you have to stay."

"Come on, Auntie," he whined from the door, "let me go with you."

"No." I shook my head. "And stop calling me auntie."

Eve chuckled. "Sorry, Auntie."

I rolled my eyes as I moved around the room. Flower was sitting on the floor playing with different colored blocks. "Why do you want to get out of here so badly, anyways?"

"Because it's getting crowded."

"Can't disagree there," I said as I swapped a different shirt into the baby carrier I was making.

"Food is even harder to come by, and I'm so hungry."

"What makes you think food is bountiful out there?"

"Because everyone's too afraid to go out there and get it."

I looked up to find Everette lazily leaning against the door. You could tell the lanky eighteen-year-old was still growing. A lean frame with arms that held a little definition to them, and long legs that made him taller than everyone. His feet were massive, like he still had five inches of growth left in him. And his frequently cracking voice aged him down. Though, his boyish face, free of facial hair could never fool anyone into thinking he was any older than sixteen. It was kind of shocking that Eve was such a late bloomer, but it didn't matter to me.

"Alright, Eve," I shrugged. "But if you're traveling with me, you've got to listen to me. It's dangerous out there."

"I know," his words were glum as vivid flashbacks of his limp body being carried into the building by a guard whipped through my mind and probably his too.

"So, you know what's out there?"

"The wrongs?" he said as he moved to the bed. Flopping on it, he picked up a block Flower had thrown earlier and tossed it in his hand. "Yeah."

"Aren't you scared of them?"

"Aren't you? And you're still going out there."

"I have to find my fiancée."

"And I'm hungry." He shrugged, avoiding eye contact with me. "I'll find food for you, me, and Flower."

"She's set." I popped my bra strap, and he leaned back and laughed. It was so weird to think that we were technically still in immense danger. However, laughing, and being away from it all made you forget, until the night came, and you were lonely. The whispers breathed into your thoughts about the loved ones you couldn't find, the darkness you outran. It all came back every night.

"I was thinking—" Eve's words were cut short when a commotion began outside.

I waved for him to grab Flower as I moved to the door to listen. It was a girl yelling, guards yelling, and other voices too. I sighed and shook my head at Eve. We'd been practicing for if this place was ever invaded, what we'd do to get out.

"What was it?"

"Sounds like a noisy group. Maybe the shelter's turning them away since it's overcrowded in here."

"Hopefully," Eve said as he lowered Flower back to the floor.

The shelter had been getting fuller and fuller. Families without a home, children wandering the streets; the invasion and the wrongs were driving droves of people to find shelter. It was a wonder that after three weeks so many people had survived. But that was partially because the news reported that the invasion had stopped for a few days when the wrongs popped up. Eventually, the Chinese forces started up again, and people have been fleeing their homes.

"Should we check it out?" Eve asked.

"No," I said flatly as I grabbed a bottle to pump for Flower. The woman who brought me pads had also brought me a pump.

"Come on, Auntie," he whined. "I'm tired of being cooped up in here with baby lotion and granola bars."

"Well, sorry we're not good company." I grabbed Flower from the floor in front of his feet and he sucked his teeth.

"That's not what I meant. Come on, just a peek." Sugar brown hands were clasped together with a pleading look on his face. I couldn't resist the innocent youthful eyes and agreed with a huff.

With Flower on my hip, I strolled cautiously behind Everette. He was a tall handsome boy despite his late blooming, who was rather friendly with girls his age. When he didn't eat with Flower and me at meals, I would spot him sitting with lonely girls, or even families with girls his age. The little flirt.

Newcomers always got escorted through the back and into an interrogation room for questioning. They asked simple questions about a person's family, whereabouts thus far, and how they got here. When they came out, they were given a meal, and then assigned a room.

Families, and women with children all got their own room. Everyone else was split by age. Anyone fifteen and below had a guard by their room all day.

Eve and I sat in the cafeteria waiting for the newcomer to arrive. Flower sat on the table, grabbing her feet and making happy baby noises in the silence. There were others sitting around at the tables, but the cafeteria was mostly empty since it wasn't mealtime yet.

As the door creaked open, Eve glanced up to watch who'd come through the door. To our surprise, it was a young girl. She was visibly shaken, with wide eyes and unkempt hair. But even in her disheveled state, the young girl was beautiful. Soft eyes, and glowing brown skin, she had taken Everette's breath away.

With a gaping mouth and a lingering gaze, he looked like a spell had been cast on him the way he was entranced with the young beauty. She sat, meekly waiting for someone to bring her a meal when Everette whipped around at the table and blurted, "Let's go talk to her."

"No," I grunted. "She's clearly scared."

"Which is even more reason we should go over there."

"She's all alone, likely taken from her family. She doesn't need a replacement family so soon. Besides, give the girl some air. She just got here."

He sighed heavily, glancing anxiously over his shoulder at her and then back at me. "You've literally given me a million reasons to talk to her."

"But the only one you need is that she's pretty."

His mouth opened and closed, his normally quick and witty response had died. But only briefly as his surprised look morphed into a smirk. "Auntie Abbey, you're still the prettiest woman ever. You know you've got my heart. There's no need to be jealous."

"Grow up." I rolled my eyes as he snickered.

"Come on, let me at least say hi."

Sighing, I gave in and he sucker punched the air with joy

before jumping to his feet. He wandered over to the girl who was sitting alone. Someone had come by while Everette and I were chatting and gave her a bowl of soup and crackers. She was just picking at the food. But eventually her appetite would return. Everyone's always does.

I've seen many people arrive here and barely eat a thing for days straight until finally, they're eating all their food at every meal. It's like the body is running off adrenaline and then replaced by fear, both of which suppress the appetite. But when you feel safe, eating and enjoying food seems natural all over again.

The small girl inclined her head to me as Eve turned and pointed at me from across the room. He was yapping away to her, and she seemed a little distracted. I couldn't blame her. There was no telling what that young girl had gone through. I felt bad for people like her and Eve. She looked to be his age, maybe a little younger, and they're experiencing such despair. It was hard for all of us, but especially kids. I looked at my own child, Flower. She was just a baby, born into the darkness of this world.

Thoughts of my labor came flooding back after weeks of trying to forget it. I lowered my head to the table and began to take deep breaths. Vivid images of Mr. and Mrs. Reinhardt chasing me after they'd changed into wrongs. Rhoda had suddenly fallen dead after mentioning that she'd heard music playing. I didn't hear any music... I didn't hear anything at all, and then she dropped dead.

Could this have truly been a virus? *No*... the thoughts were formulating when a hand pressed to my shoulder. I jerked up and away, just to see Everette standing there with tight brows and a confused grimace.

"Abbey, you alright? You're sweating."

"What do you know about the Rapture?" I asked.

"The what?"

"I've got to get to my room," I said as I got to my feet. Grabbing Flower from the table, I moved toward the door when Eve stopped me.

"What are you talking about? Where are you going?"

"Everette, I just need to be alone for a little while, alright?"

He let go of my arm, stepping back with a bewildered look on his face. "Yeah, alright Abigail."

My name on his tongue sounded foreign and distant, but I didn't have time to address it. I left the cafeteria and headed to my room to think. Putting Flower in the bed, I sat on the floor and stared at my feet. When I first got here, the shelter people got me these sneakers and a pair of house shoes. They've been all I've been wearing. I swap between the shoes, today was a sneaker day…

"What am I doing?" I whispered to myself as tears filled my eyes. "The Rapture? There's no way that happened. Rhoda and Jillian had the virus, and they didn't know it… right? God, please say something!"

I hunched over, gripping the rug as I felt a sob choking me. I was trying to hold it in at the thought of being left behind. But it couldn't be true. I glanced back at Flower; she was still here. I'd heard all my life that children would be raptured too.

"Ok," I whispered to myself as I caught my breath, "then it hasn't happened, right?" That's what I wanted to believe, but I didn't. I knew Rhoda dropping dead suddenly was odd, but I just never had the chance to think about it, never *wanted* to think about it. Now that I am thinking about it, the Rapture is the only thing that made sense. Not some virus... but I didn't know who else turned. If everyone who turned was a Christian, then maybe the Rapture happened.

But... what if everyone *wasn't* a Christian? You could turn into a wrong just from being bitten by one. By now, there were so many people who'd turned, there was no way to tell which ones were the originals—the supposed Christians—or which ones were recent victims. How would I know?

"The news has said that everyone who changed initially were mostly Americans, then Brazilians and Mexicans, and they were all carriers but didn't know it." I chewed my lip as I sat on the floor. The US and most Spanish speaking countries were heavily populated with Christians... which could mean that the Rapture *did* happen.

So then why? Why was Flower left and not taken? Why—

A soft thump came to my door. It wasn't loud or scary, just ominous.

"Hello? Eve?" I sighed as I wiped at my tears to stand. "Listen, Eve, I'm sorry about the cafeteria. I wasn't trying to push you away. I was just," I shrugged, unsure of how to tell him the truth. Religion had never come up between us, and now it was staring us in the face. Well, staring *me* in the face. I placed my head against the door, taking a deep sorrowful breath.

"Everette, I'm sorry, alright?"

When he didn't respond, I rolled my eyes and stood upright to open the door when a strange hissing noise rang out.

"Eve? What are you doing?" I snatched open the door and stared for a millisecond before slamming the door closed. A screech called out behind the door, and Flower immediately began to cry. I lunged for the bed as the wrong banged on my door, screeching and scratching on the other side.

"They're inside," I said to myself as I worked the shirts around Flower. "I've got to find Eve and get out of here."

The wrong crashed into my door loudly, and I wasn't sure how much longer I'd have before it broke the door down. But it didn't matter because I was suddenly safe—kind of. I heard my neighbor opening their door, and the wrong moved from my door to hers. The brutal screams and cries next door almost sent me into a frenzy. But I tried to stay calm.

"I've got to do something!" I hollered.

Think… think… the door!

Placing Flower on the floor atop her baby blanket, I pushed her under the bed. I took off, ripping my own door open to an empty hallway. Most people didn't stay in their rooms, they visited the cafeteria or the other community rooms, the newsroom, or the small gym to watch guys and girls play basketball. No one besides my neighbor and I knew this wrong was here. But how did it get inside?

Short steps brought me right to Jamie, my neighbor's room. She had two sons she was staying with, but the room

106

was silent now besides the crunching and choking. I didn't know how long it'd be for Jamie and her sons to turn, but I didn't care. If I could lock them inside, we could survive this. I stood against the wall, taking a deep breath and crept close along the side to peek in. I froze. Jamie was on the floor fluttering and convulsing, along with one of her sons, while the first wrong I encountered, a balding old man, was crouched like a frog, eating Jamie's youngest son. The boy was dead, his empty eyes staring right at me, his mouth hung open as blood dripped from it, over his face, to plop onto the rug. But the gory scene wasn't the only thing that froze me... it was the wrong staring back at me with the boy's torso open.

In a flash I jumped for the door, gripping the handle and pulling the door shut in just enough time for the wrong to slam right into the closed door. It was going crazy now. Banging and screeching, scratching and pounding. I turned for my own bedroom where Flower was still under the bed crying.

Tying her onto me, I grabbed the backpack Eve stole for me, and the duffle bag I came with and filled them both with all the supplies in my room. I folded the baby blanket, and rolled the other baby blanket I'd been given when I'd first arrived and shoved them both into the duffle bag. I raced quickly, grabbing the pads and diapers, pump, bottles, shoes, and clothes to fill the bag before rushing out the room and down the hall.

"Eve!" I shouted as I ran. "Eve!" When I made it to the cafeteria, he wasn't there. Panic began to settle in my heart, but I had to find him before I could leave.

"Eve!" I screamed as I rounded a corner.

"What?" He whirled around, an attitude on his face.

I dropped to my knees in relief. He was standing with the girl from earlier who'd just arrived. "Auntie," concern laced his voice, "what's going on? Why are you dressed like you're leaving?"

"Because we are leaving right now."

"What?"

"Here," I passed him the backpack, "go fill this with your clothes and any food you can find."

"But—"

"Now!"

He took the bag slowly before glancing at the girl and heading down the hall. Anxiously, I looked over my shoulder, but there'd been no movement, however, I knew that wouldn't last much longer. The only reason those wrongs hadn't broken down that door yet was because they had a child to feast on. When they grew tired of him, they'd come for us.

"Hi," I said shakily to the young girl. Her eyes were wide with fear as she looked me over. She took a step back, shaking her head.

"What's wrong?" I asked.

"They're here, aren't they?"

"What?"

"A rush of us came inside all at once. I don't know if they screened all of us."

"Something could've gotten inside."

"Something did. I swear I saw it." She began to tremble

violently, gulping down air as she tried to stay calm.

"Hey, hold on. Okay, what did you see?"

She shook her head. "I was just trying to get away from my sisters, but I was afraid out there all alone! I thought it would be safer here. Now there's one of those things in here too!"

"What's your name?" I said as I grabbed her hands.

"Acoye, but everyone calls me Coco."

"Ok, Coco," I clutched her hands, "I want you to come with me, alright? I'll keep you safe until we can find your sisters again."

She nodded as Eve rounded the corner, panting heavily. "Are we ready to—"

The screech of the wrongs rang out over Everette. The two teenagers looked like they died for a split second at the sound, which only meant that they recognized it… because they've encountered the wrongs too.

"Let's go!" I shouted. Taking Coco by the hand, I raced for the exit down the hall with Flower strapped to me and Everette right behind me.

10

Patron Saint of Victory

Breaking news went out three weeks ago stating that Syrian forces were researching the strange 'wrongs' that had appeared. The story went that a virus was infecting the world and would continue to infect the world because of all the bloodshed. The death would bring pestilence, and the pestilence will carry the infection everywhere.

More information was to come as Syrian forces made progress. But I didn't wait for China to make a statement. The very next day, another breaking news report swelled amongst the nations, stating that the virus was an infection of the brain. It attacked anyone who had brain problems or had them in their families. It was a really general statement, but it was the best we could do for now.

Since then, I've come up with things to release on the regular, challenging China who didn't have grounds to stand on. With their invasion of the USA after the five years of peace, China looked evil. They thought that evilness would strike fear into the hearts of the world, but it struck hatred instead.

A deep-seated desire for vengeance from Americans and those who relied on America so heavily were now in danger of losing everything, like Japan. And the fear that did touch some hearts was quickly turned to anger. People didn't like being afraid, and they didn't like that China had ruined the sweet peace the entire world had been enjoying.

"Hadil," I murmured as I lay beside my concubine. "Go clean yourself up and run me a bath. Have Sabiya there for me."

She sat up, dark locks flowing down to her waist over her bright skin. "Of course, Victory."

"I love you," I said as I rustled my hands through her lovely hair. She turned back, lust in her eyes as she leaned forward and kissed me. "I love you more."

We kissed again before she stood, pulling her red tunic on and left the room. All of my concubines wore red tunics when they came to see me. It was to shame them, reminding them that they are but tools for my pleasure. They weren't honorable women, and I'd never marry a single one of them. However, I wouldn't let anyone else have them either.

In their private quarters, I allow them to dress casually, and they are well taken care of. There are strict rules about mingling with the guards, however, I know they break those rules regularly. It's why I always wear protection with them and not my wives. I want an heir soon, as the world changes. I want a son to rise in my stead, and a daughter to marry her brother as the only woman worthy of him. I'd decided that after I met

Sabiya. There would never be another woman in this world as perfect as her. She will bear my daughter, an honor that is higher than bearing my son. She will preserve my legacy by producing the woman my son will need by his side.

Rolling out of bed, I looked around the stone walls. Syria was not so ancient before I became its patron saint. In an effort to please me, the Syrian forces give me whatever I ask for. A palace, I got it. Guards and women, received. A vineyard for fresh wine, workers were included.

Slowly, Syria held me as it's leader, and when Basha, the leader who took me in and raised me, offered me the head of Syria, I took it to honor him. He is not dead; in fact, he serves on my council. The transfer of power is something known only between us for now. We have chosen not to disclose my status as the true leader of Syria in an effort to keep information hidden from those who cannot be trusted, like the Chinese. I am just known as a representative of Syria for now.

In the golden bathroom, the floor had been carved out for a deep and large bathtub. Flowing water that filled the room with steam, large square pillars made of golden bricks held up the high ceiling. Sunlight poured into the bathroom, keeping the room heated. I'd designed the entire palace myself. I had a thing for being a ruler with a throne. A god with a court for subjects to enter and pay their dues.

The Syrians loved visiting Victory Palace once a month. They entered the courts with thanksgiving, singing songs of praises to me over a five-day period. On the sixth day, gifts and money, cattle and the dedication of children to my guards and harem took place in my throne room.

I sighed as I lowered myself into the tub, leaving my garments on the side. Hadil was there, in her red tunic again, using a large rod to churn the waters. The whirlpool the churning created always helped relieve my stress. I liked to bask in the waters for a while before being cleansed and rinsed by whomever had been summoned to my chambers.

The heavy door to my bathing room opened and closed after a moment. In the silence, the footsteps of my dear Sabiya rang out as she came and stood by the side of the tub.

"Saint Victory," her voice as smooth as brown butter, put me at ease immediately. "You summoned me."

"I did. Come, my love. Entice me for a while."

"As you wish, my lord."

I signaled to Hadil, she stopped her churning and nodded. Leaving the rod by the tub, she bowed and left the room without a word.

My wife, my first love of my new life began to dance for me. I met Sabiya thirteen years ago when she was just a girl. She had not yet had her first blood, but her parents offered her to me to pay off some of their long-standing debt. I had only recently been named the Patron Saint of Victory after six years of telling American secrets. She was one of the first gifts offered to me, though she was more like an exchange. But her beauty swooned me, and I could not refuse her. I took Sabiya in, and after she turned eighteen three years later, I married her.

We spent two years together in China before I returned her to Syria. Things were getting complicated in China, and I needed to show them my strength, my diligence, my fortitude, and a woman made me look weak.

When I returned home a year after sending Sabiya home and things began to work out with China, Sabiya had found two new women for me to marry and three concubines to enjoy as a gift to me. Truthfully, I'd just wanted Sabiya, but with Syrian soldiers watching, I indulged myself in their welcoming.

Bare feet stepped free from strappy sandals as she began to shake her hips. Whipping a belt from her waistband, the velvet and sequin material was laced with gold coins that rattled as she twirled and danced around. I enjoyed Sabiya's movement. She was ever so graceful, extending her legs fully, pointing all the way through the toe. She kept her back straight for stricter moves, but completely embraced a hunching position to get lower.

As her dancing went on, Sabiya moved closer to the edge of the tub. One by one, an article of clothing fell as she danced. Until finally, all that she held in her hand was the sequin belt. Her bangles had been laid down, her rings, and necklaces. The fixtures in her hair were removed to allow her sweeping mass of curls to drape her entire frame. She had so much thick hair, it sat all around her, shrinking her already small frame.

"Come," I said. Her eyes had never left mine as she danced, bearing her nudity to me in all its splendor. She nodded, taking long strides to the stairs. Seductively, she lowered herself into the tub, watching me from across the way.

"I have to say," I said as I met her in the center of the tub, "your dancing today was the best I've ever seen."

She smiled coyly. "My lord, you always tell me that."

"Do I?" I laughed as I pulled her naked body against mine. "I mean it every time."

Her gentle blush made a spark flicker in my heart. "I truly love you, Sabiya."

"And I, you."

"Can I ask you something?"

"Yes."

I swayed her in the waters, watching her gleeful eyes as we moved around. "Do the other women bother you? The wives, the concubines."

She turned her head to the side. "Saint Victory, it is your happiness that we are all hoping to bring you. Are they not enough? I will find more suitable women."

"No." I shook my head.

Every wife I had Sabiya had scouted for me. When I seemed too bored of one, she'd find me another. Concubines, however, were women she knew were desperate and could benefit from having a 'stable' home. Sex and loyalty were the only requirements to be a concubine. But as a wife, you were the pinnacle of beauty and standard for all the women of Syria. And Sabiya took finding perfect suitors very seriously.

"I'm not asking about me, my love. You have served by my side as my wife for ten long years, though we've been together for thirteen years, and I have not once asked what you think. Asked how you felt. I've only ever been focused on myself."

115

"It is my duty to bring you pleasure, that is the oath of your brides."

A chuckle escaped me as I stopped swaying us. "Sabiya, I want you to think back to your life before I married you. Before you took position in royalty. Did you like when your previous flings dated other women? Was it pleasing to you?"

She thought for a moment, a single crease in her delicately smooth skin. "Saint Victory, before you, I was raised in a Muslim family. Where our men were honored. I see no difference here. You are to be honored, despite what I feel."

Clenching my jaw, I let her go. "No." I shook my head. "I won't be like Him. I won't be like the One who requires your life but gives nothing in return."

Although He was not the God of the Muslim faith, I still felt that God Almighty had treated me the same as Sabiya's god. He required everything with no regard to how I felt. I would not be the same as Him.

"Saint—"

"It's not your fault," I held up my hand, taking a breath. Sabiya moved carefully, interlacing her fingers with my lifted hand.

"You are displeased, and you are stressed."

"They've been silent, Sabiya," I changed the subject. "They haven't said a word since the press release three weeks ago."

Her eyes were less cautious, less bewildered now. Sabiya had always kept her loyalty act at the forefront. An innocent woman whose only intentions were to serve ol' Saint Victory. However, I've found comfort in speaking candidly to her, and receiving her advice. It was Sabiya who came up with the brain-eating virus idea. And it would be Sabiya again who would help me out of this darkness the Chinese had summoned.

"I did exactly what you told me; I had the Syrian forces release a statement that our research team was on the monsters. I thought China would respond, but they haven't. I'm beginning to get worried."

"Why are you worried?" she asked.

"Because they've been silent. No retaliation, nothing. Not even their own reports."

She stood still, the warm waters still as the churning had stopped long ago, and the ripples of our dance in the water had been forgotten.

"You said once that China's silence was their strength. They used a weakness like a retreat or falling silent for their own good."

"That's right," I turned away, moving to the side of the tub. My hands gripped the tiled edge as I huffed a heavy breath. Warmth suddenly blossomed as Sabiya stood behind me. I felt her small hands weave beneath my arms as she hugged me.

"You are Saint Victory," she began, "the patron saint of triumph, of victory itself. No one can defeat you, my lord. Not even China."

"What do you suppose I do?"

"Crush them," she whispered darkly. "Crush them with their own hand. And it begins with the wolves."

I quirked a brow. "The Russians are weak. I promised Volkov I'd prove myself to him, as a brother."

117

"Do it." She dug her nails into my chest, a stinging pain that somehow brought me comfort. "Welcome the wolves into your home, give them a place to sleep and lick their wounds."

"You're saying I should have them retreat from Israel? But the resources there, we need them just as much as China."

"Exactly. If Russia retreats, no one wins. We've barely lost anything, and Russia has lost soldiers. But China has lost much. They are dependent on Russia's success."

Slowly, I lifted my hand and closed it around one of hers. "Make our alliances with the Russians, and the Europeans, who have ties to the Middle East. Syria will have the world."

"Make a deal with China."

"What?" I shifted to look over my shoulder, but her face was buried against my back as she spoke.

"Alliances with those countries align us for a future without China. But we don't know how long it'll take for our forces to be strong enough all together."

"What about Africa? I'm sure I can convince the twin princes in Egypt, the leader in Chad too."

"A deal with China buys us time to make a plan to rule without them. All you have to do is convince them that you are trying to make them look good."

Chewing my lip, I began to understand where Sabiya was going with this. "Make a deal with China to convince them we're on their side."

"You'll tell them that you'll announce that China has entered some kind of agreement to pull out of the US," she explained.

"No, they'll never take it."

"It is only an announcement," her words were like daggers in my quick response. "Leak information that China is considering a retreat. With everyone used to their retreat and silence tactics, the US and her allies will believe that China is plotting. They will ready an attack on Chinese borders in retaliation. Give the Red Dragon the wings it wants so badly, and let the Dragon have the heart of the US."

"Washington," I whispered. "So, then what is the point of the announcement?"

"To China, it'll seem like you are helping them invade the US and gain their wings. The world will come to hate China more, but they will remember you as the man who tried to tame the unruly dragon."

"The world..."

"You will become Saint Victory of the world, my lord."

"Having Russia, Africa, the Middle East, and Europe all on my side, I'll have nearly the whole world under my control."

"It will not come quickly but be patient. We will find opportunities for your victory to be relished by all," she assured me.

And I believed it.

"I am the savior of the world."

"No, something even better," she said as she retracted her hands. Her warmth was lost as she stepped away. I turned to face my beautiful Sabiya as she lifted her eyes to mine and said, "We do not need a rescuer; we need a victor. You are about to become the Patron Saint of Victory to the entire world. We

119

will be triumphant because of you."

11

Abigail

We raced for safety. Running through a grief-stricken city whose defenses weakened every day. But looking at the destruction of the city was pointless when you were running for your life.

With Flower strapped to me, I was able to run freely as I held Coco's hand. I checked over my shoulder every few paces to make sure Eve was still with us. He kept up, rushing right behind us. We'd long gotten away from the shelter and the chaos that'd erupted from the wrong getting inside; however, the wrongs weren't the only things to be feared.

Chinese forces were brutal and relentless, chasing us as we ran for safety. I was ready to scream and give up, but I had three lives to protect, I couldn't afford to give up. Pushing myself to my limits, I led our group into the woods. Ducking beneath branches and hopping over thick roots that sat above the ground. Coco kept pace with me, never letting my hand go, or tripping beside me.

By the time we'd made it into the murky forest, the Chinese forces let us go, and we could finally slow down just to catch our breath.

With his hands on his head, Eve paced back and forth between the trees. "What are we going to do now?"

"We find safety ... in the forest ... for tonight," I said between short breaths. "And in the morning, we go find real shelter. A house or something we can lock ourselves in."

He nodded, his chest rising and falling heavily. Coco remained quiet, hands on her knees as she panted for air.

"It's not safe out in the open," I said, "we need to go deeper into the forest."

"Let me catch my breath," Eve replied.

The sound of chatter and rustling rippled through the forest, and Coco's eyes swelled twice their size.

"We don't have time," I snapped as I grabbed Coco's hand, "let's go!"

The pursuit was frightening, running through a forest, knowing that the only other noise around you is the sound of the pounding footsteps of your hunters. The shouts, the barking dogs, the enemy forces had invaded, but invading wasn't enough. Killing innocent people who knew nothing of the political feud happening behind the scenes was more entertaining for them. The news reported deaths daily, but the most interesting part was that our enemy's agenda was unknown. Most countries invaded, took over parts of the land, stormed the capital, took control of resources. However, China had done nothing but kill people thus far.

A cry erupted beside me, jerking me from my thoughts and yanking my feet to a sudden stop. Coco's hand slipped from mine as she tumbled to the ground with a shriek.

"Coco!" I reached for her. Flower was crying now; I'd zoned out while we were running and hadn't heard her at all.

"My leg!" Coco whined as she pointed to her bleeding leg. It looked like it'd been split open. Possibly by a rigid root, or just a loose branch could've broken the skin. But the wound was deep, gushing blood down her leg as she cried hysterically. I was moving without thinking as I ripped my bag from my shoulders to pull out medical supplies when the howl of a dog froze me.

"Abbey! Abbey!" Eve shouted as he shook me. I was looking all around for where the howl could've come from. But there were only bushes and shrubbery, tall trees with dark leaves that hung heavily over us. I had never hiked, or hunted, had no idea how to tell which way the wind was blowing. We were trapped in a forest and none of us knew how to survive. Should we just surrender?

I looked around, as if time had slowed down. Coco was crying, Everette was yelling for me, and my little Flower... *our* little Flower...

Zion, I whispered in my heart. *I want to see him again. I want to live.*

"Abigail!"

"Yes?" I snapped back to reality, and it sounded like we were surrounded. Dogs, feet, chains, and now flames were racing towards us. The smell of burned wood raged on, and

123

when I looked around, I realized there was black smoke rising all around us.

"They don't know where we are either," I whispered. There was almost a feeling of relief, but I wouldn't let it fester. There was a chance we'd run right into our pursuers if we ran forward, but if we turned around there was not a single doubt in my mind we'd be found and killed well before we found our enemies or safety.

"We've got to keep moving," I said, "and we've got to stay quiet."

Eve looked over at a crying Coco and then at the baby strapped to my chest. "How? How can we stay quiet?"

"We have to find a way. For now, get her up! Let's move!"

Everette scrambled to get beneath Coco's arm and supported her on her injured side. I kept a hand on Flower's small body as we took off again. We were running straight ahead when the smoke began to thicken. Backtracking, we went in another direction, finding a pocket where the smoke was thinner.

"Abbey! Look! There's a cave over there!" Everette cried.

"Go!" I shouted.

Nearly dragging Coco, Eve moved toward the cave, ducking low to get inside. I was only a few paces behind after changing directions and ducked into the cave right after them. The rushing water at our feet was low, and the only light inside came from the entrance.

"Don't go in too deep," I called as I trudged from the water onto the dry side of the cave. Resting against the wall, I panted as Flower whined against my chest.

"We have to do something." Eve sounded exhausted. "For Coco."

I nodded, taking a deep breath before I carefully untied the makeshift carrier with Flower, and passed her to Eve. "Feed her," I instructed.

The tired boy nodded as he took Flower in his arms. Coco was sitting against the wall of the cave, still breathing heavily, chewing her lip and trying not to cry.

"You'll be okay," I whispered as I flipped my bag around and pulled out the medical kit I'd taken from the shelter. "I need you to keep taking deep breaths, and bite this." I passed her two cotton balls. With dirty and shaky hands, she placed them into her mouth as I pulled out the small bottle of alcohol. "Don't make a sound," I said. Her panicky head nod made me worry, but even if she whined a little, there was rushing water on the other side of the cave that would help drown out her cries.

"On my count." I took a breath and stared at the gash. Her ankle was now a crimson color from all the blood, and her leg looked swollen and bruised, like someone had *struck* her leg, not swiped it.

"One ... two ... three ..."

Coco reacted but I hadn't done anything. I tried to fake her out—keep counting to make her worry about when I'd stop rather than the pain. "Four ... five ... six ... seven—"

Shoving her head into the wall, Coco riled in pain as I poured the alcohol over her leg. She was kicking and whining

125

quietly as she held in her sobs. While she was in pain, I just went for it. Wiping away the blood and putting two paddings and a big bandage over her gash.

"All set," I whispered as she continued to cry. Sighing, I got to my feet and went to check on Eve. He was sitting against the wall cradling Flower as she sucked on a bottle.

"You did good, just like I showed you," I said as I sat beside him. He looked worried, though he tried to force a smile. Honestly, I couldn't blame him. I had no reason to be calm, to not freak out like I was going to in the forest. I felt crazy, up and down with my emotions. I was always afraid but needed to stay calm while worrying about everything. Yet, somehow, I was seated beside Eve, trying to make him feel better, not even worrying about myself. My eyes lowered to my baby in his arms…

She's why I'm so worried about Everette and Coco. She made me a mother, made me protective, even when I'm about to lose my mind.

"What happens now? We can't stay here forever, and it's cold," Eve said.

"We just have to wait them out. Coco's in no position to move right now."

He adjusted to squint at me. "Wait them out… the Chinese? They're burning down the forest to find us! We didn't run *that* far, I'm sure there's not much more to burn before they find us."

"We have time—"

"For what!?"

"To let Coco's leg heal!"

126

"I'm fine." Coco's voice was weak and strained as she took a labored breath. She was frowning deeply as she clutched her leg, eyes flitting between the two of us.

"See? She's fine. We need to move." Everette stood.

"We can't run forever," I snapped.

"This isn't a place we can stay! I can smell the smoke from here."

Staring into Everette's panicked eyes, a thought bloomed in my head, connecting the pieces of Eve's very sound argument. I knew that staying here was out of the question, I just didn't think we should go so soon.

"You're right, Eve," I said nearly to myself as I blinked away from him. "They're burning the forest down to find us. If we can smell smoke, that means they're close."

Eve nodded, and so did Coco, wearily.

"Which also means, we can still throw them off. If we start a few fires here, we can make them think someone's been through here."

"What if they still come looking?" Eve shrugged. "Can we really stay in this cave?"

"It'll be warmer with the fires all around, and they'll be burning for a while. And if gets too warm, then we'll move deeper into the cave."

"We'll block ourselves in," Coco said.

I turned and pointed. "There's more water at the end of this cave since it gets deeper. That means there's probably an exit on that side too. Come on, we need to do something and neither of you are giving out ideas. Only shooting mine down."

Eve stirred a moment, glancing down at Flower who'd fallen asleep in his arms. "Ok." His eyes locked with mine. "But we've only got two lighters. And they're just cigarette lighters, they were all I found."

"That's fine. You and I will go." I looked over at Coco. "Can you take care of Flower?"

She nodded as Eve came over to exchange Flower with her. I was about to give her instructions on how to hold a baby, but Coco didn't need any. She took Flower in her arms, pulling her close to her chest to feel her warmth, supporting her head like my daughter was her own child.

"Have you done this before?" I asked.

Coco's brown eyes gleamed with joy for half a second, but the burning memories that came with her answer weighed down her glee. "Yes, I have a little sister. We took care of her."

"I see."

"We're still going to find your family, Coco," Eve added. "She told me she has three sisters."

Coco nodded, shifting her gaze back to Flower.

"We'll find them. But for now, just look after Flower and the cave. We'll be back," I told her.

Everette and I left the cave, each with a lighter. The plan was to split up, but Eve wasn't sure he'd be able to remember his way back, and I wasn't sure I'd remember either. So we lit as many plants as we could, burning the branches of shrubs so they'd engulf in flames, and even setting our lighters to bits of

128

grass to help burn the ground.

"This should be good enough, right?" Everette asked me in a worried tone.

I nodded. "Yeah, let's go."

As we turned to run, the voice of a woman cried out, "Help me! Help me!"

Eyes larger than the moon, Eve stared at me. "What do we do?"

"Leave her," I said firmly. "This could be a trap."

Everette's mouth hung open. "What if it isn't?"

In the heavy smoke, I couldn't help but cough and cover my mouth. We'd been out there too long, there was no time to have this argument, but I could tell Everette was not going to head back to the cave without a fight. With my eyes burning and my lungs screaming, I said, "Eve, we've got to go. We can't help everyone."

"Someone helped me," he reminded me, patting his chest with both his hands. At this point, I was convinced he had lungs of steel. Eve hadn't broken a sweat. "I've got to help this lady," he told me—and then he turned and darted off towards the screams.

"Eve!" I croaked in protest, but the smoke choked me, and I wheezed out a fit of coughs.

I tried to go after Everette, limply following the sound of his footsteps. But he was too fast, and I was too weak. I could barely breathe.

When I began to feel dizzy, I stopped and placed a hand on a nearby tree to catch my breath. It wasn't enough. My chest heaved, expanding with each desperate inhale, but I felt like I was choking, sucking in mouthfuls of gravel and grit. My eyes began to burn, my throat felt raw.

"Eve! Wait!" I screamed into the black void.

Ahead, I saw a shadowy figure moving through the twisted trees. From the thin frame and lanky limbs, I knew it was Everette—but the dead giveaway was when I saw him look back. Staring. A heartbeat thumped between us, and I wondered if he would come back to me or keep going.

Everything went dark before I got my answer.

12

Keoni

We made it to a house in one piece after leaving the school through one of the only windows not surrounded by wrongs. It wasn't even much of a journey. We simply headed out, like Zion said, to find shelter.

There was nothing in sight, and everyone had begun to wonder if we'd made the right call. Zion didn't seem to be worried though. He stayed in front, and we all remained quiet until we reached a small ranch house. It was the first one on the street, and with daylight waning, we rushed for the little blue house with wide windows and a white door.

No one was inside. Sam and Winston swept the house while Zion and I checked the perimeter. There were other houses on the street, all dilapidated or burned. Doors hanging off hinges, blood staining the concrete, we didn't need to go far to know who or what had struck this street.

The Chinese forces were more than formidable, and the wrongs were wild violent creatures, nearly indestructible with a hunger for humans. I've only seen them once, but I didn't need to see them again to know what kind of damage one of those things could do.

"There are two bedrooms," Zion explained as we stood in the middle of the kitchen. There was no light except the candles lit around the room. Sam found them in one of the bathrooms and brought them to the kitchen for light. Thankfully, there was a lighter with them.

"We want our own room," Winston directed to me. He and Sam have worked with the group to get here, but they've been less than excited about it. Ever since Zion caught them *together*, they've been cranky and standoffish.

I sighed, pushing from the wall with my arms folded. I gave Zion a subtle glance, taking in his meek demeanor, though his eyes begged for me to help.

"No can do, private." I shrugged. "There are two rooms. Guys and girls."

"I don't want to stay with that creep," Winston fired off, jerking a hand at Zion.

"That creep just got you to safety."

"I should practice a bow, I guess."

I snorted. "No, soldier, but you just earned first watch duty and the couch. Now Zion has his own room. Any more complaints?"

"We're not at the armory or on base, we don't have to listen to you," Sam said. Her voice edged fear; it was weak as she spoke.

"You're right, you don't have to listen to me. But you are.

Because you don't know how to survive, and you barely know your left foot from your right. You think because one older man gives you a little attention that you're in charge?"

"I heard that's how you climbed the ranks." Winston's eyes were like ice as they met mine, but his words caused a sauna within me to shut on. I wasn't angry, just embarrassed. "Yeah," he nodded, "I heard the rumors about you and some general. That's the only reason you're even here."

"Hey," Zion said, stepping forward, "that's enough, Winston."

"No, let's talk about Lieutenant Colonel Banks," he insisted. "Let's talk about how she got her rank. How she got in charge since she's—"

"You're right," I admitted, immediately silencing Winston. "Maybe I didn't receive my rank fairly." I dropped my arms, eyeing the room. When my gaze returned to Winston's burning one, I continued, "But I am your Lieutenant Colonel, and you have your order. Anyone who doesn't want to fulfill their duty is free to leave now to find their own food, resources, and safety." I reached out and yanked on the backpack on Winston's shoulders. He hollered as I shoved him around, ripping the other strap off him until it was free.

"None of you can leave with army issued supplies or materials." I glanced at Winston's belt. "Or weapons."

"What is wrong with you? You wanna try and take my weapon too?" Winston challenged.

"I would take it," I said, dropping his backpack and stepping over it. I stood close enough to feel his funky breath on my face as I growled, "Don't make me take the one you've got concealed on your leg as well."

"You wouldn't dare," he seethed.

"I don't need a dare to successfully remove your weapons, private."

"That's enough!" Zion said, tugging my arm. "You guys, we have to work together. If you want to stay with Sam, fine. I'll stay on the couch and Banks can have her own room."

Sam grabbed Winston's arm and pulled. "Come on, Zion's right. We're all soldiers, and she is our Colonel. She has the most experience, we can't survive on our own."

"Whatever," Winston hissed as he snatched up his bag right after yanking his arm free from Sam. She went after him down the hall, and when a door slammed, I heard her open it and close it again to let herself inside.

"Colonel, are you—"

"I'm fine," I said, snatching my arm from Zion.

"Keoni," Zion called quickly behind me. He hardly used my first name, and it always sounded foreign coming from him.

When I turned to face him, Zion's blue eyes seemed to sigh before he released one from his lips. "I'm sorry," he blurted.

"For what?"

"For not sticking to what you said, about a guys and girls room. He just seemed like he wouldn't calm down."

"I had the situation under control, but thanks anyway," I said as I turned to leave.

"Under control? You were about to fight him."

Looking back, I offered a shrug, and he exchanged it for a gasp.

"Lieutenant, you can't just fight people."

"He's a dog that needs to be broken to learn his lesson. Because if he isn't broken fast enough, then that hissing he's always hearing from everyone snapping at him," I waved a hand, "it'll catch up as a hissing bullet to his head."

"I just didn't want you to get hurt."

An obnoxious laugh bubbled up my throat, it took every ounce of self-control I had not to cackle it out. Instead, I turned and headed for the room. "Don't forget you said you'd take the couch."

...❀...

I had no idea if anyone kept watch. I know I didn't. I locked myself in my bedroom and sulked. I was embarrassed that those rumors about Ollie and me had been going around, but I was more agitated that people thought I hadn't earned my rank. Maybe I hadn't earned every single one, but I had fulfilled the role of each rank to the best of my ability. I worked harder than everyone else because I knew I hadn't earned every rank alone.

And then... there was Ollie. It's been weeks now, and there's no way for me to find him, or to contact him. I've been trying not to think about him. I don't want to. But it feels like the more I force myself not to feel anything, the more I end up feeling. I can't lock him out like I used to, or maybe I just

135

didn't want to. The lines were beginning to blur, and every day it was harder to face the truth because I knew the truth. I knew that Ollie had betrayed America to save me, and even if he hadn't, this invasion was going to happen. Realistically, I couldn't be mad, but I didn't want to miss him either. So, I was just stuck in a state of limbo, hanging on until something happened. Anything.

The next morning, I rolled out of bed and onto my knees. With my hands clasped, I sat there. I wasn't sure what to say, or to think. I didn't even know why I was there. It just felt like I needed to say something to Him. To thank Him for last night. But... I felt odd. Like maybe I shouldn't. Like maybe I should assume He already knows.

"How do I even begin? What do I even say to You?"

I felt like I should've started with an apology. All the times I ignored God simply for my own sake... for Ollie. Even before Olliare, I always figured God was understanding. He knew how hard it was to be up front about your faith. He knew how easy it was for people to reject the faith because they rejected Him every day, but I was part of that group of people.

I was part of the ones who rejected Christ because of our own desires and passions. We let God take a back seat because those conversations about faith—about Jesus—they were hard, and awkward. However, there was also a bigger part of me who enjoyed the life I'd been living. There was a part of me that used 'awkward conversations' as an excuse to ignore God.

God is not like us, there's no way to pacify Him. But for mere humans, there's always an excuse that's acceptable. A doctor's note for a job or school, jury duty, mom's in town so you cancel plans with friends, and they understand. There's always an excuse, but there's not one with God. Not accepting Him because you're enjoying your life is not acceptable to God. You just spat at the foot of the Cross where Jesus was sacrificed because we refuse to crucify the flesh.

Ignoring conversations that need to be had because you know it'll push people away until they discover God for themselves forces us away from God. It just shows Him we're not willing to stand for Him. We're so conformed to the world, we're afraid to be rejected by a world who rejected our Savior and rejects us every day. We're afraid to be different when that's what we were called to be. That's all we know.

"So why?" I whispered through clenched teeth. "Why won't I just do the right thing?" There was no answer, but I wasn't surprised. I wasn't really looking for one anyway.

"Lieutenant?"

I looked up from my folded hands at the door.

"What is it?"

"Can I come in?" the voice asked from the other side.

I knew it belonged to Sam, which was surprising, considering just the day before she was telling me I wasn't in charge. Maybe she was here to kill me. Maybe she'd gotten tired of me. Today, I don't even know if I would fight her.

"Yeah," I said finally as I climbed back into the bed.

She cracked open the door and peeked inside. Her blonde hair was down, and crystal blue eyes took in the room before she came and stood at the bed. Just in a sleeveless undershirt tucked into her uniform pants, Sam looked relaxed but seemed anxious.

"What do you need?" I asked.

"What are we supposed to do about our periods?"

I squinted and looked down at my feet beneath the blue blankets. "Well, I'm not too sure, actually. I don't have the parts anymore." She raised a brow and I explained, "I lost my eye on a special mission." I touched the patch I was wearing. "But I found out later that it wasn't the only thing I didn't have anymore. I'd taken a bad hit." I pointed to my midsection, starting at my navel and going down to my hip, as I spoke. "My head wasn't the only injury I'd suffered. There was shrapnel and debris that'd been removed from my legs and abdomen." I sighed. "I had an emergency hysterectomy. So I don't have the parts for menstruation anymore. Or pregnancy."

Sam stared at me. Bewildered. "I'm so sorry," she said slowly. Her eyes darted away, avoiding mine now.

"So, you came in here looking for pads and tampons?"

"Yeah," her words were shaky, "my period should be here any day now."

She's nervous, I thought. Something was wrong... something was very wrong, and her anxiety told exactly what it was.

Adjusting in the bed, I took a breath. "How many days ago was 'any day now?'"

The room was rigid with the aching silence. Sam's eyes fleeted to mine in a panic. She adjusted her weight from one foot to the other.

"Answer the question, Sam."

"A-A week ago."

"This didn't happen these past three weeks, did it?"

"No." Her face tightened with pain as she tried to hold back tears. "I've been seeing Winston since we met at bootcamp. We snuck off twice, and on the day of graduation, neither of us told our families and went off together for a little while."

I let go of a tired breath, rubbing a palm over my face. "We need to find a drugstore, get you a pregnancy test. That's the only way to know. Does he—"

"No," she said quickly. "Please don't tell him."

"Is he hurting you?"

"No." She shook her head quickly. "I just don't want anyone to know."

"Alright."

"Thank you, Lieutenant Colonel Banks."

I nodded and she left.

Sam was pregnant, or potentially pregnant. What would we do if she was? *That would be such an inconvenience.*

Getting out of bed, I got cleaned up in the bathroom. Gurgling a drop of hand soap with water was the worst idea I've ever had, but it was better than nothing. Pulling on my uniform jacket, I got ready and left the room for the kitchen.

Zion was sitting in the dining room, his jacket hanging on the back of his chair. Arms lined with muscles and a few scars were stretched out as he lazily twisted the knobs on a hand radio. He obviously wasn't expecting a response with his lax

139

demeanor.

"Morning," I said as I placed a hand on his shoulder.

Tired eyes snapped to my hand, and then up my arm to my eyes. "Morning, lieutenant. Is everything alright?"

"Yeah. Kinda…I-I don't really know."

He frowned now, adjusting to look up at me with earnest eyes. They were just as dizzying as the day I found him relaxing in the back of my weapons class. Looking away, I pulled my hand from his firm shoulder and took a seat beside him.

"You want to talk about it?" he asked.

"I would, but I promised I wouldn't."

"You promised yourself?"

My eyes slid to his as I shook my head. His brows reached for his hairline before he nodded and casually changed the subject. "So, how did you sleep?"

"Fine. And you?"

"I slept alright. That couch wasn't that comfortable."

"Really?" I chuckled. "Then I'm glad you offered to take the couch."

"Why is that?"

"Because I noticed the raggedy thing and sentenced Winston to it on purpose. But you took it instead. You deserved a bad night of sleep for that."

He leaned back in laughter, nodding as his honey gold skin flushed red with joy.

"Alright, that may be true. But tonight, I'm taking my chances with the floor."

"Hopefully that goes well." I paused and looked down at

the dirty floor. "But all the dirt and dust, and dried blood. I don't know if you want to sleep on that."

"That's true…" Zion looked down at the floor, then glanced up at me and we laughed together.

"We need to try to find more supplies," I said when the chuckles subsided. "And we need to figure out what we're going to do about Washington." I had plans to avoid the topic since Zion and I had an unspoken agreement to let Ollie's letter go, but Sam's urgent needs forced it. I wanted to be angry that the last part of Ollie was gone, the letter he'd left me was torn, leaving only the directions, but it was okay. Because now only Zion and I knew the truth. That was better to me.

"Right," he said in a quiet tone, "I forgot about Washington. We still need to get to Charleston before we can even think about getting to Washington."

"That might be more difficult than we thought, if things don't go right."

"What do you mean?"

"I wish I could tell you." I sighed. "But I'm sworn to secrecy."

"Should we really be keeping secrets at a time like this?"

"You have a point." I waved a finger at him. "But I don't know. I told Sam I'd keep it a secret."

"Sam? What kind of secret can she possibly have?"

I rolled my eyes and sat back in my chair. "A bad one—I'll tell you that much."

Zion squinted at the table, and then a crooked smile appeared on his handsome face. "What… is she pregnant?

Because that would be horrifying." He was laughing when he looked up at me, but I never faltered. A blank stare was all I could offer him as his smile slowly began to fade.

"C'mon, Banks," he chuckled nervously, "I was joking."

I didn't speak.

"C'mon, Banks!" he snapped.

"Lower your voice," I grated out.

He sucked his teeth, dropping his head. "We cannot afford a kid right now. That will slow us down so much."

"I know, that's why we've got to find a test before—"

"Sam!" Winston hollered suddenly.

Zion and I blinked at each other before rushing to our feet and heading down the hall. When I shoved the door open, I found Winston standing in the middle of the room with a knife sticking out of his forearm.

"What's going on!?" Zion snapped before I could.

With a laugh, Winston turned to face us. "We were playing darts with our knives. Sam kept missing so I came over and pointed to the target. She threw the knife and hit me instead."

"What kind of an idiot are you?" I looked over at Sam who was leaning against the wall.

"S-Sorry," she mumbled, dropping her gaze to the floor.

"Why are you throwing knives?" I yelled. "This isn't a game! We're under attack, you know that, right?"

"Goodness," Winston mumbled as he turned away.

"Seriously?" I stepped aside as he moved for the door.

"I'm going to find some bandages. I don't want to use up ours if this dump has some."

I shook my head, my attention returning to Sam. "Why?"

Zion tsked her before turning and leaving.

Gently closing the door behind him, I crossed the room to her. "What actually happened?"

"He… Well, he said he was in the mood. But I didn't want to do it." She gulped audibly. "He tried to force me, and I stabbed him."

Sighing, I reached out and rubbed her arm. It was pebbled with goosebumps. I wanted to go out there and wring Winston's neck for trying to force himself on to her, but the fact that Sam was willing to make up a lie about throwing knives for fun instead of telling the truth of what'd really happened said a lot about how much she still cared about him. It left a sick feeling in my stomach.

How could she care so much that she'd be willing to overlook the pain he caused her?

I felt torn. Should I go confront Winston or stay and comfort Sam?

I took another glance at Sam and noticed how nervous she looked. Eyes bulging, hands clasped together, standing perfectly still yet shaking all the while.

"It's going to be alright, Sam. I promise. Let me go see how he's doing."

She nodded, forcing a tightlipped smile. Just as I was going to leave the room, Winston hollered out again… except this time it wasn't like he was in pain, it sounded like he was afraid.

"Help me! Someone come quick!"

I raced from the room, my feet pounding the ground,

letting every stride bring me closer to what sounded like a scuffle. The house wasn't big, one straight shot, but I was frozen in my tracks when a screech echoed through the entire house.

It was a cry I couldn't forget. The sound of a pig squealing, oddly echoed by the sound of a car horn, loud enough to sound like it'd screeched through a microphone. The sound was the most terrifying thing to hear, something that could literally stop your movement. You didn't know if you wanted to hear more because it was so strange, or if you wanted it to stop because you were utterly terrified. However, Winston's cries got my feet moving again and when I rounded the corner, the horror I'd hoped I wouldn't see was playing out before me.

Winston was on the ground fighting a wrong, trying to keep it as far away as possible. He was screaming, I don't even think Winston knew he was screaming. His words were slurred together, and he looked like he'd seen death.

"Winston!" Sam screamed behind me.

I turned and caught her just before she lunged into the messy fight. "Zion! Zion!" I called frantically.

In what seemed like seconds, Zion was there with a gun raised.

"I don't have a clear shot!" he yelled.

"Just shoot!" I screamed.

He fired. The bullet grazed the wrong, and it snapped its head up at us, as if the creature hadn't noticed us all this time. It opened its mouth to shriek but Zion fired again, this time, lodging the bullet right in its head.

"Let me go! Let me go!" Sam screamed as she tried to break free from me. "Winston!"

He sucked in a breath, turning over weakly. My eyes darted around, looking for a bite mark when Zion said, "The closet, the wrong must've been in the closet."

"What?" I looked over, still holding Sam who was riling in my arms to get to Winston. The closet door was open and there were scratches all over the inside of the door. "No one checked the closet before?" I screamed.

"Please," Winston croaked, "please... tell her..." His body ticked and I knew he was changing.

"Zion, shoot him," I ordered, my voice a breathy whisper.

"No!" Sam jabbed her elbow into my chest, and I reflexively let her go.

Cradling my chest, I hollered at her, "Sam! Get back! He's changing!"

"I don't want to hit her!" Zion yelled.

"Baby," Sam was on the floor, cradling Winston as he began to twist and writhe. "I'm right here. Tell me, tell me what you want. I'm so sorry. I'm so—"

"Tell my wife Mary Anne that I love her!" Winston croaked out his last words and then grunted as his head flipped back and his body began to violently shake and tremor.

"Move, Sam!" I charged over to her, hooking my arms beneath hers and dragging her back.

"Don't shoot," Sam said calmly as she slipped free from me. With speed I didn't know she had, Sam ran at Zion and tackled him to the floor.

Zion fired the gun, but the shot was off—thanks to Sam—missing Winston completely.

"Stop it, Sam! What are you doing!?" I lunged onto her as she fought Zion, punching him and swinging on him to get his gun.

"We have to kill him now!" I screamed.

"Let him become a wrong! Let him be the monster he's always been!" Sam shouted as the three of us tussled. Some kind of way, the gun sprung loose from Zion's hand and all at once, we stopped at the sound of Winston's screech.

I wouldn't look at him.

"Get up!" I yelled, pulling Sam to her feet by her shirt. "We've gotta move!"

The world was a blur as I took off for an exit. With Winston on our heels, and the house being a straight shot, there wasn't a whole lot of places to run.

"My room!" I screamed to the others as we raced away from Winston. He was clumsy, running after us like he wasn't used to his new body. But that worked for us as we all piled into my room, barely getting the door closed before Winston slammed against it.

"This is your fault!" Zion screamed.

"It's *his* fault!" Sam yelled back. "He still loved her!" She began to sob. "In the end, he still loved his wife instead of me."

I shook her by the shoulders. "Stop it! We need to get out of here." I pointed to the window. "We'll go out the back and run until we find safety. Got it?"

"I… I don't have any shoes," Sam said.

146

"You'll have to go barefoot for now," I told her, then I turned to the window. "Come on, let's go!"

13

Zion

We made it through the window with Sam running barefoot. There was nothing we could do for her, and I don't think Colonel Banks would've wanted to do anything for her anyway. Considering this was technically Sam's fault. If she hadn't fought me, and let me kill Winston while he was changing, we wouldn't be on the run. But when he asked for us to deliver a message to his wife, Mary Anne, Sam wanted something more sinister than death for him.

"I think we can stop," Colonel Banks said as we slowed in the street.

Sam was hunched over, breathing heavily, when I hollered, "This is your fault! We were fine! Now we've got half the supplies and four weapons, including one gun! How do you think we'll survive?"

"Stop yelling at me! This isn't my fault!"

"It is!" I screamed as I marched up to her.

"Zion!" Banks called as she got between us. "Stop, Zion,

148

come on. We shouldn't fight."

"No, maybe we should! Maybe we should fight and throw knives at each other so there's one less mouth to feed and maybe the rations will last!"

"Zion!" Banks yelled in my face. "Hey!" She grabbed my face as I panted. I was so fiercely angry. We were fine in that house. We could've hunkered down and figured out a real plan. Now we've got to find shelter again, and with only one gun, that could be a problem.

"They didn't check the house," I said through breaths. "They didn't check every crevice like we said. And a wrong was in there."

"I know," Banks said as she held my face. She nodded; her wide eye filled with worry as she tried to calm me. I stared at her brown eye before my gaze slid to her patch. She'd already been through so much, probably survived off less than what we have right now. The thought brought a calming feeling over me.

Taking a deep breath, I closed my eyes. When I opened them again, Keoni was just standing there. She didn't look as worried anymore, her brown skin was smooth again, the wrinkle of frustration from earlier was gone now.

"Are you okay?" she asked sincerely.

I nodded, and she nodded along with me. "Ok," she said, patting my cheeks. She stepped back and turned to Sam who was whining on the ground.

"You don't get to cry," Banks said coldly. "Get up. We've got to find shelter and we don't have all day to look for it."

Slowly, Sam got to her feet, sniffling and wiping at her eyes. "Where can we go?" she said gently.

"Not much further than here," Banks said. "You'll get blisters if you haven't gotten them already. We need to find supplies too, and shoes for you." Banks dug through her pocket and pulled out a piece of paper.

"We still need to get to Charleston. If we can take shelter and recover for the rest of today and then tomorrow, we can probably make it to Charleston within a day or two of that."

"Alright," I agreed.

Sam didn't say anything, she just nodded sheepishly as she wiped at her nose.

"Good. With no objections, let's move."

"How can we just keep moving?" Sam said softly.

"What do you mean?"

"We need to take a moment to acknowledge that Winston is..."

"We're not hung up on him, and quite frankly, you shouldn't be either," Banks scolded.

"That's not fair." Sam's voice warbled in misery. "You just want to keep going like it doesn't matter that he just died!"

"Why are you having an outburst right now?" I snapped. "We don't have time for this. You caused this problem, and you're causing us *more* problems because we've got to find you shoes and protect you because you've got no weapon and you're pregnant!"

Everyone froze. Banks whipped her eyes to me... I'd said too much.

"What did you say?" Sam asked quietly.

"Nothing," I looked away from the two women. Flat feet smacked the concrete as Sam approached Banks.

"You promised..." she whispered. "You promised you wouldn't tell anyone."

"I didn't tell him. He guessed it," Banks clarified as her eyes darted to me.

"It doesn't matter! I didn't want anyone to know!"

"Guys, it's probably not good to stand out in the open yelling like this," I tried to offer but Banks whirled on me so quickly, I had to take a step back.

"Don't start handing out orders now! I told you we should leave five minutes ago before you shouted at Sam, *again*!"

"You're just mad that Sam knows that I know that she's—" My words were cut off when a gunshot went off. Banks and I ducked, dropping low to the ground. A cry ripped from Sam, as she fell to the ground beside us.

"Sam!" I hollered. She was lying on the ground clutching her shoulder. More shots went off around us as Banks and I moved to grab Sam.

"Get her up!" Banks ordered.

"It hurts!" Sam whined.

"Come on!" I shouted, grabbing her by the arm and pulling her to her feet.

We rushed down the street, dodging bullets and keeping our heads low.

"There's a warehouse up there! Let's get to it!" Banks screamed.

"Roger!" I screamed back.

We stayed low to the ground, sprinting from car to car to take cover between gunfire. Sam and I sat against one car while Banks found her own. Sam was breathing hard as I peeked around her to see Banks pulling her gun out. The magazine fell from the gun before she locked it back in place. When she finally caught my eye, she signaled to me to wait, then she moved to the end of the car and counted down from five.

"Get ready to move," I whispered to Sam.

She nodded, clutching her shoulder. The sound of Chinese banter rang out, gunshots, and pounding footsteps played background to the hollering voices.

I glanced back at Banks, and she mouthed the numbers, three ... two ... one!

Jolting to my feet while gripping Sam, we made a break for it as Banks fired at the soldiers rushing towards us. She hit two of them before ducking back down behind the car to reload.

"Keoni!" I screamed. "Come on!"

"Just go! I'll catch up!"

"No!"

"That's an order!" she hollered before standing up and firing at the approaching men. There were six of them rushing right towards her.

"Come on!" Sam pulled on me, turning me away from Keoni. I didn't want to leave her with just one gun and a knife on her hip, but I knew I couldn't help without a gun myself.

I had no choice but to leave.

Tripping behind Sam, we ran for the warehouse. It was

only a few feet away when a screech pierced the sky, like a bullet ripping through the air, hissing its fury before lodging into a target. I stopped immediately, looking back to where we'd left Banks.

"I'm going back," I said to Sam.

"No!" She pulled my arm, but I shoved her off.

"Get into the warehouse. Have the doors open for us because we're going to come rushing with those things on our heels. Got it?"

She swallowed and agreed.

Parting ways, I raced back to the Lieutenant Colonel.

Please, God, let her be okay.

Pumping my arms, my legs dug deep into the ground as I raced back for Banks. Where we left her wasn't too far away, however, when I returned, she was missing. I was going to yell for her, but I was afraid of who might hear.

Weaving between the discarded cars, I looked everywhere for Banks, then I stepped between two cars and froze. There was a wrong looking right at me as a Chinese soldier riled and flung his body beside him. The skin on what used to be a woman was hanging down, brushing against the concrete. Rotted teeth, and eyes that were dead with yellow pus all around them bulged at me. In a crouched position, like some kind of rogue animal, the wrong snapped its head to the side with a pronounced popping noise.

"Oh no." I turned on my heels, bursting with new energy as I ran from the creature.

It screeched and cackled behind me before it rushed at me.

153

"Zion!"

I looked around for the voice.

"Zion! Get down!"

Without knowing where she was, I dropped to the ground, rolling under a car when two shots went off. There was a second screech, and I covered my ears. It sounded like the cry of a lonely woman, while somehow the whine of a bat was intertwined with the voice of the woman.

Squeezing my eyes closed, I tried to keep my breathing steady as I listened to the wrong run. They were clumsy things, running with all their might, crushing their own bones at times, but they felt no pain. So even as they toppled over, they continued to move, racing towards you. They would chase you even if their spine was broken. Slumped over, the decaying wrong that was once a human would come for you no matter what.

"Hey!" I heard Banks scream.

My eyes shot open, and before I could do anything, a shot was fired, and out of the air a wrong slammed into the ground beside the car I was under. Slapping a hand to my mouth, I feverishly crawled from beneath the car, backing right into the open. I didn't care if I was found or not. Staring at the wrong lying on the ground, I wanted to panic, but there wasn't a reason to with a bullet in its head.

"Reinhardt," Banks' voice was nearby as I turned to find her. She came and slid down beside me, pulling me into a tight embrace.

"Why?" she whispered. "Why would you come back?"

"I couldn't leave you," I replied as I held her.

Pulling from our embrace, Banks patted my face. "We've got to keep going."

"Sam's at the warehouse. I told her to have the doors open for us."

"Good. Then let's move."

"Wait," I grabbed her arm as she stood. A look of surprise shimmied across her face as I held onto her. "We have to stick together this time."

"Ok, then get on your feet." She extended her hand to me, and I took it.

Banks held onto my hand as we raced through the demolished city, heading for the warehouse. Just like I'd instructed, Sam had the doors open.

"Sam!" Banks hollered as she ran in front. "Sam!"

Sam appeared the next moment, cradling her shoulder. "Come on!" she screamed for us.

Thankfully, no wrongs and no soldiers were on us as we reached the warehouse, squeezing between the doors. I turned and helped Sam push the doors shut and pull the big wooden plank into place to lock it.

14

Claudius

We'd been traveling for days, looking for Coco. I was ready to give up, but her sisters were determined. Coco ran off, thinking she'd killed Kingsley who's been quiet since the whole thing went down. She didn't say much as we traveled, not even if she was tired. She ate the least, drank the least, and spoke the least. I know she's blaming herself for arguing with Acoye, but there's nothing that can be done now. Coco was gone and we had no idea where to even search. I wasn't sure we were even in Springfield anymore. It was hard to tell with all the devastation everywhere. I wondered how much of America had been invaded by now.

Little Lyla had been struggling to keep up. So, we had to take shelter in a small barn. Lyla's coughing has gotten worse, her body looks weaker every day. I was thankful though for her sickness two days ago when her coughing fit brought us to this barn. I needed to rest my leg before it just completely gave out beneath me. Thankfully, on our travels, we've secured more medical supplies. Not enough to create a cast, but we did find a medical boot that fits a little uncomfortably, but it was better than the makeshift poles I was using. And we also found two bottles of aspirin.

"We can't stay in this barn forever," Chemistry said as we sat around the fire. We burned one every other night to preserve the wood and shrubbery we were able to find nearby.

"I know. We need food and water," I agreed.

"We need to be safe; we need to find Coco."

Chemistry dropped her head, squeezing her knees a little tighter as we sat on the ground around the fire.

"Chem," I tried to sound sympathetic, "we'll find her."

"Will we really find her? We've walked all over, Cloud, and we haven't found her at all. And it's my fault. I wanted to be mean, and I was trying to protect my sisters." She hiccupped.

"Chem, calm down. We can still find Coco."

"How?" She snapped her head up, tears were trailing down to her chin. "How can we find her? Tell me!"

"Chem, you'll wake Lyla," I said sternly.

She pressed her lips together as she tried to hold in her tears.

"Should I just accept it? Accept that she's gone? Will that make this easier?"

"It'll never get easy," I said as memories of Keoni bloomed in my head. "However, accepting she's gone is okay. Just don't accept that she's dead. Being gone is not the same as being dead. I know my fiancée is out there somewhere. I've just got to stay alive to see her again."

"But your fiancée is another soldier," she sniffled, "of course she'll survive."

Chemistry and I had gotten kind of close. Well, technically, we're all closer since I never told Chemistry anything in private. While we walked, looking for Coco, I'd tell the girls stories about Keoni, stories about my fiancée who was the strongest woman I knew. Lyla was a little jealous, but Chemistry really admired Keoni.

"Acoye isn't a soldier, but she doesn't need to be one to survive. You just have to be smart, know to keep warm, drink water, eat food, and stay out of sight. She knows this from traveling with us and it's kind of human instinct. She'll be alright."

Chemistry bit her lip, pushing her dreadlocks from her face. "I've always said Coco was actually the strongest of us all because she wasn't afraid of being afraid. She could let the fear in, and still somehow manage. But I can't let an ounce of fear in, or else I'll never be sane again," Chem admitted.

"You sound like a real soldier," I joked.

She looked through the fire at me, tears reflecting the golden flickering flames as she wiped at them. "A soldier? I could never be one."

"Anyone can be a soldier with the right training. You just have to want it bad enough."

"I guess."

Reaching my arms up, I stretched a little as Chem asked, "How's your leg?"

"Well, actually, I think it's getting better. When I checked on it today, the swelling had gone down a lot, and there's more room in this boot now." I pulled my leg up and she laughed gently.

"That's good. At least one of you is doing better." She looked over her shoulder and I followed her gaze to spot Kingsley wrapped in a blanket with Lyla. The two were asleep, Lyla's small chest rising and falling.

"I think Lyla's the real soldier," I said as we turned back to the flames. "That little girl, she's survived so much already. I feel like I've got to protect her to see her get stronger."

"When did Ly grow on you?"

"Honestly," I laughed as I reflected on the day she found me in that shed. "Lyla saved my life. I owe her, she just has no idea that she saved me."

"It's funny, one small girl saved the life of a general in the United States Army. You think anyone would believe that?"

I chuckled. "Maybe. But I think the one person who'd never believe it is Lyla."

She nodded, her free dreadlocks swaying with the motion. "Probably not. She's funny that way. And I think when she grows up, she'll still be the same."

"Selfless, you mean."

"Yeah."

The fire continued to crackle as it began to dwindle. There was maybe enough material to make one more fire, which meant we could possibly survive two more nights out here since we started a fire every other night. When there was no fire, we huddled close, keeping Lyla as warm as possible. But it was starting to get cold, and in no time, the winter chill would be here. Snow would fall, and survival would get that much harder.

"Winter is waving at us from a distance. I think we need to find a good place to stay. Reinforce it and get as much food as possible to hunker down there. We've got to tough the winter out from inside."

Chemistry sighed. "You think we can find enough food and water to hold out for months?"

"I want to believe we can, but we probably won't be able to. So we'll have to go looking for food."

Chem grunted. "Your leg, and Lyla's lungs? Please."

I dropped my head, laughing silently to myself. When I raised it, I found Chem smiling again, and it was good when she smiled. "That's why I'm going to teach you how to hunt and teach you what to look for. Until my leg gets better, and Kingsley's head is straightened out, it'll fall on you, Chem."

She clung to herself, hugging her knees as she shrugged slowly. "I don't know if I can do it, Cloud."

"You have to," I said casually. "If you don't, we won't survive. And you'll never see Coco again."

She took a deep breath, her eyes watching the flames. "Alright then, I'll do it."

15

Patron Saint of Victory

"Bastion, have you heard anything from China yet?"

"No, they haven't said a word."

I sighed, digging my nails into the stone chair. "Why aren't they answering? Have you told them that we're trying to work with them?"

"Yes, sir, I told them exactly what you said—that you want to discuss a plan to change the way the world sees China."

Shaking my head, I blew air between my lips and sat back. "Anything else to report?"

"The Russians, they've asked for your help. All the forces in Israel right now are weary. They're being utterly destroyed out there."

"What kind of help can I give them from here? Syria needs all its warriors; we can't lend a hand in any capacity. Not anymore than we've already helped."

It was my idea to invade Israel, to pinch the US, force them into a corner and allow the Chinese to have their way with

America. Israel is a land of resources the world needs, they're sitting on a melting pot; we need what they have in order to keep the entire world afloat. Gas, oil, even water had gotten more difficult than ever before to find. But Israel has wells of oil, gas lines we could tap into, fresh water sources that could help the thirsting world. If we didn't gain those resources, the world could wink out like a dying star.

But that wasn't the only reason I wanted Israel; it was just the only reason I'd told the council. Syria had wanted Israel all along. Since the Biblical era, Syria has suffered at the hands of Israel, but my people have never stopped thinking of ways to conquer them. Now, I have risen to power, and I plan to take Israel, not just for my Syrian people, but for my own sake.

Israel was *His* chosen dwelling place. I want to crush and annihilate them. I want to utterly wipe them from the face of the earth, leaving the ground stained with blood. No one will remember them, and God will be forgotten... just the way He forgot me.

I will make this world mine, make them hate Him, and see God for what He really is.

A sham.

God is not the Great I am... I am. I am. I am.

"Russia wants resources—anything to keep them in the fight." Bastion's deep voice pulled me from the crevices of my mind.

I studied my sandals as I sat in the council room, thinking over Israel. "What if we pulled out of Israel and then went back in?"

"Pull out so they can fortify their already strong defenses?" Bastion frowned deeply. "My lord—"

"If we can make a treaty with China, it'll look like they are retreating from America, but they're really just preparing for another attack. A bigger, deadlier one. What if we do the same thing with Israel?"

"You mean have the forces retreat to launch a second attack?"

"Yes, but this attack couldn't be like the last one. It'd have to be different... more cunning. They'll expect another invasion, but what if we walk through the front doors? What if we befriend them?"

Bastion folded his arms, scowling heavy brows for a moment. "Befriend them? How?"

"A treaty, just like China."

"A peace treaty." Bastion's voice held a question in it, but he was headed in the right direction.

"Yes, that's it," I confirmed. "A peace treaty with Israel. No nation can invade Israel ever again, under my ruling here."

"You'd have to establish your ruling."

"Not if we can get everyone to sign the treaty. If I get China to sign a treaty, people around the world will see me as a leader and expect the rest of the world to follow whenever I do something. So, if Syrian forces sign that peace treaty with Israel, everyone else will too."

"Well, that might work," Bastion conceded. "But, number one, China hasn't agreed to a meeting with us. And number two, the world may think you're a leader but, sir, the others here won't."

I sighed, standing from my chair. I moved around the long oval table, tapping each chair as I walked. "A council, made of everyone."

"Like the United Nations?"

"Even better. We'll decide things for the world. Everyone will listen to us since the world is in a frenzy and we're the only ones trying to do something about it."

Bastion nodded, dropping his arms to his side. "This can work, but where do we even begin?"

"With China," I said as I stood directly across the table from him. A small patch of light was splayed on the table beside Bastion. "We've got to get them to agree to that treaty. It'll help me win the world, and all the heads."

"And the Russians? What do we say to them?"

"Hold off on them. Make them suffer a little more. Then it'll really seem like I've saved them from this war."

"As you wish, sir." Bastion nodded. "I'll get right on getting word again to China about a meeting."

"Good. We need this, Bass."

He looked at me, a stern expression on his hard features. "I'll make it happen. No matter what."

"Thank you."

He smiled. "Of course, sir. We've come too far not to see everything we've dreamed of come to pass."

"Very true."

He nodded, taking his leave. Bastion was my most trusted ally besides Sabiya. After rescuing him, he and I worked out

164

the plan to make America fall. To fight the injustice we experienced by the same country, being left to rot. Becoming a prisoner of war, but never anything more than that. Never anything more than a cluster of names on a banner for people to mourn and wish we'd return.

If they only knew how selfish America truly was. How she cared more for what she looked like and not for who she was. The backbone of America is her soldiers, yet every day, prisoner release deals are made, and soldiers remain prisoners of war, while others walk free. It's like being a prisoner of war was a badge of honor, just one we never got to wear. America wore it for us as she mourned along with her people, while never truly helping the ones who kept her free.

I returned to my seat at the head of the council room. I looked at all the empty seats, imagining every single one of those belonging to someone under my control.

Power... I had never cared for it until I realized this was my chance. My chance to defeat God, to show Him that the precious world He loved more than me will never love Him more than I did. I believed in impossible situations, yet He has still forsaken me.

Taking a slow breath, I blew the angry thoughts away. I needed a clear head to think everything through. Anger would get me nowhere. The moment China agrees to a meeting, agrees to this plan to make them look better, I'll already be turning the tables in the region. The Western world is falling apart, there isn't going to be much left of it once China's invasion is over.

Americans will flood the north and south of their land, clustering in Canada and South America. When those countries' resources become scarce, hunger, anger, and civil wars will break out. Half the country will want to help the refugees, the other half will want them gone for resources' sake. A weak and a warring country will be easy to entice.

The doors to the council room opened and Bastion returned, but there was a panicked look in his eyes. He marched down the center of the room and stopped short of my seat.

"What is it?" I demanded.

"Our forces, Russian, Egyptian, everyone wants to pull out of Israel. There's some sort of pestilence in the air."

"Pestilence? Like a sickness?"

"I don't know what to call it. But they're rotting, right on the battlefield. The medical tents smell petrifying, bugs and birds won't stay away because of the strong stench. It's like the smell is calling to them. But there's something else." He paused, nearly lost for words.

I gripped the edge of my stone chair, pulling myself forward on it.

"The pestilence," Bastion went on, "we don't know if they're carrying the same virus as the wrongs. If this is an early stage. The only thing we know is that the wrongs decay, like their skin begins to sag. But these soldiers, they're rotting. The flesh is peeling right off the bones. Tongues rotting right out of their mouths." He shook his head. "It's almost worse than the wrongs because they're not dying and changing. They're

166

fine one minute, then the next they're in horrifying pain, eyes falling from their sockets. And Japan," he stood there a moment, his eyes finally lifting to mine. He looked like death had come for him. "They were sending soldiers to America, bringing some back. A plane crashed close to China and there's been an outbreak that China's trying to contain."

"What do you mean an outbreak?" I could hardly speak.

"Sir, China's borders are crawling with wrongs right now."

"It's spreading." I stood. "Those Japanese idiots went to help America and brought that virus here! We had it under control until they screwed everything up!" Spittle flew from my mouth as I yelled. I wiped it away and took a deep breath.

The eastern world had mostly contained the wrongs, had even developed programs to study them. Now, with an outbreak of them in China, the most crowded place on earth, we were about to see death like never before.

"We need to stop the spread right now," I said. "Who knows about China and how did you find out? We don't need everyone freaking out about this."

"Just me and the forces on the battlefield know about the rotting soldiers. China is trying to keep a low profile. They didn't really tell us, we found out that a Japanese plane went down on Chinese borders. The group of spies we've got there in China reported that wrongs had landed in China and they're trying to contain it."

"Good, they're trying to keep that quiet. They don't want us to know—which can work to our advantage. We can still use this chaos, demanding peace with China and Israel." I

167

stopped. "Bastion, is it just our soldiers dying over in Israel?"

"No reports of Israeli bodies rotting have come through," he admitted weakly.

"Very well." I clenched my jaw so tight my head began to ache. *He* was protecting Israel, I had to do something. But I couldn't. Not yet.

I need to believe in the peace treaty and trust that it will work out. *I am the patron saint of victory.*

"Bastion, right now, Syria is my top concern. The world comes second. Once the Syrian border is secure, and we've got a screening process, we can share that with other countries. But we have to serve home first. Understood?"

"Yes, sir. I'll get right on this."

When he left again, I stood, silently thinking over the pestilence and the wrongs outbreak. I wondered if God had sent the pestilence. It only made sense if He had. But there were heaps of bodies lying all around Israel, there was a chance that the pestilence came from all the death… though I knew that wasn't true. That's what we'd tell people, that's what we'd feed the media, however, I knew it was God. He was fighting for His people.

I smirked, slipping a hand into the pocket of my linen pants. Gazing out my window, I whispered, "You can protect Your people, that small land. But I will protect mine, the entire world."

16

Abigail

I inhaled, eyes shooting open. I was staring up at a rock ceiling, and the fuzzy memories began to come back. I'd passed out after inhaling all that smoke when Eve and I went out to try to throw off the Chinese soldiers who were after us. I slowly sat up, glancing around. I wasn't sure how I'd gotten back to the cave.

"Abbey, you're up." Eve scooted over to me, helping me sit up.

Gripping my head, I felt dizzy as I stared at my legs. "How long was I out?"

"A few days," Coco said as she sat on my other side holding Flower. I wanted to reach for her, but the sudden movement made me cough roughly. Catching my breath, I noticed Coco's leg, and remembered the gash in it. However, the bandages she had on now weren't the ones I'd put on her. They were fresh, clean bandages.

I blinked away, back to Eve. *"Days?"*

He nodded. "But that woman," he pointed ahead at a woman sitting with her back to us. A braided ponytail, long and thick, hung down her back as she sharpened her knife.

"Who is she?"

"Have you told her yet?" the woman's voice called over her shoulder, echoing through the cave.

Coco's grip on my hand tightened as the woman turned to face us. Regal brown skin, long lashes, full lips, and a charming smile. She looked seemingly harmless, but Eve's and Coco's tense reactions to her told me otherwise.

"Who are you?" I asked.

"Call me Whisper."

"Whisper? Where did you come from?"

"The name's not my given, it's just what people call me. But that kid there, Everette, he saved me a few days ago."

I turned and looked at Eve. His eyes swept the cave as he avoided eye contact with me. Probably thinking of how he'd abandoned me in the woods. I wanted to yell at him for it, but there were other issues to address.

"You brought her in here?" I asked slowly. "Over my *daughter*? While I was unconscious?"

"It's not what you think," Coco spoke up. "He rescued her."

"She was screaming for help," Eve cut in. "And I found her being attacked by a Chinese soldier. We fought him off together, and she helped me bring you back. She even hunted for us the next day and cleaned Coco's wounds." He pointed towards the strips of meat sitting on a stick on the floor of the cave.

"Then why are you so afraid of her?" I asked.

"Because she's..." Coco's voice trailed off, but the woman filled in what Coco couldn't say.

"I've been bitten."

Whisper stood, long legs lifting her up. She rolled up her sleeve, revealing a bite mark, and then lifted the brown leather jacket she was wearing, revealing more bites and scratches— even one on her neck.

I could feel my eyes bulging from my skull as I reflexively backed into the wall. She had been *seemingly* harmless when she turned with a smile, but now I thought my heart might fail me. She was a wrong... wasn't she? The air was tense, but only around Coco, Eve, and me. Whisper was completely relaxed, like we shouldn't be afraid of her.

"Why? Why haven't you changed?" My voice was shaky as I squeezed Eve's and Coco's hands.

Whisper adjusted her clothes, smoothing out the wrinkles in her jacket. "Because I'm covered."

"What?"

"I'm covered," she repeated. "They can't pass that virus on to me."

"What are you talking about?" I snapped.

"The wrongs." Whisper pointed to the mouth of the cave. "They bite you and transfer a virus to you. It takes over your body in seconds to a minute."

"I still don't understand why you haven't changed!" I was

yelling as the fear swelled in my chest. Flower began to cry, and Coco tried to bounce her to quiet her down, but Whisper wasn't bothered by the baby as she went on to explain, "I told you; I'm covered. Do you know anything about the Bible? The Rapture?"

"What does the Bible have to do with this?"

"Everything." Whisper leaned down and picked up her knife. She inspected it a second before placing it on her hip. "Revelation chapter eighteen, verse eight, it details a plague that comes in a single day. The world—"

I shook my head, shaking away the thoughts I'd had right before we left the shelter. I was thinking that everything that'd happened had something to do with the Rapture, but I didn't want to believe because that would mean we were all left behind.

"Don't screw with me!" I hissed angrily.

Whisper smiled again. "Oh, I assure you, I'm not screwing anyone. Those creatures, they're all plagued. They're all the living dead, walking around, attacking everyone in their sight. Every sound they hear, they hope it's something to eat."

"How," Eve spoke, his voice wavering, "how do you know all this?"

For the first time since I'd awakened, Whisper didn't look so smug. Her eyes dropped to the cave's floor, and her voice was tainted with glum. "I studied in Jerusalem for some time when I was younger. I'd learned so much about the Bible, interpreting it, living, eating, and breathing everything in it. But I came back home, and I stopped believing for a while. For too

172

long."

"Why?" Coco asked as Flower finally hushed and began to fall asleep.

"Well, my husband wasn't a Believer, he just went through the motions of Christianity. Which kind of put a damper on my faith. But it wasn't until my daughter died that I completely stopped believing. She had a painstakingly long battle with cancer, and eventually she passed."

Whisper looked over at Coco, a grim smile on her face. "She wasn't much older than you, probably. But when this invasion began and then people started disappearing, I knew I had to bury my grudge against God and start believing again. Because these next seven years would require it."

"Next seven years? What are you talking about?" Eve asked.

"Hold on," I snapped, "I really don't care about your backstory, or your faith. I need to know why you haven't changed. Why are you special? Are you immune?"

"No." She sighed. "Anyone can be protected if they believe. If they allow Him in. But it can't be for the wrong reasons. You can't just say, hey Jesus, protect me because there's a plague. There needs to be sincerity there."

"You're seriously telling me that because you believe in Jesus, you're not changing?"

"Technically, yes." Whisper nodded. "That's exactly what I'm saying. Like I told you, I studied the Bible, the End Times, the seals, and all that for a very long time. I know that it sounds crazy, but—"

"No," Coco's voice wasn't shaking. Her eyes were sealed to Whisper as she said, "I'd heard once that when the Rapture happened the world would fall apart. That Jesus would really be the only way to survive."

Whisper brightened. "That's right. The Rapture happened, and everyone who was taken left their earthly bodies behind. Those empty vessels turned into wrongs."

I swallowed. I'd heard of the Rapture, had even believed in it for a while. But I never counted on it actually happening anytime soon. Sure, the world had gotten drastically worse, but things get bad before they get good sometimes. That's what I'd always been told. However, the Rapture was the only explanation for the sudden death of Zion's parents.

Mrs. Reinhardt literally dropped dead, and then changed.

Scratching my head in the silence, I tried to make sense of what Whisper had told us.

"Let's say this is true," I started. "The Rapture happened, and the bodies left behind turned into the wrongs. In what way is this a plague? And why are there children left behind?"

"Some kids disappeared, others didn't. The moment a child can choose right from wrong is the moment they can choose to sin or not to sin. Which means they can choose Christ."

"Then why is Flower here? She doesn't know anything." I stared at my infant daughter, too young to even speak. How could she choose right from wrong? How could she choose Christ?

Whisper glanced over to my baby, and she looked like she

pitied me for a moment. "Children born after the Rapture have to live it out."

I went silent, trying to think, and Whisper noticed my confusion.

"If she had been stillborn, then I would've assumed she was born just as the Rapture happened. Not impossible, but that's some perfect timing. However, the Rapture *did* happen in the blink of an eye, unless the child exited the womb right at that moment, they were—"

"Flower was born seconds to a minute after..." I trailed off.

I brought Flower into seven years of chaos. I wanted to cry; I could feel my mind tearing apart as Whisper started speaking again.

"As far as the plague goes, you must understand that Believers never really die. However, the pestilence circling right now is a judgement on America and the world."

"I don't follow any of this," Eve said sourly. "And I don't believe that the Bible is the answer to the problems we're having right now."

"You should," Whisper said flatly. "The Bible is not an ancient book of scribblings from old people. It's a guide, it's information—holy divine information. It points us in the right direction, literally outlining the future. Yet, we somehow still choose not to believe it."

"It's all encrypted, how are we supposed to just take it and believe it?" I said roughly.

Yes, I did believe, but not to this extent. I knew God was

175

good, Jesus was the answer, and the Holy Spirit was the power. But the prophecies and the things no one really explained, how was I supposed to just believe that? Especially now that I'd given birth to Flower. She'd have to choose between right and wrong and she only had seven years to do it.

"Ok, let me try to explain this to you all." Whisper cleared her throat, glancing around the three of us and Flower. "What happened is a release of a virus. It's a brain eating virus. It makes you drop dead so that it can take over the host." She rolled her wrist as she further explained. "In this case, the body is the host. And the virus will keep eating until the brain is gone. That's why those things don't die from being shot anywhere but in the head. You have to stop the virus. And this thing, this virus, it doesn't want to die."

"That's why it bites, right?" Coco asked.

"Yes. The wrongs bite to pass the virus so it can keep living. It's like God struck the bodies of the raptured ones with one single virus fighting to stay alive."

"Why would He strike the bodies of Believers though?" I asked. "That makes no sense."

"They're dead." Whisper shrugged. "I doubt anyone in heaven cares what happened to their discarded bodies right now. I doubt they're even thinking about *earth* right now."

I nodded slowly. I suppose it made sense.

Whisper went on, "This virus is the beginning of God's judgement. Pestilence is to strike the earth, and it is to strike Babylon hard. Making everyone a wrong is too easy. God made the ones He raptured a wrong to attack the earth. He wants the judgement to be felt, all these years of longsuffering and putting up with our mess. God is finally retaliating on the wicked."

"So that means, God used Believers to judge the nonbelievers?" Coco asked. She seemed intrigued with the convoluted story, but she was just a girl. So, I cut her some slack.

"Exactly." Whisper nodded.

"Wait, who's Babylon?" Eve asked as he adjusted beside me.

"Who do you think Babylon is?" Whisper replied. "The scriptures describe Babylon as a 'her.' A woman with perverse sexual desires who spreads that perversion all over. A woman with luxuries at will. Power, more power than everyone else. She's an immoral woman, one who loved her wickedness and evilness."

"Babylon is a modern country full of evil, described as a 'she'? I don't know."

"Why do you even care?" I said to Eve, but he never got to answer. His eyes had grown timid when he looked at me, but Whisper cut in and said, "Babylon is America. America has always been a female country, with Lady Liberty as our leading lady. Our judgement is just beginning. The day where we fall all at once has only begun. The morning sun is just rising, and when it sets, America will cease."

There was a moment of silence as we all sat blinking. No one moved or spoke. Even Whisper just stood there, gauging our reactions.

"You really want me to believe this?" I asked. "Believe that this is a plague from God, America is suddenly Babylon, and in twenty-four hours, America will no longer exist? But every other country will stand? C'mon," I shook my head, "there's no way any of this is true."

"Why? Why can't this be true?"

"It's already been twenty-four hours, way more than that, and America's still standing,"

"Not a day in our time, a day in *God's* time."

"Alright then, explain to me why some people don't change with the bite. Are they all covered like you said?" I fought back. I wanted anything but the Rapture to be true. It would hurt too much to know that we've all been left behind.

"No," Whisper answered. "They still die, their body just isn't a good host. The virus kills them instead of taking over."

I gritted my teeth, remembering my neighbor's youngest son from the shelter who didn't change. He lay dead on the bed getting eaten away. The thought sent a bubbling anger up my spine. I was ready to freak out when I screamed, "This makes no sense!"

"It makes perfect sense!" Whisper shouted back. "America is being invaded, we're experiencing a plague that's going to wipe out our economy and our people. Our livestock—everything is going to be whisked away! Have you seen the other countries? They've all got allies helping them, trying to contain the wrongs and share resources. But who's helping the US right now? No one! Because they can't." She finally took a breath, calming down for a second before she said, "No one

178

can help America if they've got ties to the country invading it. China has set us up to fight this battle alone. But God purposed for the US to lose this war."

"Why though?" Coco asked shyly. "Why is He so mad with the US?"

"Because we've forgotten Him," Whisper answered. "We've ignored His pleas for righteousness, and we've entertained the world, influenced them with sexual immorality—tainting the earth called God's creation." She stood there a moment, glancing around at all of us. "The Rapture broke America, even if we won't say it. In an hour," she looked up at the ceiling of the cave, "in a single hour, your judgement has come."

"What does that mean?" Coco asked.

"It means that the fall of America will happen so quickly there will be no recovery. In the hour that the Rapture happened, America began her spiral. Even if we fight the invasion, we will never win. But the Rapture had to happen. God called for His people to come out of Babylon so they wouldn't experience the judgement."

"How can we trust anything you said?" I asked. "Sure, you know the Bible, but what about the wrongs? How do you know all this?" I was asking out of anger, out of hope that maybe this could explain away the things I didn't want to understand. However, it all made sense, perfect sense. How could I come to terms with being left behind?

"The wrongs, the virus that's attacking. That info came from a friend across the way. He's studying them. I was able to make contact with him before the power grid went out, and he's told me a lot about the wrongs."

Eve sighed, slumping against the wall. "Even if this is all true, I still don't know if I can believe it. I don't even understand how you're covered and what you're covered with."

"All you need to understand is that we're living in the tribulation, and you won't survive it if you don't believe," Whisper said firmly.

"Fine," I said forcefully, "you're absolutely right. Now what? What can we even do if any of this is true?"

"We need to find better shelter first. The city is a few miles south of here, we can make it in about two maybe three days," she said as she leaned down and grabbed her bag.

"So we're just supposed to follow you?"

Whisper looked over at me and shrugged. "You don't have to. I'd like it if you did, but there's no reason for us to travel together."

"I think we should stick together," Coco began. "Even if we don't necessarily understand everything Whisper said, she can hunt really well. We'll need food, fresh water, and she can help us."

"I do understand what Whisper is saying," I admitted. "I just don't believe it." I used the wall to get my feet beneath me. My legs felt wobbly as I faced Whisper. "If you can help us get to safety, then I don't see why we can't travel together."

Whisper smiled. "Glad to be tagging along."

She extended a hand to me. I stared at it, before turning

back to Coco and Eve.

"Let's get our things and prepare to leave," I said, taking her hand.

17

Zion

"Ok," Keoni said as she sat beside me, "I spy with my little eye, something dark."

I squinted. "Something dark? Ki, that's everything."

She laughed beside me. The warehouse didn't have working lights. So the only time there was light was the daylight that came through the small windows during the day. At night, we cracked the door and burned the chunks of wood lying around. I wasn't sure what the old warehouse used to be, possibly a place where wood was handled since there was sawdust and huge machines with planks of wood in them. Everything looked like people were in the middle of working and just left.

"Ok, it's big and it's dark."

"That doesn't help either," I snorted.

Keoni and I had gotten closer the last few days we've been in the warehouse. Initially, we were just going to stay here for a little while, but since Sam had blisters and then came down with a fever, we've been stuck here.

Keoni and I have found nothing useful to do besides play games or see who can count the highest. We were able to use the pens and papers from the offices—where we found a loaf of bread, candy, and three bottles of water—to rewrite the directions to Washington since I left mine at the old house, but Keoni had a copy.

Keoni laughed, patting my shoulder gently as she leaned against me. "Ok, I'll give you one more clue—it's expansive."

"What kind of clue is that?"

"Come on, Z." She bumped her shoulder with mine playfully. "Look out there, and tell me what's dark, big, and expansive?"

I stared at her for a minute before glancing back at the empty warehouse. There was wood, an old campfire we'd made, and Sam lying beside our bags.

I squinted when I finally guessed, "The wall?"

"Yes!" she exclaimed.

I leaned back and laughed. "Keoni, there's no way that the wall is a fair one!"

"Oh come on, but you guessed it. That was a really good one."

"No," I laughed, "that was hard."

"Not harder than the pile of dust you made me guess."

"Ok, maybe that was kind of a bad one."

Keoni laughed, leaning against me again, but I welcomed her warmth, her laughter, her joy. She was so different from the woman I thought she was. Colonel Banks always seemed so rigid, despite her beauty, she was only focused on the mission. Which in this case, you really couldn't blame her. But there were these pockets of laughter we'd share, and she was always so fun. Now, it's not little pockets, or glimpses into who she is. Lieutenant Colonel Banks had allowed me to see the real her, and she was a very nice woman.

"Alright," I nodded. "My turn. Let's see. I spy—"

A thud rang out from the side door. Keoni and I looked at each other before scrambling to our feet.

"Cover Sam," she whispered as she pulled her gun from her hip. Keoni moved quietly towards the door where the thudding was coming from. Before she could open it, the door swung open, sending Keoni stumbling backwards.

"Hold it right there!" we yelled in unison. "Don't move!"

"Please don't shoot!" a woman called back.

"We have children, don't shoot!" another woman's voice rang through my entire body.

I recognized that voice. Slowly, I stood as Keoni waved them inside. An older woman, dark skinned in a leather jacket stepped inside with her hands raised. A boy followed, with a limping girl holding onto him. And then one more person stepped inside, a woman. There was an infant strapped to her chest, and her hands were raised. Chocolate brown skin, wide eyes that could stop my heart were blinking around.

"Abigail?" my voice cracked.

She looked past Keoni, finding me in the low evening light. "Zion?"

"Is it really you?" I stepped forward.

184

Pulling the child from her chest, she passed it to the boy, and moved closer. After a moment, she squealed and charged into me.

"Abbey!" I cried.

She sobbed as she clung to my neck. "Zion! Zion!" She was inconsolable, but I wasn't too far behind. I didn't know if I'd ever see Abigail again, and here she was, clinging to me, weeping as we embraced.

Peeling apart, I cupped her face to see her. She was beautiful as she cried, blubbering that she loved me and missed me. I couldn't formulate words; I couldn't do anything but stare.

"I'll get the others settled in," Keoni said as she came over. She patted Abigail's shoulder, and Abbey turned and thanked her. Keoni gave her a sweet smile, and then passed it to me before heading back to the others.

"How did you get here?" I asked when she finally began to calm down.

"It was so hard, Z." She hiccupped, clutching a handful of my shirt in her hand. "It was so hard."

"I'm so sorry I wasn't there." I pulled her into my chest as we lowered to the floor.

"It doesn't matter. We're together now! We're together again! I was so afraid this day would never come."

"So was I," I whispered.

"I have a surprise for you," she said as she pulled away from me, wiping at her tears. Looking over her shoulder, she flagged down the boy who was holding the baby.

"Is that… is that our daughter?" I asked slowly.

She looked back with the widest grin on her face. "She's perfect, Zion."

I hugged Abbey again. "I'm sorry I wasn't there to help you."

She lifted my face, pressing her forehead against mine. "I'm just happy we're here right now."

The boy cleared his throat, jerking us apart. "Here's Flower," he said awkwardly.

"Thanks," Abbey whispered. He nodded, eyeing me an extra second before walking off.

"Who's the kid?" I asked.

"That's Everette, well, I call him Eve. He really looked out for us out there."

"Really?"

She nodded. "Enough about him, look…" She passed me the baby. She was tiny and light brown with a little hair on her head.

"Goodness, we made her."

"She looks just like you."

"I was going to say that to you."

We laughed as I gazed at our sleeping child. She was precious, the greatest gift I'd ever received. But looking at her brought a wave of sadness over me.

"This world, they don't deserve her. Why did she have to be born right now?"

"Zion," Abbey whispered, "don't see it that way. I needed her to keep me strong while we were separated. She's a blessing."

"She is," I agreed. In my heart, I whispered gratitude to God as I rocked our little Flower.

...✿...

That night, Abbey and I spent all our time together glued to Flower. We didn't sit around the fire, and we barely spoke with anyone. Abbey and I needed to talk but our words fell short. We ended up spending a lot of time in silence. Not sure what to say, or how to even talk about what we've been through. Thankfully though, everyone gave us our space.

I caught that kid, Eve, glancing over his shoulder every now and then, checking on Abbey. The two must've been really close. He never looked at me, only at Abbey and then at Flower. I didn't know if he hated me or not, but it honestly didn't matter. He was just a kid; he was protective because he had to be. I appreciated him, though right now really wasn't the time to tell him that. He'd just feel like I was taking Abbey from him.

The following morning, I woke up with my family by my side. Flower was asleep on a blanket, and Abbey and I were tangled together beside her. When I opened my eyes, I realized I was happy. Even in this situation, I was happy.

Rolling over and pecking Abbey on the cheek, I moved from the floor to head out back to the bathroom. When I opened the door, I found Sam outside, vomiting vehemently.

"Sam!" I exclaimed as I ran to stand beside her.

"Sorry, it's just a bug."

"Let me get you some water." I moved for the door, but that older woman from yesterday was standing in the doorway now. There was something strange about her. Something I recognized. Like if I looked in the mirror, I'd see it in me too.

"Is she sick?" the woman asked, her eyes on Sam.

"Yeah, she's got a fever," I said.

She glanced up, then went right back to staring at Sam, craning her neck to get a better look. That's when I noticed what looked like a bite mark on her neck. "No something else is going on," the woman said.

"Have you been bitten?" I stepped back.

"Yes," she said plainly.

"Abbey! Keoni! Get up!" I backed away from her, and she sighed.

"I hate explaining this every time," she grumbled.

"Explaining what?" I snapped. "That you're a wrong!"

"I hate explaining how I've been bitten but never changed."

Just then, Keoni burst through the door with Abbey on her heels.

"What's going on?" Keoni asked.

"She's been bitten!" I yelled, frantically pointing.

Keoni's eyes bucked. "What!"

"Wait." Abbey squeezed out the door and grabbed my arm. "She's alright. She's got some kind of cure for the bite.

She says it's a covering."

Keoni ripped her gun from her belt and aimed it at the older woman. "You need to start explaining, right now."

"Calm down," she grumbled. "If you noticed I had bite marks, you'd notice they were fading. Healing." She turned to Keoni, shoving her gun away. "If you want to know the truth, come inside." The woman stepped through the door and disappeared inside.

"Why didn't you tell me you were traveling with someone like that?" I snapped at Abbey.

"I don't know. We didn't really talk about that yesterday. We reminisced, enjoyed each other's company."

"Yes, Abbey I was there. I know what we did. I just don't know why you didn't mention a woman with a bite mark. That's kind of important. More important than reminiscing."

She frowned, shoving me back a little. "You're so rude." Rolling her eyes, she turned and headed inside.

Keoni snorted, standing there with a gun in one hand and a smirk on her face.

"Shut up," I grumbled as I pushed by her to get inside.

The woman was standing in the middle of the warehouse as I took a seat on the floor beside Abbey, though she wasn't talking to me. Keoni helped Sam inside and laid her down before sitting beside her.

"Now, I'm only going to explain this once," she held up one finger. "My name's Whisper. Got the nickname from the mission trips I did in the Middle East. Rescuing Jews from hostile nations and getting them back to Jerusalem."

189

"I don't care about your backstory, just tell us about the bite marks," Keoni called.

Whisper rolled her eyes and said, "I've been bitten. But I'm covered, so the virus that's plaguing the world right now doesn't affect me."

"What exactly are you covered in?"

She leaned down and opened her bag. Pulling out a bottle of grape juice, and a pack of crackers.

"What's that?" Eve asked.

"Communion."

"Not this again," Eve grunted.

The young girl beside him raised her hand.

"Yes, Coco?" Whisper acknowledged.

"Communion is made up of the Body and Blood of Jesus Christ, isn't it?"

"Yes, that's exactly right."

I watched in silence as she held up the two parts of communion, remembering when my mother wanted me to perform communion in my dad's absence. He'd gone to Washington to speak with the president when Israel was invaded, but he returned before I was needed.

"The Body and Blood of Jesus possesses healing properties, and protection," Whisper said.

"You're telling me," Eve spoke up, "that grape juice and crackers are going to prevent me from changing?"

"I'm telling you that the Body and Blood of Jesus Christ will protect you and heal you if you believe. Grape juice and crackers won't do a thing for you."

190

I thought for a moment in the silence. A conversation between my mother and I happened a while back where she mentioned something about the Blood of Jesus being our protection in the End Times. But if any of this were true, that would mean we were living in the End Times right now.

"The Rapture," I spoke up, "has it happened?"

Whisper raised a brow. "Yes, son. It happened a while back. It's what kicked off these wrongs."

I looked at Abbey, but her eyes shied away from me. "Abbey, what's wrong? What do you know?"

"Something happened when you left," she began softly. All eyes were on her as she spoke. "Rhoda, she'd been helping me give birth. And then," her voice began to tremble, and her eyes filled with tears, "then she stopped suddenly and asked if someone was playing music. She said she heard trumpets, Z. And the next moment, she fell to the floor and began to change."

My breath hitched as I stared at my fiancée.

"And then Jillian came upstairs," Abigail continued, "but he wasn't himself. He and your mother had changed into wrongs."

"No," I whispered. "No, that can't be right."

"It is," Whisper said to me. "If your parents were Believers, then your mother heard the trumpets announcing the return of Jesus Christ. The Rapture took them away. Leaving their bodies without guidance. The virus took over the body as its host once God sent the pestilence."

"Stop it!" I shouted at her.

"You need to hear this, boy. Because you're like me."

I wiped at my tears. Abbey tried to comfort me, but I pulled my arm from her. I wasn't mad at her—I was just frustrated with the whole situation. "What do you mean I'm like you?"

"You're going to save a lot of people, preach to a lot of people, and make it farther than you think. I can see the calling resting on you."

Swallowing, I realized that she saw in me what I'd seen in her when we met at the door. I had seen something spiritual.

"You shouldn't mourn your parents, they're better off than you are right now. You need to listen to me carefully," Whisper said.

"Why should I?"

"Because I have the cure that you'll have to tell people about."

"The cure?" Keoni spoke, catching my attention. "What do you mean the cure?"

Whisper smiled. "The cure, the protection, a guarantee of your survival is through communion, through the Blood of Jesus."

"What if you don't believe?" Keoni asked. "Is there no other way?"

"No one comes to the Father except through the Son. He is the only way. His Blood is the only protection," Whisper said calmly.

"She's right." I stared at the ground. "My mother, she said that once. She said that death cannot conquer life because the life of the flesh is in the blood. So Jesus' Blood is life."

Whisper nodded. "That's right. Blood holds life. The virus attacks to stay alive, but it can't live if you're living too. This virus is special because it needs a dead host. That's why it kills you and changes you in the next instant."

"And Jesus conquered death. Which means, you can't die if the life of Jesus flows through you because of His blood." I placed a hand to my mouth, remembering the conversation with my mother. "Oxygen…" I looked up at Whisper. "My mom said that the breath of God is the oxygen of the Blood of Jesus. God is the life of Christ. So the virus can't kill us, it can't even pass to us, can it?"

"Nope. Our immunity comes through communion. So even if we're shot and killed, our bodies won't change after death."

The room was stiff with silence, everyone taking in what Whisper explained.

"Well," Keoni shrugged, "can we just take it?"

"Communion? Yes, but you won't be covered if you don't believe. Like Eve," she pointed to the boy who was holding Flower. "He doesn't believe, he thinks this is mere grape juice and crackers. Taking communion in a state like that can cause more harm than good. You must first repent of your disbelief, find sincerity in your heart to believe earnestly in Christ, and then take communion."

"That's a long process," Keoni said.

Whisper laughed. "It doesn't have to be. Whenever you guys are ready, we can take communion. But until then," she opened her bag, "I'll hang on to this."

"Wait a second," I said, "we should take communion to Washington."

"That's stupid," Eve spoke to me for the first time just to degrade me.

"What do you mean?" Keoni asked.

"I mean that if this is the cure, and our country is in disarray, people will believe right now and take communion. We can have soldiers distribute it and—"

"You think they're going to believe that?" Abbey questioned. She wasn't shooting me down—at least, I don't think she was—she was just genuinely confused.

"Well..." I gestured toward Whisper. "She's got bite marks. They'll see her and know that what we're saying is true. It's why we can believe, right?"

"Who said I believed any of this?" Eve snarled.

"Eve," Coco patted his leg, "don't be so aggressive." The boy calmed a little, avoiding eye contact with me.

"My calling is not to Washington," Whisper spoke. "But, when you go to Washington, and you *will* make it, amongst those who travel with you, one of you all will be bitten, but you won't change."

"Hold on," Keoni interjected, "say that again? We're going to be bitten?"

"Yes," Whisper responded casually.

"I need a break from all this," Abbey said as she stood.

"Good, let's take a break and reconvene at another time," Whisper said.

194

As I stood to follow Abbey, Keoni tapped me on the shoulder. "Hey, can we talk?"

I glanced over at Abbey, but she didn't look like she was in the mood to talk, and I really didn't feel like apologizing for being a jerk earlier, so I agreed. Following Keoni into one of the back offices, I shut the door behind myself.

"Listen, if what that lady says is true, then I think we should go to Washington."

"Alright." I shrugged.

Keoni snorted. "Zion, your fiancée just showed up. We can't travel with a baby."

"But we can travel with Sam who's pregnant?" I said defensively.

Keoni didn't say anything, looking off at the file cabinet in the corner.

"Goodness, you want to leave Sam too?" I shook my head.

"She's a risk, we cannot take risks. We have to get to Washington, and figure things out from there."

I stared at her. "I just reunited with Abbey. I can't just leave her."

"Fine," Keoni shrugged, "then I'll go on my own. You've got a set of directions."

"Wait—" I grabbed her as she tried to leave. "Keoni, I don't want you to have to travel alone. Give me a day or two with Abbey, and then we can go. Only if you promise we can return here to Abbey and stay."

Keoni looked me over and sighed with a nod. "Fine. We'll go and come back. Take the information we have and get back here to your fiancée."

It wasn't until that moment that I realized how hard it was for Keoni to watch me with Abigail when she had no idea where Olliare was. But, Keoni was dedicated to the mission, she put her feelings on hold until there was enough time to explore them. Even if she missed opportunities to find him, saving this country came first for Keoni, and it needed to come first for me again. But seeing how Abbey had to survive on her own, I didn't know if I could put the mission first now.

"Are you sure you're okay with this?" I asked as I reached out and rubbed her arm.

"I'm fine, soldier." Keoni gave me a tight smile, but I knew she wasn't fine at all. Her voice had hardened again, squeezing the pain out so she wouldn't feel a thing. "Go see your pretty fiancée," she told me. "Make love to her at least once before we leave so you won't be cranky." She punched my arm before she opened the door and left.

Standing there, I looked up at the ceiling. "God, please be in the midst."

18

Patron Saint of Victory

China agreed to a meeting with us. They don't want us to know how badly they're struggling. The spies reported the outbreak is still spreading, but China's not doing a bad job containing the wrongs. They're fighting them off with skilled snipers, but with their growing numbers, snipers would only last so long. The last five days have been grueling for China, but I have a plan to offer them help since they're spread so thin.

"Bharat, Adnan, welcome," I said as two Indian men dressed in their robes and traditional attire entered the dining room, glancing around with curious faces. I'd invited the Indian leaders to dinner to create a concrete plan to win China over in my meeting tomorrow. I needed something that would help them win America and still protect their people.

"Please sit." I offered two chairs, and the men obliged me, sitting beside each other. "Bastion," I called as I moved to sit across from them, "please serve dinner at once."

"Of course, sir," Bastion nodded.

When he left, I noticed the two men staring at me. But I already knew why they were looking, so I tried to act oblivious.

"Do you like the décor?" I asked. "The blue tablecloth, and traditional sculptures of the Hindu gods. That was my idea." I chuckled. "I wanted you both to feel at home."

"The décor is very nice," Bharat Tilak spoke with a thick accent. "But … your seat. It's across from us."

"We're equals," I leaned forward, "there's no need for me to sit at the head of the table. You know I'm not the real leader anyway. Just a stand-in, the one who makes things happen around here."

Adnan laughed.

"You two are the leaders of India, and I am a leader here in Syria. Why should I sit higher than you?"

"You make a fair point," Bharat said warily.

"So, let's forget the politics right now and enjoy the feast."

"Ok," Adnan agreed. His copper skin and salt and pepper beard made the well-dressed man look old and tired. He didn't care though, because a feast meant women, and I knew between the two of them, I'd be able to get at least one drunk on a good time.

The door of the dining room opened, and Sabiya stepped inside. She was wearing a long black gown, dawning gold accents across the bodice. Over her shoulders was a matching black cape, made of fine silks with a golden trim. Her hips swayed as she led a line of women into the dining room. With a satin ribbon around her head, Sabiya looked like every bit the queen I would make her once I became ruler of the world.

Sabiya was my only wife to attend tonight's feast. The rest were to wait in my chambers to relieve my tension after this dinner. The trail of women she brought inside were some specifically picked out for tonight's events, and others were concubines Sabiya wanted to get rid of. Entertaining another man was strictly against the rules Sabiya set for the palace women. Tonight, anyone who even laughed with either man would need to find another suitor to live with. Which is why we're offering these women to Bharat and Adnan to take home as gifts.

"My lord," Sabiya spoke, inclining her head to me first, then she turned and bowed to our guests. "Dinner is ready, but I thought it would be more entertaining to fill your table first."

"I see no issue. Gentlemen, what do you think?"

"Bring her," Adnan said greedily.

"Sorry, she is *my* lady. However, these women behind her are all for you." I motioned toward the ladies escorted in by my lovely wife. Each woman bowed, holding a small gift in her hand. Adnan gleamed like he'd suddenly became the big bad wolf, ready to devour every woman before him. Bharat seemed impressed, but he was more contained than Adnan.

"Ladies," Sabiya said to the fleet of women, "find a spot and entertain your guests."

"Yes, Lady Victory," they said in unison.

I like that ... Lady Victory.

The women found their way around the table, crowding the men in their own traditional clothes or the traditional clothes of Indian women. Adnan was looking all around, giving

199

compliments to each girl that passed him. Sabiya placed a hand on my shoulder before bowing once more.

As she turned to leave, Bharat called to her, "You are not staying for the fun?"

"My lord, Saint Victory has not permitted a night of fun for me. But I assure you, leader Bharat, and Adnan, tonight you will have your fill of delight. Poison shall be on your tongues as you indulge in the passions of these women."

Adnan clapped. "Who's going to poison me!" The ladies giggled around him.

Sabiya nodded once more, excusing herself. Her use of the word poison was perfect. Adnan and Bharat would defile themselves tonight with women they did not know. My fleet of women would surely poison them with lust, weakening them and giving me the favor I needed.

"Let Victory be yours," Sabiya said as the doors opened behind her, and men filed out with steaming dishes of food. Sabiya backed out of the room, catching my eye once more before she turned and left.

Truly, I love her.

...❀...

By the end of dinner, many of my women were comfortable. They strolled the dining hall topless or naked, laughing and dancing for our guests. Adnan had entirely discarded his dignity and robes, *indulging* himself with a concubine at the head of the table. I had expected as much, which was why I'd kept

200

a keen eye on Bharat instead.

He'd surprised me. Rather than spending time with as many women as possible, Bharat only kissed a few ladies and found a particular spark with a single woman in the corner of the room. Even now, they were still huddled together, drinking, raising their silver goblets, and toasting. I watched them a few moments more before taking a deep breath. It was time now for the main event, and unfortunately, the women and alcohol would have to go for the night.

"Attention." I clapped. My fleet of women gave me their attention, even the one who was busy with Adnan. "I'm sorry to interrupt, gentlemen, but there are things that must be discussed tonight."

The women obeyed, pulling on their clothes and covering themselves as they all moved to the door they'd entered through. Bharat held the hand of the woman he'd been whispering with as she stood to leave. He watched her with desire in his eyes as she sashayed away. Adnan hurriedly dressed himself as he watched the women go. The doors opened and Sabiya stepped out, my heart lifting once more as I saw her.

"Gentlemen, I hope you are full. Lord Victory," she directed her attention to me, "may the rest of your night be grand."

"If it is what you wish, then I will grant it."

"It is, my lord."

"Then tonight it will be grand."

Sabiya curtseyed and turned, leading the women out of the

room again. When the door shut behind them, Bharat and Adnan returned to their seats.

"Did you two enjoy yourselves?" I asked.

"I did," Adnan said happily before he grabbed his cup of wine and chugged it.

I sipped my own as Bharat said, "Tonight was like no other."

"You flatter me, gentlemen. I'm glad I was a good host."

"But now you want something, right?" Bharat asked.

"I do, sir."

"What is it?" Adnan demanded.

Clearing my throat, I stood and folded my hands behind my back. I took my time walking the length of the table, my cloak dragging the floor behind me as I explained, "China is in a bit of trouble. They need more men."

"Then let *China* ask for more men," Bharat countered.

"Hold on." Adnan shook his head. "Why does China need more men? We've given them our men and our sons. Our loyalty and hard work. Why do they request more?"

"America's defenses are much stronger than they anticipated."

"China's feud with America is not our problem!" Bharat shouted as he stood.

"Oh, but it is," I stopped walking as I stood at the head of the table. I looked at my seat, defiled with the gross sweat and fluids of another man with my own concubine. "You are owned by China, and you will give them what they ask. If you don't, I will make it known to them that you betrayed them

202

this night and ate dinner with me without their knowledge."

"You can't do that!" Adnan was shouting now, but I held up a hand.

"I won't, but if I have to, I will."

"What more do they want?"

"Their forces are split right now. Dealing with a problem in their land and dealing with America and Taiwan. China may be big, but they are not strong—not widespread like this. They need a stronger army to invade the US and Taiwan. And they need support in their country."

"Why are they sending a request through you?" Bharat asked as he lowered himself to his seat. Adnan never stood, only scowled darkly as he listened.

"China knows nothing of this meeting. I'm requesting this of you in exchange for a seat on a council I'm building and the women you enjoyed tonight. There's also a fleet of gifts prepared for you for your departure."

"The women from tonight," Bharat said slowly.

"Forget the women," Adnan grunted. "What is this council?"

"Nothing more can be said. But you are the first to know."

"I accept," Bharat said after a moment. "I accept right now."

Initially, I thought it would be his vote that would be the hardest to get. But he was just a man infatuated with a woman he desperately wanted to see again as his reward for his cooperation. As expected, he'd been poisoned by her hypnotic beauty.

"Hold on," Adnan objected. He was still scowling, though it had softened a little. "How can we trust you? How can we trust that tonight won't get back to China?"

"You now know of a council I'm building. If I turn on you, the information I've given you can be used against me. Creating a council behind the backs of the nations seems treacherous, doesn't it?"

"It does, indeed," Adnan said. His scowl had eased a little more as he took a breath. "This council, why offer us a seat?"

"Do you accept?"

He clenched his jaw, looking over at Bharat who'd already sold his soul for a chance at a love he never had before.

"Yes," Adnan grated out, "I accept."

"Good, your fingers will be pricked. A blood seal of your seats." I pulled a small dagger from my sleeve and crossed the room to them. Bharat extended his hand first, I pricked his finger with ease and placed his hand on the chair he was sitting in.

"This is your seat," I said, cleaning my knife.

I looked up at Adnan. He was hesitant, but just a drop of blood would seal this for me.

"Adnan," I extended my hand. He looked at it a moment, causing a frenzy of emotion to ripple through my body. I didn't stop stirring until he placed his hand in mine and I could breathe again.

Pricking his finger, I placed his hand on the arm of the chair he was seated in.

"Now," I whispered to him, "if you tell a soul, your blood

is here as proof of your allegiance to me."

He ripped his hand from mine, ready to bark at me, but the door to the dining room opened, and Bastion stepped inside.

"Sir, the departure fleet is ready."

"Perfect." I looked back at Adnan who was fuming again. "I look forward to working with you."

...✿...

Last night went better than I thought it would. Bharat went home with that woman tucked under his arm, however, Adnan left in anger. He no longer wanted to speak with me, but it wouldn't matter for now. The only thing that mattered to me was my meeting with China today to secure myself as leader of the new world order I was putting together.

"Reema," I called to one of my wives. She opened my bedroom door and stepped inside. "Remove these concubines from the room and retrieve Sabiya. I must see her at once."

"Yes, sir."

Reema was my fourth wife—older than Sabiya, closer to my age, and we didn't see much of each other. She was here when I needed her, but nothing more than that. We haven't slept together in years, but she's comforting to talk to when I am lonely. She was also motherly, something I think some of the young brides and concubines needed. I've never wanted to get rid of Reema, though she brings me no sexual desire. She brings motherhood to my fleet and gives Sabiya a break sometimes at running the castle when I'm not available.

Draping the concubines in red, she gathered the girls and led them out of the room. "Sabiya will be here shortly," Reema said in her kindly voice.

"Thank you."

Out of the bed, I went to the showers instead of the bath. I stood in a glass box as women poured water over me. It rushed down the drain I stood over, and the women used big brushes to scrub me down over the top of the glass box. When they were finished rinsing me, I stepped out the box, and they wrapped me in warm towels before sending me off to my chambers again.

Inside, Sabiya sat quietly on my bed. She looked dazzling as her rich brown skin was freshly oiled, and she'd been rubbed down with what smelled like lavender petals.

"My Lady Victory," I said as I came over to the bed, "I have one more meeting. What do you wish for me?" My hand traced her face and down her neck.

"For you, my Lord Victory, I wish success and honor."

"Because you have wished it, I will make it happen."

"No, my lord," she reached up and touched my arm, "because you are my victory, you will have all that you wish for."

"Sabiya," I whispered as my eyes took in her plump lips. "I want to make love to you right now, but I must wait. So we will make love tonight, if you will have me."

"I will have you, my lord."

I held in the excitement bursting through my chest. Sabiya

and I rarely slept together. I was preserving her, keeping her body as my idol. I worshipped it when we made love, and I could never treat another woman as good as I treated Sabiya.

"And tonight, I will try for our daughter. I have tried for my son all week, but you are the only one who can bear daughters to me."

"I will bring her into this world for you, Saint Victory."

Leaning down, I kissed my wife. I wanted to continue kissing her, to kiss her until she could no longer breathe, but my meeting was on the horizon, and I needed to be ready.

"Wait for me here," I whispered as I pulled away from her. She nodded, blue eyes half lidded with passion.

After dressing and leaving Sabiya in my chambers, Bastion walked me to the council meeting room where the Chinese officials waited. Stepping inside, I walked to my seat and sat in my stone chair.

"Jun Sun, General Yang Pen, welcome."

"Skip the openings," Jun spoke darkly, "what are we here for?"

"Someone leaked reports," I said plainly. "You've got an outbreak."

Jun gasped, looking over at Pen. "Who told you?"

"So it's true," I stood from my chair, walking down the steps to the table. "A little plane went spiraling down near your borders and a bunch of wrongs that survived the crash infiltrated your land and infiltrated Japan—which is like a wasteland now." I shrugged. "So it seems like you've got a lot of problems."

"We don't have problems." Jun nearly jumped in his seat. He'd always been a nasty man, but now I didn't have to be bothered by that. Before, when I needed the Chinese, I had to accept his behavior. But now, China's going to need *me*.

"Seems like you do," I said casually. "America's capital is still intact. Taiwan is fighting back pretty hard too. And now you've got wrongs on your borders. You're spread thin."

"So what do you propose?" the general asked.

"I propose you get men from India. Fill your armies, guard your borders."

"The way yours are?"

"Mine are guarded quite well." The border of Syria was guarded by a wooden fence with pointed stakes that allowed wrongs to jam themselves on there. There was also a team on rotation, shooting and taking out wrongs regularly.

"Why are you telling us this? Why are you helping us? You didn't seem to want to help us when you got your information out there about the virus." He scoffed. "Your doctors, and all your fake reports—that happened without us. Seemed like we were warring too."

"China can't fight everyone, and I'm the only one who realizes this. So I want to capitalize on it. Make a treaty, and retreat to launch a bigger attack on the US. Even if you finish your invasion of Taiwan and then return to the US, it won't matter. The US will be even weaker because of the wrongs. And they don't have much power over there to know about the retreat. They'll still be living in fear."

Jun sat still, giving Pen a sideways glance. "We will not retreat."

"Then you forfeit Taiwan and America, *and* China falls to the wrongs. It's a matter of time with China being so crowded. There's no way other people aren't already infected."

"The same can be said for you."

"True." I nodded slowly. "But Syria is small, we'd sniff out the wrong, deal with it and protect our people much faster than you ever could. However, we're not talking about Syria, we're talking about China."

"I think," General Pen started, "I think he's right. If we can regroup, you know we can beat America, Jun. We just need to regroup and relaunch."

Jun pressed two fingers to his temple. "Who else knows what condition China is in?"

"Just me. I've kept a low profile."

"I don't want a peace treaty," he said firmly. "I just want a treaty. We want a standstill, but we don't want to make it look like we're weak."

"Fine." I nodded. "Call a ceasefire. That way, it'll seem like you are considering peace talks with the US."

Jun slammed his fist on the table. "We are *not* weak!"

"No, but you will be if you don't regroup," I pushed.

"We have no intentions of speaking with America," he seethed.

"I will speak with them. I'll talk to them for you. We'll make it look real, like a mediator. And who better than an

American to talk to America? Resurfacing right now will make America look horrible and the spotlight will be off of you."

"What do you mean?" General Pen jutted his chin at me.

"I mean a prisoner of war, fighting on behalf of America after they never came to save him? The world will soak that up, maybe even call for China to cancel the ceasefire and attack the US again for the outrage of not rescuing me in the first place."

Jun adjusted in his chair, nodding a little like that worked for him.

I took a deep breath and knocked on the table, catching their attention. "What's it going to be, gentlemen?"

Jun and Pen looked at each other and nodded in unison.

"I will bring this information back to our leader," Jun said. "He will make the final decision. You will hear from us by the evening."

I smiled. "Very good. Glad we talked."

19

Abigail

Zion lay with his head in my lap as Flower slept quietly beside us. After learning the truth from Whisper, Zion's been so clingy. I wasn't sure what was going on with him, but I didn't mind his clinginess. We'd been apart for months; to suddenly be together again with our daughter now, everything felt right. It felt complete. Though Eve hasn't liked it very much. Coco told me yesterday that Eve was complaining that Zion was smothering me. He hasn't said more than a few words to Zion since we've been here. But I really didn't have the time to work out Eve's frustration at my fiancée. I was focusing on Zion, Flower, and getting my heart right with God.

Communion. We learned that was the cure. It was the protection that would heal us and keep us safe from death if the virus was transferred to us. At first, I couldn't find it in my heart to believe it, but I knew I needed to. And deep within, I was afraid that the cure couldn't be that simple. Believing was all I needed to do, yet I was struggling.

Zion wasn't though. He said he'd gotten closer to God since this whole thing began. He told me about God's message about the wrongs being strong at night. Whisper overheard us and joined in.

She explained that wrongs thrive off three things: sound, darkness, and blood. The wrongs are essentially blind. It's like walking around with your eyes closed. So it's not dark, but you still can't see. They're not really looking at you when they give you their attention. They're listening. And they rush at the sound of even heavy breathing if they're close by. And since they're functioning as if they just had their eyes closed, the daylight actually bothers their eyes, but the darkness is soothing. Making them stronger and faster, not fighting with the sapping heat of the sun on their eyes.

However, beyond sound and darkness, blood is the strongest tool for them. They actually fall dormant if they don't get blood. Though the virus is a brain eating monster, killing their host on contact, the purpose for them is to spread the virus so it never dies. A bite transfers the virus into the bloodstream, taking over the entire body at once. The virus overcrowds one body, and needs a release, so they attack to spread it. With the brain always at risk of completely decaying because of the overload from the virus, they bite to release the virus elsewhere, keeping the host and the virus 'alive.'

Just the smell of blood can wake a dormant wrong. Zion thinks that's the reason behind a wrong that he and Keoni and Sam ran from. He said it came out of the closet. With wrongs reacting to sound, and his team being in there making noise, it would've made sense for it to attack much earlier than it did. But, when one of the people they were traveling with— Winston—went near the closet door, he was bleeding, and the smell of blood probably shook the wrong from its dormant state.

There was much to take in, much to understand, and to hold onto. However, it was necessary for survival. We needed the information; all we could get in order to know how to fight at least one of our enemies. With the Chinese, we weren't sure how to fight them. But being armed with the information we have about the wrongs, our chances of survival against them just went up.

"So," Whisper said as she came over and sat beside us.

Zion lazily opened his eyes, nodding at Whisper.

"We can't stay here forever," she said. "You both know that. Therefore, we need to decide what we're going to do before the supplies get too low."

"What do you mean? We'll just get supplies and stay here." I shrugged. "It's the safest we've been in a while."

"I agree," she nodded, "but it's dangerous to stay in one spot too long. And I need to go find an old friend of mine."

"An old friend? Where are they?"

She hesitated. "In Jerusalem."

Zion looked bewildered as he sat up slowly. "Jerusalem? Like Israel?"

"Yes."

"Oh, well," he turned and looked back at me, his appearance hadn't changed much. Still handsome, even with his scruffy hair that was growing rather long. His eyes were filled with worry as he asked me where I wanted to go.

"With you, of course," I answered without hesitation. "To Washington."

He just looked at me before sighing.

"I'm going to take a walk. You guys talk and let me know what you want to do," Whisper said as she stood and left.

When she was gone, I looked at my fiancée, thinking of the deep sigh he just let out. "Zion? What's going on?"

"You know I love you, right?" he said to me.

I nodded.

"And you know—"

"Z!" Keoni called as she wandered over to us.

Z?

A slender hand rested on Zion's shoulder as the womanly military lady said, "Do you…" she paused as she looked over at Flower. "Goodness, Z, you two made a cutie." She shook him, and Zion blushed as he looked down at Flower too.

"Thanks, Key."

Key? Nicknames? What happened to last names only in the army?

"Of course." She was all smiles until she glanced over at me. I must've been frowning because the next minute she said, "Sorry, am I interrupting something? I didn't mean to just barge in."

"No." Zion shrugged. "What's up, Keoni?"

"Well, I was going to ask if you were free. I found an old map in one of the offices and I thought we could take a look at it together."

"Oh," he looked back at me and then at Keoni. "Well, Abbey and I *were* discussing something."

"Sorry," she squeezed his shoulder, and I clutched my own pants. "Why didn't you say something?" She turned to me, flashing her stunning smile, and pointed to Zion. "He literally just told me I wasn't interrupting something." She laughed, and I forced a small one out myself. It sounded more like a grunt.

"Listen." Keoni patted Zion's shoulder again and I thought I'd scream. "I'm going to just take a look at it myself. I'll tell you my findings later tonight if you've got time."

Zion looked transfixed. Intrigued by her every word, nodding along like he wanted to actually go look at a stupid map instead of staying and talking with me.

"Sorry to interrupt," she said to me again. Her smooth voice added to her magnetic personality. Zion was always laughing when he was with her. Whenever they started the fire together, they'd laugh their heads off. Her pushing him, Zion enjoying it. He even sometimes bumped his shoulder with hers, whispering about a joke only they understood. Something had changed in my fiancée, and it happened well before he returned from bootcamp.

The military life changed Zion. When he returned, he was more reserved, though he did seem to love me more, he was still distant somehow. I tried to ignore it, but I knew for certain the military had discarded the old Zion and replaced him with a man who found a love in the brotherhood of being a soldier.

It's funny, the military was supposed to love *families*. It was supposed to support them. But they tore them apart more

215

often than not. Wives and husbands filing for divorce during or after a deployment, children without parents for months at a time, families losing loved ones.

The military took Zion and placed him in an environment entirely controlled by them. Their rules. Their beliefs. And told him that everyone in the room beside him was more important than anyone else. So, when he looks at Keoni, he wants to be with her, to serve beside her. When he looks at me, he just wants to protect me, nothing more. And even then, he only wants to protect me because the army said so.

I don't even know if that's bad. I used to consider myself at least a little patriotic. But now? The way Zion looks at Keoni… it's not even with lust. Admiration maybe? Something deeper has developed between them over these few weeks. Saving each other, confiding in each other. A new relationship blossomed between them, and they have no idea that's what happened.

Keoni pats his shoulder because he's a soldier, not because she likes him. Zion hangs on her every word because she's his commander, and the line between work and life faded when he left me to save America. But Keoni understands what I don't. She understands him in ways I never will. How can I love him or marry him when he's in love with the military?

Maybe he isn't. Maybe I'm overthinking, but from the looks of it, I think I'm right.

"I'll catch up with you later, Keoni," Zion's voice drew me from my thoughts.

"Alright, Zion." Keoni nodded at me as she finally turned

and left us.

My eyes stayed glued to Zion as he watched her leave. He was smiling, like he was the happiest man in the world. Keoni had crossed the room, leaning over to talk to Sam. Brushing hair from her face, she glanced up, noticing Zion still watching her. And she smiled at him, blushed even... and Zion? He smiled back.

"Earth to Zion," I snapped. He could barely take his eyes off Keoni as she talked to Sam who was lying down. It was like they'd developed a secret language that only they knew every time they looked at each other. It's been this way since we arrived. Zion hasn't even kissed me. He's kissed my hand, my cheek, my forehead, but not my lips. He's been so absent, coming alive only when Keoni invites him to do something. All along, I've been trying to ignore it, but I can't any longer.

"Is that where you want to be? Over there, with her?" I asked.

Now he gave me his full attention. "Abbey, sweetheart, what are you talking about?"

"I'm talking about Keoni, the only person who has your attention."

"That's not true." He shook his head like he didn't want to hear this.

"It is true, Zion. She comes over here, placing her hands all over you."

"She touched my shoulder, calm down."

"Calm down?" I was ready to snap at him, but for the sake of not drawing attention, or waking Flower, I took a breath.

"Are you sleeping with her?"

"No! Why would you even ask that?" He was taken aback, offended, meaning he didn't see anything wrong with his behavior.

"Have you seen the way you two look at each other?"

"Abbey, we've been *surviving* together. We may seem close, but Keoni's engaged, just like us. She wants to find her fiancée too. Get married. We're not interested in each other like that."

"You sure act like you are interested in each other."

"Well, we're not," he said flatly. He sucked his teeth, grunting as he turned away from me.

"Don't turn away," I hissed. "We still haven't figured out our travel plans."

"What plans? You've got to stay here because it's safe."

I stared at him. "You're kidding me, right? You're seriously suggesting that you go galivanting off for the military *again*. Run down to Washington and then come back?"

"It's not galivanting in the least bit," he said sourly.

"That's not the point," I said between clenched teeth. "How long am I supposed to wait? You want me to sit here and wait for you to possibly come back from Washington on *foot*? Zion we're talking months! Years even!"

"It won't take that long," he stressed, "but what am I supposed to do? I can't protect you in the long run, in the grand scheme of things. If I can get to Washington with the information I've got, we can save the country, Abbey. This is bigger than you and me."

"Then take me with you. I want to be together, Zion."

218

He stopped, his eyes moving to look at Flower. "We can't… we can't travel with—"

"Don't you dare," I snapped. "She is your daughter!"

"I know that! Don't you think this is hard for me too? You think I just up and decided I'd go all the way to Washington without you, leaving you *again*, easily? No! But I know what has to happen for you to be safe. To give Flower a chance at a better future."

"Shut up," I forced out. "You sound like a brainwashed idiot! Zion, America is as good as dead! Stop trying to save her!"

"I'm trying to save *us*!" His voice came out as a dangerous rumble. "So what, we just sit by and let America fall? Newsflash, Abbey, she hasn't fallen." He flung his arms open. "Which means there's time to save her, or to at least give us an opportunity to get a better fighting chance. When America goes down, so do we! I'm just trying to prolong the fall."

"You're trying to fight God," I corrected.

The tension between us was stifling. I could hardly take it.

"I'm not trying to fight God," Zion hesitated for a moment, but regained himself the next second. "I'm trying to run on the fumes of His mercy before that's all gone too. What don't you understand? This is for us."

I shook my head, looking down at Flower. "You want to save us? Stay with us. But you can't because of your duty to this dying country, and because of her." I looked over at Keoni who was nodding as she talked with Sam still. Zion looked over at her, his eyes shifting from a glance to a gaze the moment his eyes landed on her.

"I don't know what you're talking about," he said as he turned back to me.

"I think you should go."

"Abigail, hold on. I said I'm coming back; I'm not just going to leave you."

"Yes..." I nodded, raising my eyes to his. "Yes, you are. And if you won't leave, then I will."

"Abbey, you have a child, it's safer for you—"

"Our child, Zion! Flower is *our* child," my voice began to tremble, "not *a* child."

"That's not what I meant."

"I don't care."

"Abbey, come on. I'm her father."

"She doesn't know that. You haven't been here in all this time; she won't even remember you by the time you get back. So do her a favor and leave before she's more conscious. I don't want her missing the man who left her to chase after his dying country."

"Abbey," he called as I began packing our things up. "Abbey—" He caught my arm. "Please, I love you."

I shook my head. "You love America. You love Keoni. But you don't love me, Zion. Not anymore. But I'll always have a part of you in my heart." I touched Flower. "And I'll never forget you. I will always love you, Zion."

"Baby," he said, his voice hitched with emotion. I closed my eyes, as he took my hand. "Please," he whispered now, but I shook my head and pulled my hand from him. Then I leaned

220

over and picked up my sleeping Flower. Tucking her blanket into the bag, I slipped it onto my shoulder and stood.

"I've traveled and protected Flower myself all this time. I'll keep doing it. I'm going to Jerusalem with Whisper if you change your mind."

"Abigail, don't do this." Zion's eyes filled with a burning mist, the same one burning my own eyes. We'd fought all this way to find each other, just to separate... for good.

"Goodbye, Zion."

He shook his head, but I didn't wait for a response. I headed into a back office, where I stayed for the rest of the night with Flower. And when the morning came, Eve got me for breakfast. I stepped out the office and realized that our team had shrank a little.

Zion and Keoni had left during the night.

20

Chemistry

Stay quiet. Move quickly. Stay focused. Cover your tracks. Know your limits. Those were the five things Cloud drilled into me. Keeping track of time was something I had to learn how to do by watching the sky. I needed to be able to tell how long ago an animal had died or passed through an area, how much time had passed since moving from one location to the next. Time, it was the criminal of winter. If you wanted to survive, everything had to be done quickly and precisely before the cold invaded your body.

"I was able to find two weapons, another blanket, and two bottles of water. The house looked like it'd already been raided," I reported.

"You did good, Chem," Cloud complimented as he picked up a gun. He turned over the weapon, checking it before releasing the magazine. "Fully loaded. Good picking."

"There was a little ammo too." I dug through my bag and set down five magazines.

"Good. This will help us, a lot."

"It's almost noon," I said. "I need to get going so I can be back before the sun sets."

"Do you want to take King with you?"

"I don't think Kingsley's going to want to come. She's been taking care of Lyla anyway, so it's best if she stays."

"Alright, then take a second weapon and ammo." He pushed a handgun towards me with a magazine. Taking the gun, I slipped it onto my hip and put the magazine in my bag.

"Be careful out there, Chem."

"I will."

Leaving the barn, I started down the street towards some shrubbery. So far, I haven't brought home much food. I was able to get into a pharmacy, it had already been raided, but there was some medicine there for Lyla at least.

I found more bandages and medical supplies, had even found some clothes for everyone to change into and whatever didn't fit we burned to keep the fire going. And it hasn't been too hard to find water bottles lying around.

Whenever I enter a store, they're always there, like they slipped from the pack. But food was scarce. Shelves were emptied, homes were in disarray. It's like we've been last to the party every time. So, we stayed at the barn and Cloud's helped me get better with my aim. He's helped a lot lately.

Losing Coco took a toll on all of us. Lyla's beginning to catch on that Coco's not coming back, Kingsley's still blaming herself, but I'm the one to blame. I was being forceful with Kingsley when I didn't need to be. Yes, she's got a thick skull, but I could've let her find out the hard way that Cloud was no good. Or maybe she never would've found out.

Cloud has changed. He's been nicer since Acoye left us, and even with his broken leg, he tries to do what he can. Starting the fire, entertaining Lyla, keeping watch. He'd hunt for us if he could, but his hobbling would be too loud. And if something went wrong, or he ran into a wrong, he'd never make it back. Right now, we need everyone in our group. King helps Ly, I hunt, and Cloud teaches me and keeps busy doing everything else.

One of the things Cloud has taught me is staying small and silent. He couldn't demonstrate very well, but keeping your body tucked, and moving swiftly—not fast or running—actually helped you stay quiet. When you move too slow, you give the ground, or the floor, enough time to catch your full weight and react to it.

There are some instances where it can't be helped. Stepping on a twig, walking over a creaky floorboard, those are things that are just going to alert people to your surroundings no matter what. But it's what you do after your position is given up that makes you successful—or dead.

Taking a breath, I moved into the shrubbery off road. I checked my surroundings, being sure to take in land markers so I wouldn't forget how to get home. In an area like a forest, it was harder to place land markers, so you made them yourself. Pulling a pocketknife from my front pocket, I carved an 'A' for Acoye, representing that I'd been there before. But each A would be different. The 'A' I carved in the first tree is upright.

Every few trees, I'll carve them sideways, indicating what direction I needed to follow to get back home.

There was never a guarantee with hunting, but food was getting low at the barn, I'd have to catch something even if it was just a squirrel. From sticks and shreds of clothing to cans and string, Cloud taught me how to make a few traps and snares. Today I'd take the time to actually set a few up and check back on my way back home to see if I caught anything.

It was about finding the right spots, a perfect tree branch, or an opening in a tree. Burying traps in the ground beneath lots of leaves, finding and recognizing trails which was easier than I thought. It's been a lot to learn so quickly, but we needed to survive, and I was determined to bring something home.

We only had one assault rifle with a few magazines of ammo. I only took one spare with me today, but I was hoping I wouldn't need it. Keeping the weapon close to my chest, I moved through the forested area, looking for animals and places to set up my traps. There wasn't much out there it seemed, but I was hoping to find something. Stopping at a tree, it was broken in half, the trunk snapped at a weird angle. There wasn't much disturbance around the massive tree lying in my way, but small animals could travel along the tree and not disturb anything.

I swung my gun around to my back and pulled my bag to the front to retrieve a can with three holes in it. One tall stick, a piece of rubber I'd taken from a home workout studio. It was actually a resistance band, but I took the set, hoping Cloud could use them for making a better homemade cast. Later that day we found the boot, so we just held on to the rubber resistance bands. Thankfully. Aside from the rubber and stick, I had string and a few smaller sticks that Cloud carved for me.

One stick went in the back hole of the top of the can. Then there were two more holes at the opening of the can. That's where I tied some string through the holes and worked a stick that went into another opening on the can. I cut the band, using the rubber as the resistance for the trigger. Wiping sweat from my head, I continued to assemble the snare as I remembered what Cloud said about traps and snares.

"Do you think it's easier to kill an animal or to remove the body of a dead animal you've caught?"

"Um…" I didn't know how to answer as Cloud sharpened a stick beside me. He'd shown me how to use a spring pole out of small trees, and how to build a grass wall to keep an animal on the path you wanted it to follow.

"A trap does just that—traps an animal. If your trap fails, the animal gets out. Your dinner is gone. If you take too long to check your trap, the animal can chew its way out. But a snare, it's meant to kill an animal. Instantly. So, I'll ask you again," green eyes lifted from the stick in his hand, "can you kill an animal or remove the dead body?"

Obviously, I chose to remove the dead body since I only brought snares along with me. I was hoping to catch bigger game, but I was fine with just the snares for now. It took me maybe two hours to make two squirrel snares from cans and another two hours to make a wire snare for rabbits. I found one path that I was certain was for rabbits or some other small

226

critters. The flattened grass was a trail leading the animals through the forested area. If you weren't looking for it, you probably wouldn't find it.

Shoving broken sticks into the ground along the trail, I set a wire snare between two trees. After setting my can snares and wire snares, I carved an 'A' into a tree trunk and moved deeper into the forest. Usually, I appreciated the silence, since my sisters were always so loud. But being alone out here, with nothing but my own thoughts, was more chilling than anything I'd ever experienced.

I clutched my weapon as I moved, looking for a sign or something of an animal. Everything looked fine, no disturbances like the way Cloud described them: smoothed grasses were animal trails, lots of broken twigs and trees indicated something moved quickly through there and you follow that path to see if anything was at the end of that trail. Lots of dead plants also indicated something's moved through there, ruining the plants.

I tried to go over everything in my head as I walked. It was beginning to get cold, and the daylight would be gone. I needed to start heading back, but a trail caught my eye. It was small, but the grass was very flat, like it was used a lot or used by a heavy animal. Quietly, I moved along the trail, trying to avoid twigs and crinkling anything. I stopped when I noticed tracks. I leaned down, taking in the oddly shaped heart imprint. Up close, it was clear the pair of tracks had another set right on top of them. They didn't perfectly cover the first set, but it was obvious what animal the tracks belonged to.

"A deer," I whispered. Claudius had told me that deer tracks were the easiest to spot since deer usually stepped their back foot nearly exactly where their front foot stepped.

The ground was wet, the tracks could be fresh or old, I couldn't tell. But I could at least follow it a little, just to see where it led. Carving an 'A' on a nearby tree, I moved quickly along the path watching the tracks. They continued straight, and I stopped abruptly when I walked right up to a deer standing in a clearing. Its head was low, nibbling on the grass.

I took a deep breath, slowly lowering myself to the ground. Raising the gun, I took aim, all I needed to do was fire a shot. It didn't have to be perfect, but I needed to wound it, keep it from moving.

I looked down my sight, keeping the deer's shoulder in view. I knew I probably couldn't hit the head, and I didn't want to take a chance. But if I fired, and didn't exactly hit where my gun was aimed, I'd still hit the deer in a generally good area on the body.

The deer looked up when I cocked the gun, its fluffy ears wiggling as it looked around.

Can I do this? I wondered. *Can I kill an animal?*

"It's either kill or be killed. And every time you choose not to kill an animal, you exchange your life for theirs. You think their life is worth more than yours and everyone you're fighting for? Don't make that mistake."

Claudius' words wracked my brain as I stood there holding my gun. With shaky hands, my finger moved to the trigger.

Three... two ... one ... I fired.

The deer leapt, tripping over itself, and took off running. I got to my feet and raced after it, running as fast as I could. I kept my eyes straight ahead, swapping my rifle for the handgun I'd found earlier. I fired at the deer again. Two more shots and it fell over onto the ground. Birds erupted from the trees, and the world around me that had been silently watching me was suddenly alive. Tiredly, I trudged through the brown and green grass, until I walked up to the deer. It was panting hard, its frame moving rapidly as it struggled.

Kneeling in front of it, I knew I had to kill it. I had to stab it, or I would let the animal die a terrible death. The stress it was feeling, the horror. Looking at me as I took its life.

Trembling, I leaned over and hurled beside the dying deer. I dug my hands into the soil, gagging as I stayed hunched over. I stared at the ground as tears slipped from my eyes.

"I'm sorry," I panted.

I wiped my mouth and pulled the knife from my hip. I couldn't hesitate, if I waited any longer, I'd chicken out and then we'd starve. So I stabbed the deer with a grunt, and it stopped moving.

Falling back on my butt, I stared up at the sky, wondering if there was a God, why was life so hard? Why did all this have to happen to me? My whole life had been hard, and now this?

"Why do You hate us!?" I screamed at the sky. "What am I doing?" I scolded myself the next second like I was crazy.

Pulling the knife out of the deer, I dried it on my leg and put it away. There was rope in my backpack that I used to tie around the neck to drag the deer.

I trudged along, walking slowly back through the forest. With all the noise I'd made, I wasn't surprised that my snares were empty. I stopped three times in the forest, exhausted and sweaty. The deer was heavier than it looked, and now that it was dead, the weight had increased. Each step felt like my last as I followed the A's back to the road.

I stopped, falling over for another break. The barn wasn't much further, but I really didn't know how much more I could take... until a screeching noise pierced the quiet streets.

My eyes shot open, and I looked around. The noise sounded distant, but it was loud enough to strike fear in my heart and light a new fire under my butt.

Picking up the pace, I dragged the deer back to the barn, ragged and exhausted. When I finally made it, I tripped into the big red enclosure, lifting a weak fist and pounding on the door. When it opened, Kinglsey blinked at me.

"Ollie! Come help!" she hollered.

21

Claudius

"You didn't gut it?" I asked as Chem sipped water. She was sitting against the barn still panting from dragging an entire deer back all by herself.

"I couldn't." She shook her head.

"Chem—"

"I couldn't do it!"

"Alright." I held my hands up defensively. "I get it, this was probably really stressful. But you made some good shots. Nothing that can harm us has been punctured."

She nodded, wiping at her tears. I can only imagine how hard it was for her; hunting, setting traps, and getting back home. Despite her agitation and exhaustion, Chemistry did really good.

I looked over the deer. A shot in the shoulder and then another lodged right in the back of the head and neck area. And there was a stab wound in the throat. I looked over at Chem, she was still wearing her red jacket and black gloves, sipping water. Kingsley took Lyla to the bathroom. We were using the furthest side of the field for the bathroom. Ly was afraid of the deer when we brought it in, hysterically crying, causing Chemistry to scream at her. The whole ordeal was taxing, even for me.

"Chem, what happened with the deer?"

"I tried to hit it the way you said, not too high not too low in the shoulder area. I aimed for the neck and traced down to the shoulder, but the deer took off. I had to chase it."

"Which is why there's a second shot."

She nodded. "I tried to hit the head, but I just hit the neck."

"You paralyzed it. So then you had to finish it."

"I don't know what happened."

"You did good," I said. "This will last us a while. But we need to gut it right away."

Setting her water down, Chem took off her jacket, and laid it on the stack of hay. She rolled up the sleeves to her black turtleneck as she came over.

"I'll hold the leg open, but you've got to do the cutting."

She took the hunting knife from her hip and sat shakily on the deer as I held his legs open. Chem traced her hand along the beautiful white fur of the deer's belly, a softness in her eyes. "I was so scared."

"I know. I'm sorry I couldn't be there."

She shook her head. "I think it was better I did that alone."

"Do you want my help now?"

"Yeah." She flipped the knife around in her hand and

looked up at me. Brown eyes were still fearful, but she tried to be strong, and that was more than I could've asked for.

"Alright, it's been a while since the animal died, so the deer is probably a little bloated and the cutting might be harder. But if you work quickly, it'll be fine."

"Ok."

"Alright, lift the tail, and you're going to have to ring the anus."

"What?" She looked back at me, and I sighed.

"Yes, you've got to keep the anal sack from spilling."

"No." She shook her head, passed me the knife, and stood. "Here."

"Chem, my leg is broken. I can't get into the right position to gut it."

"Well, then I guess all this was for nothing! I'm not ringing his anus!"

"Chemistry! Come on! We'll die! We've got no food! You have to do this. We don't have a choice anymore."

I could see the anger and the tension on her face. Every line and wrinkle in her forehead spoke to the hunger and the stress we'd all been going through. Life on the run had not been easy for us. We haven't encountered any wrongs, but we've struggled to find food, we've struggled to find shelter, we've struggled to stay together. How much we've been through has been less than fair in my opinion, but who's counting the ducks and deciding what's fair and what isn't?

"Come on, Chem," I said with a sigh. "We've got to do this. I … we all need you."

She took a deep breath and snatched the knife from my hand. "What do you mean ring the anus?"

"You need to find the anal hole and cut around it. Then you've got to start cutting him open."

Chemistry struggled. She was beyond exhausted, probably not even hungry anymore. I remember how often I wasn't hungry after my father made me learn how to gut, skin, and butcher all the animals I hunted. Initially, he just went crazy when I made a clean shot. But when I was consistently making clean shots by high school, I started gutting.

I remember the first deer my dad made me gut. He'd killed it, and though I'd watched him gut a deer thousands of times, it was nothing like doing it yourself. Being careful what to cut and what to avoid. Keeping all the guts intact so the stomach acid and the colon wouldn't empty into the body cavity.

King checked on us midway through and vomited. She was the only one with free hands, so she had to clean it up herself. Despite how sick she was feeling, I gave her instructions to find sticks and the things we'd need to cook the deer. She'd have to take our only flashlight and Lyla, but by the time Chem and I were through, I was certain she'd be back.

"That was disgusting," Chemistry said as she rubbed her hands in the dirt. I was working the deer's front legs, sawing them at the knees with the saw from the barn. The old place must've still been functioning before the invasion. There were tools, and a stench that was still pretty heavy in the barn.

"How do you know all this stuff?" Chem asked me.

"I hunted when I was a kid but being in the military and

234

enduring a lot of different things, you learn how to survive. Or you make a way."

She was silent, but I didn't bother to look up. As I sawed at the knees, I could feel the tension in the barn twisting into some uncomfortable conversation about my past. However, Chem surprised me by asking about something else.

"How long do you think it'll take for the US to be completely invaded?"

"That's not possible. We will fight this."

"And what if we don't?"

I clenched my jaw, slowing the sawing. "We have to," I whispered. The barn was still again, and I wanted to forget that Chem had ever asked that question.

As a soldier, I was taught to always believe in my country, but my faith in the US dwindled every day. Every day I didn't see Keoni, every day Acoye was running around or possibly dead, every day we suffered and struggled to survive, I wondered how much longer until we reached victory. How much longer until things got easier? That was the real question Chemistry wanted to ask, and that was the only question I was searching for an answer to.

22

Keoni

"We've been out here for two days, and you still haven't told me why we left in the middle of the night."

Zion huffed, ignoring me.

"Zion," I stopped walking, and he kept going. "ZION!"

"What?!" He snapped around. "Why do you think I left my fiancée and kid!? They don't want me, Keoni! They're done with me! Because I decided to follow you!"

I took a step back. "So it's my fault, then?"

"Yes! The whole invasion is *your* fault! Because you couldn't stop—" his words caught in his throat. He was just standing there, blinking at me.

"What couldn't I stop doing?" I challenged, though my voice was weak and shaking.

"Key, I didn't mean it like that." His voice was soft again and he sighed. Rushing his hands over his face, oceanic eyes opened beneath his hands. They were apologetic, like he truly regretted what he'd said or tried to say.

"It's true, I didn't stop a relationship that never should've happened," I admitted. "But I love him, and I'm not going to let what happened between you and your fiancée make me stop loving him." I adjusted the straps on my pack and pushed by him.

"Keoni, wait—" He grabbed my arm.

I stood there looking ahead at the road. I couldn't look back; I think I would've slapped him if I had.

"I didn't mean to say that. I was just—"

"No, that's how you really feel."

"It's not. Please, I was just angry. I didn't really mean any of that."

I swallowed, turning to him. My hand burned, begging me to slap him, but I clenched it instead. "I'm going to pretend you didn't mean it, but I'm not going to act like you didn't say it."

Snatching my arm from him, I kept moving. We'd covered a lot of ground in the last two days in mostly silence. I was fine with continuing all the way to Washington like that.

We'd finally made it to Charleston, and you could hardly tell. The city lines were gone, all of Missouri looked the same, ragged and scorched. Buildings were toppled over, cars were crushed, streaks of tar and burned rubber lined the streets. I'd never seen so much destruction in my own homeland, and it kind of left me saddened. All the homes I'd destroyed in other countries, children and mothers moved from their place of living to seek refuge. War was painful, and it was ugly. I don't know why we did it, or why we were conditioned to love it.

Every soldier wanted to see combat, at least, every older soldier did. They wore their tours around their necks as badges of honor. Forgetting the body count that came with each one. We know it's us or them, but why?

I stopped walking. When did I begin to feel this way?

"Key—"

"Don't touch me." I pulled my shoulder away from Zion's hand. We weren't cool, we weren't friends again. He didn't need to know anything I was struggling with. I was a fool for letting my guard down and believing he was different.

I'd believed Zion was a good kid, and I believed out of everyone he would understand me. He was furious when he found out that Ollie knew the truth, but he wasn't mad *at* me. However, that must not have been true. From my own experience, things barked at you in the heat of the moment are often the way someone secretly felt. I wouldn't allow myself to care if that was truly how Zion felt. I was going to Washington to save what was left of my country, and with the hope that somehow Claudius made it there too, despite the conflicting feelings I had for him.

"How long are you going to act like that?" he asked behind me.

"Act like what?"

Zion grunted. "I apologized, Keoni. What more do you want?"

I rolled my eyes, looking back at the city ahead of me. "Let's follow this road, it looks like there are houses further down the way. We need clothes. We need shoes. We need supplies. Let's see what we can find, rest tonight and get moving in the morning."

Zion didn't respond and I didn't wait for one either. Walking through the city, we followed the road until it took us to a gas station relatively untouched. Zion went around back, and I stood at the front, peeking inside through the broken glass windows. There were cans of food on the floor, water, and the freezer door was open... the lights were flickering. There was power here.

Whistling for Zion, I hopped into the window and moved quickly across the white tiled floor. The shelves that would've been neatly stacked any other day were tipped over and stacked against each other. As I made my way to the freezer, I stopped at the bathroom. Ripping the door open I shoved my gun inside first while I stepped into the doorway. There was one toilet, and a porcelain sink. The silver piping snaking out from the white wall beneath the sink looked wet... like there was condensation on the pipe. I swiped a hand across the pipe, there was moisture along the tips of my fingers.

"Zion!" I screamed. "Zion!" I lifted the faucet handle and water began to run. Jumping for joy, I screamed again, "Zion!"

He burst open the door the next second, his knife raised and eyes wide open. He looked between me and the sink, a fraction of a second ticked by before he screamed too. He raced over, shoving a hand into the running water, he drank right from his cupped palm.

"There's power! There's water!" he was shouting at me.

"I know!" Throwing my hands around his neck, I held

onto him. I wanted to scream, I wanted to cry. There was relief in knowing water was running and power was working.

As we peeled apart, Zion stopped me. He kept a hand on the small of my back while my own hands rested on his chest. "Keoni, I'm sorry. What I said back there was hurtful, and it wasn't right. This invasion would've happened with or without your relationship with the general. They just used that to get under your skin and his, and what I said was so wrong. Will you forgive me?"

"I have to, don't I? If I want to get right with God."

He lifted a shoulder. "But you don't want to forgive me."

My eyes studied his. He was truly sorry, and I could forgive him, but that wasn't the problem. "The truth is, I blame myself too. And when you said that, I felt like I was looking at my own reflection."

"I'm so sorry, Keoni."

Patting his chest, I nodded. "I forgive you, Z."

He pulled me close, hugging me tightly. "I can't lose you too," he whispered.

Wiggling one of my hands free, I wrapped an arm around him. "I'm not going to leave you, Zion. We'll make it together."

After a moment, he finally let me go. "We should see what we can find."

"Come on," I said before turning the water off.

The gas station was in pretty good condition. Though the freezer section was pooling with tubs of warm ice cream because the doors had been left open (all but one), the rest of the store was alright. Zion and I secured the doors first, locking them up. With boxes from the back, we taped pieces of them over the windows and the door to keep people from seeing inside. We didn't plan to stay for longer than the night, but it was a good idea to board up the place to keep people from disturbing us.

I walked through the store with a shopping basket, picking up the canned goods lying around. There was a microwave here, and a miniature oven, which meant the frozen pizzas that survived in the freezer that hadn't been left open would be enjoyed. We'd walked into a goldmine for food, I just wished there were weapons. But just knowing that this city wasn't as bad as it looked stirred hope and fear in my chest.

I was making my way to the front to meet Zion when I spotted something—grape juice.

"Communion," I whispered. "Z? Did you happen to find any crackers?" I wandered to the front where Zion was sitting on the counter holding a little hand mirror.

"My facial hair looks rough," he said.

"It looks fine. We've got more important business to handle."

"Like what?"

"Like, did you find any crackers?"

"Yeah? Like three boxes of them."

I held up the grape juice. "Look what I found."

He lowered the mirror and his eyes locked on the grape juice immediately. "Communion."

"Exactly. We can have it for ourselves."

"Alright, we'll do it tonight. But first, look at this." He

hopped down from the counter and went around it. I followed him into the back office, watching as he went over to the large brown desk cluttered with papers and sticky notes. Zion tapped the black mouse and clicked around.

"There are news articles going out regularly," he said.

"What?" I leaned over the desk beside him. He scrolled the search engine, revealing articles written about all that had been going on. People explaining their theories, headlines about pastors who suddenly dropped dead and then came back to life as a monster.

"And look at this." He pulled up a video that'd been uploaded three days ago. It was of a woman begging for people to help her. She said she was in Nebraska, and there was a huge food shortage. People were hoarding food, stores were empty.

"I thought China invaded?" I whispered.

"They did, but they only invaded important places. Places that held resources and power. Like the borders, the coasts, the capital set up in Springfield—"

"And Washington, DC."

He nodded. "Yeah." The hue of the white screen glared against Zion as he scrolled the comments. People were putting their locations, saying the same thing had happened to them.

"They're creating another civil war. They want the US to make herself fall from the inside out," I said.

"But why haven't they taken over the capital yet?"

"Because we're still fighting. We're still fighting along the borders, along the coasts. We're not giving up. Springfield's defenses weren't as strong as Washington's. But I know

242

somewhere back there, our soldiers—our *comrades*—are still fighting."

Zion closed the browser and pulled up another one.

"What are you doing?"

"If what you say is right, that we're still fighting, then maybe there's a way we can get in contact with someone from the military." He pulled up the military portal and logged in. He pounded the keyboard, writing messages to everyone he could think of, explaining the situation we were in.

"I'll leave this up, so if someone wants to chat or replies back, we'll know."

"Okay."

...❀...

Zion and I ate pizza and drank soda. Zion chugged almost a whole two liter of soda and couldn't stop burping. There was a lost and found bin in the back. I found a new pair of pants, and a hat. Zion found a full outfit. Sweatpants, boots, a shirt. We decided to try the clothes on, and for the first time in months, I looked at myself in the mirror.

I'd been keeping my hair pulled back in a tight ponytail to keep my new growth from looking tacky. But since I didn't know when I'd get to do my hair again, I splashed water on it to get it to shrink up. Thick curls seized off my shoulders as I used a shirt that was too small for Zion and too big for me to dry my hair.

I didn't have any products, but water was enough to at least make the curls come back. Twisting my afro textured hair into a small bun right on the top of my head, my hair looked neater.

"Keoni, you coming out?" Zion called.

"Yeah, yeah," I said as I picked up my uniform. It was dirty, *filthy*. We'd traveled through so much dirt, ran all over. I stared at the digital pattern and my rank in the center of my jacket. I placed a hand on it, remembering when Ollie told me I was moving up a rank.

"Come on, Key!"

"I'm coming!" I snapped at the door. Swallowing the memories, I ripped open the door.

Zion was standing there, looking down at me. He looked kind of different. My eyes traced him. I knew his outfit was different. Seeing him out of uniform was strange, but not as strange as he looked now.

He rolled his eyes. "I trimmed my facial hair. Made my beard look kind of nice."

"That's what it is! You trimmed your beard but not your hair?" Zion's hair was growing in a lot. There were curls all over him, but he'd been keeping them tied away.

"I kind of like my hair. Once it gets really long, I'll start cutting it."

"You look nice, Z," I complimented.

"So do you. I like your hair." He reached out and touched the bun on the top of my head which made me laugh.

"Well, if you're ready now," Zion shrugged, "we can take communion."

"Oh yeah," I nodded, "we can."

He motioned for me to follow him to the front. On the counter, there were two crackers sitting on a plate, and two coffee cups with grape juice. I took a moment before I made it to the counter to think about everything Whisper had told us.

We had to accept Christ and believe in Him. I accepted salvation as a kid, but I didn't really understand it. I just did it because my mom said it was good for me. But now, I was staring at devastation every day. Was it alright to come back to God now? Was it fair? I was only coming back because I had nothing else to believe in. That didn't seem right to me.

"Zion," I called.

"Hmm?"

"I don't think I can take this yet. It's not right. I don't think I should just take communion and be covered now. I don't think it's fair."

"To whom?" he asked as he leaned against the counter. A tall strong frame, that was the only part of Zion that hadn't changed. That was mostly because Zion did pushups every morning and planked. I started joining him back in the warehouse. His face had matured because of his beard, his hair had grown, he'd lost his fiancée. So much had happened to him, but despite all that, Zion returned to God.

The day I saw him murmuring to God at the school, I thought he was just eccentric. And I didn't really know how to feel. But, lately, it's been feeling like God is giving me reasons to come back too. Surviving impossible situations, making it to Charleston in one piece and finding all this food. Running water, heat, and electricity. I feel like these are miracles, but I just don't understand God very much. Why bless me? *Me?*

I turned away from God long ago. Why would He still care? And to come stumbling back to Him for my own sake … That was shallow.

"I feel like it's not fair to God," I admitted.

Zion pulled his shoulders up slowly. "There was a story that I clung to my entire life, the prodigal son. The story of a kid who gets his inheritance early, and when he runs out of money and out of patience with his new dead-end life, he returns home. He goes back just to be a servant to his father, yet his father welcomes him home with open arms."

"I remember that story."

"The prodigal son isn't unique because that's the story of all of us." Zion pushed away from the white and red counter and opened his arms. "When we return to God, we usually have a reason. The prodigal's reason was because he didn't want to keep living the life he was living. He wanted basic necessities. He wasn't pitiful or sorrowful, but he had been humbled, and he was genuinely desperate."

Humbled and genuine. Desperation. I believed I could feel all those things, except genuine. So, I asked Zion, "How do I feel genuine again for God? I feel like I'm using Him if I return now."

"Do you want to believe, or do you just want to be protected?"

"I want to believe, but I just don't know how."

Zion smiled and stepped forward. His large tan hands took

mine and held them. "Keoni, I want you to reopen your heart to God. What you feel right now is genuine. Uncertainty is genuine. The only way to feel something different is to let God inside."

"It's cheating though, isn't it? Wanting Him now when I had a chance before?"

"God doesn't see it that way, and you shouldn't either. He sees you the way the father of the prodigal son saw him. He was happy he returned. Key." He squeezed my hands. "God doesn't feel cheated that you want to return because you're afraid. He's happy, *genuinely* happy, that you've found shelter and peace in Him. Besides," he shrugged, his smile turning a little smug, "the world is only going to get worse. You really think you should be hesitating on this?"

I laughed, feeling a little relieved. "I guess not."

"Good. Let's pray together and ask God to accept us again into His beloved. And after prayer, we'll take communion. Sound good?"

My cheeks lifted, and I smiled up at Zion. Relief washed over me, like God wanted me to know that this was okay. This was the right—no—the *righteous* thing to do.

Without a second thought, I nodded. "Yeah, Z, let's do it."

23

Abigail

"We can't take her," Eve said as he leaned against the desk in the office. "She's too much of a liability. She could pass whatever's wrong with her to us. My vote is not to take her."

"Mine too," Coco agreed with her hand raised.

Whispered nodded. "Alright, that's three to one, Abs, we've got to leave her."

"She'll *die*," I stressed. "We can't leave her here."

Whisper rolled her eyes, moving from the wall she'd been standing against.

"Where are you going?" I called after her. She didn't respond, she just left the office and we all followed behind her. Whisper made a beeline for Sam, who was lying asleep on the warehouse floor. Keoni and...

I stopped walking. I couldn't bring myself to say his name. The last few days have been the hardest of my life, even harder than fighting his parents to survive. Harder than *surviving*. But only because for so long, part of the reason I wanted to live was to see him again. Now he's gone and he's not coming back because of me. I forced him away, but he could've chosen to stay. Saving his family wasn't enough. He wanted to save the world.

"Hey, Abbey?" Eve's hand was on my shoulder. "You alright?"

"Yeah." I patted his hand.

"Abigail," Whisper called to me. "Come here."

"What?" I asked as I came over. Sam was trembling. Her skin had paled beyond belief, and she'd stopped eating the day Keoni and... I took a breath. The day Keoni and Zion left. I wasn't even sure she knew where she was.

"Look..." Whisper turned Sam over and lifted the patch on her shoulder. There was a bullet wound with yellow gunk sticking to her bandages. It was still bloody and fresh looking.

"What is that?"

"She must've been shot."

I stepped back. "When? How long ago?"

"Who knows?" Whisper shrugged. "But her body has been sick for a while. Too sick to fight and heal. This should've been healing for how long she's been here."

Leaning down, I took in the chills on her body, the way her skin was pebbled. The wound was fresh, and it looked like she'd been keeping the wound covered with a single bandage. Who knows the last time that thing's been changed?

"She's very sick," Whisper went on. "The best thing we can do is make her comfortable."

"She's pregnant, Whisper."

249

Her eyes widened and she looked down at Sam. Whisper deflated. "How do you know?"

"Zion told me."

She shook her head. "We still can't—"

"She's pregnant! There's a child within her!" I said hotly.

"Her body is too weak for a child!" Whisper snapped back. "She'll more than likely miscarry, if she hasn't already. Abigail, there is nothing we can do for her."

Eve came and placed a hand on my shoulder, but I shrank away from him, hissing, "Don't touch me."

"Abbey, come on," he said gently, but I didn't want to be around anyone.

"You're all wicked and evil! If that was Flower and me, would you all just leave us for dead?"

"When there's nothing that can be done," Whisper said firmly, "then you must keep moving. No matter what. No one said we enjoyed doing this, but we don't have a choice. So either get on board or get off, but you can't slow everyone else down."

I whirled around, leaving the group to go back to the office with Flower. She was lying on the desk, playing with the air. Closing the door, I flattened my hands against it. I just felt like we were doing something so wrong, yet I knew they were all right. Sam was too sick; it was even fair to say she was dying. She hadn't recovered in the slightest, just gotten worse. Even the blisters on her feet hadn't gotten better. But I just couldn't come to terms with leaving her, especially knowing she wasn't fighting just for herself, she was fighting for the little baby

250

inside.

When I look at Flower, I feel the pain of losing Zion. But I also feel the pain of protecting her and the joys of her future. Sam will never get to experience that. Her body is failing her, and thus failing her child. A woman's easiest battle is carrying a child. The hard part begins when they're born. Because the moment they begin to grow is the moment you must prepare for them to leave you.

They're gifts, lent to us from God, to be raised until He calls them. Samuel was called at a very young age; Caleb was known for his work at an older age. You spend all this time preparing for their arrival, just to begin preparing for their departure once the child is born. Sam would never get that, and I was to blame. Zion, Keoni, Whisper and Eve, Coco, and in part, Flower too. We were all to blame.

Lifting Flower from the desk, she blubbered happily, smiling cheerfully at me. I trembled, seeing Zion in her eyes, knowing he was gone, and Sam would be too.

"It's going to be okay. I promise. I'm not going to let anyone hurt you. Ever." Flower clawed for me, giggling as she got hold of my face. It was funny, maybe she knew I was feeling sad, or maybe not. But when she grabbed my face, she pulled on my cheeks, forcing me to smile.

"Abbey," Coco called outside the door.

"What?"

"Whisper said we should get ready to leave soon."

"Okay."

She patted the door, and I heard her footsteps trailing off.

251

I sank to my knees, cradling Flower. "God, I know it's been a while since we've spoken. But I need You right now. Please, come back into my life. I'm so … so scared and broken. Please," I sniffled, "help me."

We set off, leaving Sam with a bottle of water, a pack of crackers, and a knife. If she ever woke up, she could at least defend herself if a wrong or someone else tried to break in. I hoped, deep within, that she wouldn't wake up. That she wouldn't have to wake up and figure it all out on her own, the way I had to when the Rapture first happened. But if she did wake up, I hoped she would survive.

The first three days of travel were hard and long, but by the fourth day, walking seemed to get easier. As the weeks passed, we seemed to get faster. Staying close, keeping Flower quiet, and being watchful, that's what it took to make it. We were a large group, so we were noisy by default, but we did our best. As we traveled along, we found random places to settle. Sometimes we didn't even settle in a building, just right out in the open. It was getting cold though, and Flower was waking me through the night. She was getting irritated from the cold; her skin was breaking out too.

"How much further?" I asked as we sat around a fire one evening.

"Maybe two days, including tomorrow," Whisper answered as she held up a map. "If we keep the pace we've been moving at, we'll be ok."

"I'm exhausted," Coco said, rocking Flower. Coco seemed particularly attached to Flower. She was always willing to carry her for me. Sometimes, for a full day, Coco would keep my daughter strapped to her chest and walk without a complaint. She's never said much about her past to explain why she liked taking care of Flower besides the time she mentioned her little sister, and I've always been too afraid to ask. Sometimes it's better to forget, at least that's what I've been telling myself lately. It was easier to forget Zion than to remember him and the pain that came with the memories.

Eve leaned back and stretched with a groan. "I was thinking—"

"Shh! Do you hear that?" Whisper said as she pulled her gun from her waistband. The older woman jolted to her feet, glancing around.

"I don't hear—"

Whisper hushed Eve again. Moving from her seat by the fire, she stepped between Coco and me with her gun raised. I signaled to Coco and then Eve. He nodded, grabbing his backpack and Coco who was already tying Flower to her chest. I grabbed a gun from my bag. We'd found it along the way. Eve had wanted it, but it was safer for me to have it.

Whisper looked back at us, and I nodded, signaling we were ready. We had to stay ready, that was Whisper's constant advice. Before we left the warehouse, she made us practice our

253

signals to each other.

"Come out! Show yourselves!" Whisper demanded loudly.

A few seconds of tense silence ticked by before a man stepped through the bushes with his hands raised. His clothes looked tattered, and his hair was disheveled. He looked like he'd been running longer than we'd been traveling. "Please, I just smelled the fire and followed it."

"Are you alone?" Whisper asked.

The man looked around the group and lowered his arms. His demeanor shifted from frazzled to menacing the instant he lowered his hands and I screamed, "Run!"

"You're not going anywhere," the man said as men and women stepped from the bushes. A woman in a winter hat stepped out, shoving a gun in Everette's face. He threw his hands up and a man snatched his bag. Coco's eyes were as big as the moon as she clutched Flower, holding my whining daughter against her chest. I was ready to retaliate when I felt a gun press into my back.

"Don't move," the husky voice hissed. We were surrounded, and every single one of them had weapons. We were going to die here if we didn't do something.

Whisper looked around, she was shocked, undoubtedly blaming herself for not hearing the movement. Whisper had done a lot of work in her day, some of which included missionary work, moving groups of people to safety, like the Underground Railroad.

"What do you want?" she finally asked.

"I want all of your supplies, and that girl there, she's

254

pretty." He pointed to Coco.

"Not happening," Whisper said calmly. "You can have our supplies but not the girl."

The man stepped forward, a dark expression taking over his aged face. "You're not in a position to negotiate."

"And you're not in a position to pass out demands."

He chuckled, glancing around his group that laughed along with him. "And why aren't I in a position to make demands, darling?"

Whisper glanced back at me and gave me the slightest nod. That was all the signal I needed to know we were about to be in a fight for our lives. When she turned back, she said, "Because you're a dead man." Her gun seemed to fire before she finished speaking, sinking a bullet into the man's head in the blink of an eye. A frenzy of gunfire broke out around us.

"Run!" I screamed as I jabbed my elbow into the man who was pressing a gun into me. I swung my gun behind me, firing in his direction with the hope that I'd hit him. I couldn't tell if I had shot anyone because everyone was screaming. But above the chaos, my ears seemed to only tune in to the cries of Flower.

I searched for her as I fought my way through the frenzy. Out of nowhere, I was tackled, shoved into the dirt, and wailed on. I screamed, trying to get a few good hits in, but the woman was wild. Kicking and scratching, pummeling me. But I couldn't give up, so long as I heard the sound of Flower's cries.

Suddenly, the woman was shoved off me. She went flying into the dirt beside me, and I sat up immediately, glancing

255

around as I gasped for air.

"Get up," a man reached out his hand and I took it. I didn't know who he was, but he was helping me, and I needed it. "Come on!" he shouted.

"I can't leave my daughter! Coco!" I whirled around. "Coco!" I couldn't see anyone or anything as the fire flickered, and the figures moved about.

"We've got to move!" The man grabbed my hand and pulled me along. I only went because I didn't hear Flower anymore, and Coco was nowhere in sight.

Rushing along behind the man, we raced through the woods, the darkness getting thicker as the fire faded in the background. We just had to keep moving. We didn't know if anyone was following us or if we were safe. I didn't even know who I was running with, but I'd figure that out once we were safe.

The man I followed led me back to a different campsite. We walked up to a fire in the middle of a large group. There were all kinds of people dressed for the winter sitting together around a fire. Some wore puffer jackets while others wore pelts like they'd fallen out of the Middle Ages.

"What is this place?" I asked.

The man turned around, as breathless as I was and said, "Just a campfire. These people, they're traveling north to Canada for safety."

"Where's my daughter?" I looked around for Coco, walking through the big camp. They had tents, and food. It was like these people had gotten a heads up on the invasion and were completely prepared for it.

"She may not be here, or she'll be here soon. What does she look like?" the man asked behind me.

"She's a baby, strapped to a girl—" I sucked in a breath, trying not to cry.

"Alright," he said, "we'll find her."

"She could be anywhere!" I cried and dropped to my knees. "I'm an idiot for leaving her. I just left my own child! I'm not fit to be a mother at all." I sobbed endlessly into my hands. I'd just lost the last piece of Zion I had, my last hope, my everything. I lost my child, traded her for my own freedom. How could I?

"It's too dark to go searching now, but in the morning, we'll look for her," the man reassured me.

"She could be dead," I whispered as I pulled my knees into my chest.

"Or she could be alive and well. You won't know until the morning. You should get some sleep until then."

"How? How can I sleep when she's out there?" I finally gave the man my full attention. Hazel eyes seemed orange with the firelight around. His square jaw, free of facial hair, and his light hair that coiled from the sweat on his forehead. His face held a calm expression, maybe a look of boredom. I felt like he wanted to scowl at me, but for my sake, he didn't. Instead, he said flatly, "It's your choice, but you can't go searching tonight and draw attention to our camp."

"Draw attention?" I waved a hand around. "You're relaxing in the middle of the forest with a bonfire! You're drawing attention to yourselves!"

"We're letting enemies know we're a big group, big enough to be unafraid of their threats."

"And the wrongs?" I shrugged. "What about them?"

He casually held up his gun and looked it over. "We're prepared for those too."

I shook my head. "You have no idea what you're up against."

"No, but I'm ready to find out."

"Unbelievable."

"You should be more grateful," he scolded. "I saved you. This camp is your safe haven until you decide it isn't anymore. The only reason those guys didn't kill you when you walked up is because you were with me. So, a 'thank you' would be appreciated."

I scowled. "I'm *not* thankful! I lost my daughter because of you!"

He groaned, shoving his weapon into his holster. "Get up." His words were hotter than the fire burning in the middle of the camp. But I didn't move as he stood. I wasn't going to let him push me to do anything else. He forced me to leave and now I'm here safe without my daughter.

"I said *get up*," he repeated.

"No."

He snatched me up by my arm, a tight grip on it with his large hands. He pulled me along, though I fought and tried to pull away from him. We moved through the camp, everyone's eyes on us until we reached a tent. Whipping open the flaps, he tossed me inside onto the sleeping mat. I hit it, turning over quickly to snap at him. "What's your problem!?"

He didn't respond. He simply zipped the tent closed and began to undress. He removed his jacket, revealing a military uniform beneath it. There was a patch in the center of his chest, it looked identical to the one Zion had. Maybe he knew him.

Peeling away a sticky shirt, the man revealed all of his tan skin. He looked like a peanut butter cup with winding tattoos up his arms and across his chest. They were thick bold lines that reached around his fingers.

I watched him, moving to a basin sitting on a stand. He splashed water onto his chest, and then over his neck and hair. I was shocked, wondering where all this stuff came from. As if he read my mind, he glanced over at me. Hands clutching the rim of the basin, muscular arms were straightened as he spoke.

"We raided an armory that was invaded. Killed a bunch of dragons, took all the supplies we could carry. And what we couldn't carry, we put in a wagon and dragged with us." He grabbed a towel, turning towards me as he dried himself. "What's your name?"

"Abigail," I said.

"Diaz," he replied.

"Is that your first name?"

He raised a brow, and I pointed at his uniform.

"No," he grunted. "My first name is Evelyn."

I nodded.

Diaz grabbed a bowl of fruit and extended it to me. "You should eat something. If you want meat, you'll have to wait.

We just ran out. Our hunters were going out but since we're planning on leaving soon—"

"You were drafted?"

He blinked, lowering the fruit bowl. "Why?"

"My," I paused, "my friend, he was drafted and the patch on his jacket was the same as yours."

Diaz glanced down at the jacket and back up at me. "I was drafted a few months back. Did some training. What's your friend's name?"

"Zion Reinhardt."

He snorted. "Reinhardt? Yeah, I knew him."

"Oh…" I nodded.

"Well, you can have the sleeping bag. I'll pair up with someone else for the night. Don't leave until I come for you, understood?"

"Why?"

He sighed like I had annoyed him. "Because there are rules. And I broke them by bringing you here without asking. That means my rations, and everything else, will be split with you. So you better not bring me trouble. Got it? Do as I say, and we'll find your daughter. Trust me, the sooner I can get you out of here, the better it'll be for me."

"Why did you come to our camp?"

He was holding the tent flap open, ready to leave when he stepped back. "We came because we heard gunshots. We didn't want the fighting to reach us, so we went and reached them first."

"Then why save me if you knew the consequences?"

"Would you rather I let you get beaten to death? Because that's what was happening."

I looked away. There was suddenly a burning sensation in my cheeks, and it wasn't from the pain I'd been feeling from all the blows I'd taken earlier.

"Clean yourself up," Diaz ordered. "Dress your wounds and eat. I'll be back in the morning."

24

Abigail

Evelyn returned in the morning. The tent flaps opened, and the sun peeked in before Diaz stepped inside. He was wearing a white shirt with cargo sweats tucked into black boots. He wasn't a very tall man, but his striking face and tall attitude made up where his height lacked.

"I'm ready to find my daughter," I said before he could even speak. Not that I assumed he would.

"Good morning," his voice was flat. He didn't even look at me, just walked around me to a bin in the back of his tent. I didn't explore anything last night. I just sat on the sleeping bag for over half of the night, and then I fell asleep. When I woke up, I finally dressed my wounds like he'd instructed.

My eye felt sore, my lip was busted, so I had the pleasure of scraping dried blood from it this morning. Every part of my torso and face hurt, and when I felt down my neck, there were scratches there from the tussle. Some on my arm too. But the scratches brought back memories of Sam, and briefly, I

262

wondered if she made it.

The bin behind me slammed shut, jerking me from my thoughts. Diaz was standing in front of me, putting a gun belt on.

"You need to eat, then we'll go looking for your daughter."

"I can't waste any more time," I urged, "please, just let me go look for her. I stayed like you asked. It's morning, so let me go."

Evelyn lowered himself to squat in front of me. The tension that was on his face yesterday, coolly hidden behind the look of boredom he pulled off, was there again today. He was as stressed as I was, probably not about my daughter, but just surviving in general.

"I said we'd go, and we will. But if you don't have the strength to look for her, you'll die and you'll never find her. Eat, and we'll leave." He stood without another word and left the tent. It was unzipped, so I figured I could leave.

Stepping outside, I blinked back the sun. It was shining so aggressively. With a hand up shading my eyes, I walked through the camp. It was quieter this morning than it was last night. Tents and sleeping bags were all over. I stepped around them, hoping I didn't disturb anyone. I followed the smell of food, something hot, which I hadn't had in a while. We'd been surviving off jerky, crackers, and water. Whisper said she wouldn't hunt because it was too much to carry since we were almost to the shelter she'd been taking us to.

The smell of food brought me to a cart with ingredients on it, nothing out of the ordinary, it all looked like chopped flowers and grass, probably wild spices and garnishes.

"Hey there, are you hungry?" The kind voice came from a girl around Eve's age. She had cat-like eyes and fiery red hair. She was plump and beautiful.

"Um, yes, a little," I replied shyly.

"Come, I'll make you a bowl of porridge. Leo!" she called.

A man tripped out of a tent behind her. Green eyes against his creamy skin and blonde waves. He was as golden as wheat and looked out of place. He was… oddly beautiful, the only thing missing was a crown on his head.

Long strides brought the princely man to me. He raised a blonde brow. "Can I help you?" his snarky voice pestered.

"Don't be rude," the girl said. "She wants porridge, Leo."

"We can't go giving porridge to everyone, Faire."

Faire sighed, placing a hand on her hip. "Why are you so mean?"

"I'm just trying to protect what's ours."

She rolled her eyes, but before either of them spoke, I added, "I'm really not hungry. I just needed a little strength to keep me going."

"Well," a big man, thick with muscles and everything else, stepped out with a haggard old woman. "There's enough food for everyone. Have whatever you like," he rumbled in his deep tenor.

"Thank you—"

"Abigail!" I spun around in fear, it was Diaz marching across the camp. He grabbed my wrist and snatched me forward. "Why did you leave my tent?"

"So, she's yours?" Leo asked over my shoulder.

Diaz looked like he'd spew poison into my soul if I said a word. Returning to his normally unbothered self, he looked up at the people behind me. "She is." He pulled me into his firm chest. "Sorry to bother you all. She got away from me."

"Better keep a leash on her," Leo sneered.

"*Leo*," Faire snapped.

"Sorry," he muttered.

"Let's go," Diaz whispered through clenched teeth. He gripped my arm and turned me. We walked in silence for a moment before I tried to wiggle free from him.

"Let me *go*. I'm tired of you snatching me around."

"I told you, if you cause problems, there will be problems for *both* of us."

"How was I supposed to know those people are problems! You left!"

"To get you food," he snarled as we walked.

"Well, you should've said something instead of just waltzing out and—"

"Diaz," a voice called from behind. He stopped, turning us to face a girl. She had smooth brown skin and shoulder length curls that were pinned back on one side.

"Yes, Fox?" Diaz answered calmly.

"Dart, Kohl, and I were going to head to the end of the forest to gather more berries. Can we go?" Her eyes flicked over to mine, taking me in quickly. "Who's this?"

"A friend," he grunted. "Listen, take—"

"Fox," the girl extended her hand to me. She had slender

fingers with silver bracelets around her wrists. "It's my codename. Ramah says we shouldn't go by our real names out in the open."

"Oh… Uh…" I shrugged one shoulder, half afraid to spare a glance at Diaz. He was so angry the air between us was hot with his rage. But he held it in as I said, "I don't have a codename." I took the girl's hand and she laughed, brown cheeks pulling into a baby doll's smile. In my heart, I hoped Flower would be this precious when she got older. Fox looked like a teenager, probably sixteen, but she still had some of her childish cuteness in her adorable dimples. She didn't belong in this messed up world. Not any more than Flower did.

"That's alright," Fox laughed. "Diaz doesn't have a codename either. He's against it."

"Alright," Diaz cut in and we dropped hands. "Take Kaiis with you, he's rested enough."

Fox blushed. "I'm going to tell him you used his real name," she teased, but Diaz only rolled his eyes.

"Just take KI and be back by evening."

"Ok," she was turning to leave when she stopped and glanced back at me. "See you around."

I nodded and the pretty girl flounced off, her curly hair bouncing all around as she trotted. Diaz grunted beside me, cutting through the lighthearted mood as he turned to leave. I walked quickly to catch up to him as we returned to his tent.

"That girl, she asked your permission to leave," I said.

"I vouched for her friends to stay here at the first camp our group made. Nobody wanted them aorund since they were a bunch of kids, but we came to terms," Diaz explained without looking at me. "The kids helped with gathering food to make up for being useless."

"I see."

He handed me a plate, there was fruit and grilled vegetables on it. I didn't know I was hungry until the food was sitting in front of me. I grabbed the vegetables with my bare hands, eating carrots I normally didn't like and the grilled tomatoes that always gave me acid reflux. I'd completely stopped eating them when I was pregnant with Flower.

"Slow down," Diaz said, handing me a canteen. "You'll make yourself sick."

"T-Thanks." I took the canteen and sucked down the water. It tasted so fresh, but that was probably because Eve wasn't slobbering on the top like he always did when he guzzled water. I hated drinking after him, but I always spared Coco the repulsiveness.

"I took a walk this morning," Diaz said. "Back to the campsite where I found you. There was no one that way. A few dead bodies, no children though, all adults."

My heart wanted to fail, but at least knowing Flower (and Coco) weren't dead gave me a little hope to hold on to.

"Do you know where your group was headed?" he asked. "You could try to find them if you know where they could've run off to."

"We were going to a shelter. It was two days away. But I don't know the exact location."

"How long has your group been walking?"

"Weeks, three maybe. It felt like more."

"From where?"

"I… I'm not sure. But the shelter was on a beach, I think Virginia Beach."

"Well, you're in Virginia, the Suffolk area. Virginia Beach is a straight shot from here, not too far. Two days of travel is probably right, possibly three. If your group slowed down, or went looking for you, that's probably three days for them too. I can take you there and return."

My eyes widened. "What?"

"I said I can take you—"

"No," I held up a hand, "I know what you said, but why?"

"It's mostly for my own good. I brought you in, I get you out safely. It's easier for me this way. One less person means less resources being used. Which is why we don't pick up free loaders. Everyone's got to offer something. If you don't, we can't take you in."

I finally understood. Evelyn taking me in was a problem since I really didn't offer their group anything besides tears and an empty belly. They weren't looking for extra mouths to feed, they were looking for extra hands to help, if they were even looking at all.

"What if your group leaves you?" I asked, feeling guilty all of a sudden.

"We're not planning to leave for another five days. I'll only be a day behind them. With our large group, I'd catch up in no time. Besides, I know where we're going. I'll have enough supplies to take care of myself."

"Oh my goodness, thank you," I lunged forward, wrapping my arms around his neck.

He grunted.

"Alright." He pushed me off and stood. "Finish your food. The faster you finish, the faster we can leave."

...❀...

Evelyn wasn't much of a talker. We walked in total silence. He wore a backpack full of supplies, and he was able to snag some supplies for me too. It would only be two days, so I didn't need much. All while we walked, I wondered if I'd find Flower along the way. A clue, anything. I could only pray that we'd move quickly enough to make it there.

With little conversation and mostly being left to my own thoughts, Diaz and I arrived in Virginia Beach. The place looked like a flaming tornado had hit it. I wasn't sure if anything was even alive here. It reeked... like a stench had laid claim to the air and nothing could get it to leave. You could almost see the stench, almost touch it. But that was because there were dead bodies in the streets. Some had decayed a lot, some looked relatively fresh. I stared in horror as we walked the streets. I could've vomited, but thankfully, my food stayed in my belly.

"We've got to be careful," Diaz whispered as we walked. "The coastal areas were heavily attacked during the invasion. It's likely the Chinese are still here."

"How do you know so much about this?" I asked in a quiet

voice.

He scowled at me, as if I should somehow know the answer already. "I was in the military."

"You were a private."

"I was still dispatched, given information. Does my rank suddenly make me not a member of the military?" He'd stopped walking, his glare eating away at me.

"No, sorry," I said weakly.

He grunted, turning away again. "Let's keep moving."

"Why do you always act like you're in charge?"

He shook his head and kept walking. I gritted my teeth and stomped behind him. Zion was not like this, but this guy. With his fragile masculinity or something! He was so annoying, despite how kind he was to escort me. I was thankful for his help, but I won't miss him when he's gone.

We arrived at a red brick building. It was trimmed in black; the way Whisper described it. It took us hours to find it since that was the only description I could remember, and the fact that it was supposed to be a shelter.

It *was* a shelter—a women and children's shelter. However, the shelter was a little scary. Big with not a single window on the outside. A metal door that looked like you were locked in once you went inside. I was beginning to wonder if I was at the right place. And, if this *was* the right place, had it always been a shelter?

Taking a breath, all I could do was try. I knocked on the door and waited. Evelyn stood behind me, his weapon drawn.

There was a sound, like thumping footsteps, and then the

hatch in the door opened.

"Who's there?" someone asked from the other side.

I recognized the voice. "Whisper?" A lump immediately formed in my throat. "Whisper! It's me, Abigail!"

"Abs?" The hatch closed, and the door unlocked. Creeping it open, Whisper peered out. "Abbey!"

She stepped out and I squeezed her tight. I didn't exactly like Whisper when we first met, but right now none of that mattered. We'd traveled together, got separated, and now we were reunited again.

"Are they all here?" I sniffled as I stepped back. "Is Flower here?"

"Yes," she nodded, "her and Coco arrived yesterday. They were in bad shape, but they're better now."

I dropped to my knees, weeping right at the front door. "Thank you, God," I whispered.

"We need to get inside," Whisper said, trying to help me up. "Sir, come in."

Diaz took a step back. "I just came—"

"Come inside," Whisper demanded. "There are others watching. Traveling alone is not an option."

Diaz grumbled something and came inside with us. There was no one upstairs. Just an empty room. No furniture or furnishings. Nothing but space and walls. Whisper led us over to a corner of the room and knocked on the tiles of the floor. A knock came back, and Whisper began picking up the tiles. Below was a hatch with a ladder.

"Come on, everyone's downstairs."

I couldn't descend the ladder fast enough. When I got to the bottom, a man with green eyes and dark hair helped me down. His olive skin and charming smile was a nice welcome, but I wasn't concerned with that.

"Where's my daughter?" I asked the man.

"Likely through those doors. I just need to make sure you're healthy and don't need to see our medics."

"I'm fine," I snapped. "I want to see my daughter."

"Hughes," Whisper called as she came down the ladder. "She's with me."

He nodded, a tight smile on his face as he stepped aside and let Whisper, Evelyn, and me through the door.

"Abbey!" Everette called from across the room. He stood from a table, tears soaking his eyes. He looked good, with fresh clothes and clean hair.

"Eve!" I raced to him, and we embraced in the middle of the room. "I thought I'd never see you again!" I cried. I could feel Eve trembling as he held me.

"Abbey?"

That voice.

I stepped from Eve's embrace to find Coco sporting new bandages and a sling. Her left arm was broken, and just beneath her shirt, I could see the bandages around her abdomen. But, in her right arm was my little Flower. She had a cut on her face, but I couldn't care less. They were both alive.

"Coco," I was weak again, sitting on the floor before I knew it. She approached me, and as she got closer, I could see the bruises on her face, and one of her eyes was bloodshot.

272

"Coco," I whispered again.

"We got attacked, but I protected her." She extended Flower to me in her one good arm, but I snatched her close too. She'd given everything to protect my Flower, and now I owed her my life. Doubly. I owed her for Flower's life too. She gave almost everything to protect my baby... *my* baby, while I ran for safety. Coco was stronger than me. And I will never forget that. I'd do everything I could to become as strong as this little girl.

"Thank you, Coco. Thank you so much," I sobbed.

25

Patron Saint of Victory

The evening came and went with no word from China. In fact, many evenings came and went. But I couldn't give up, so I had to pinch China when the moment was right. The USA was a sitting duck, nothing more. The country wasn't going to last much longer, and China knew that.

China began reallocating more resources towards their fight with the US and pulling away from Taiwan. Their presence was still felt, but it was much weaker than ever before. With more pressure on the US, it would crack soon enough. If I could just bandage the US for a little longer, somehow get them to believe in a ceasefire, then I could move forward with my original plan.

"Israel is the goal," I said to myself as I stood in the window of my chambers. "America is a pawn."

"Victory," Bastion's voice called from behind the door.

"Enter."

"My lord, we are ready for departure."

274

"And Sabiya, is she ready to assume leadership in my stead?"

"She has been prepared with instructions."

"Very well." I turned to face Bastion; he inclined his head as I made my way out of the room.

The hall to Sabiya's personal chambers was long. Onyx pillars holding up gold encrusted ceilings and ivory walls. The rouge carpet that consumed every step, so it seemed like you were walking on air, carried you all the way to her grand door, hand carved from a single stone.

"Sabiya, my love," I said.

The door opened, rolling smoothly across the thick carpet. "Lord Victory," she replied as she stood in a white headdress and long white robes. "Your preparations were followed; I have outlined the details you stressed to your assistants who will help me in your absence."

"Just don't do too much work." I stepped into her room and slipped my hands to the small of her back. "I want you ready to try again for our daughter when I return. I got word from our doctors; they said your test was negative."

"I'm sorry, my lord." Her eyes shrank away from mine as a sullen look took over her face. "I don't know what's wrong with my body."

"You're too stressed, always picking up the slack for me."

"No, Lord Saint Victory, your work is my burden to share. Though I do not see it as a burden, but an honor."

"Raise your head when you speak to me," I said calmly. "You are my wife, and the head of Syria in my absence."

"Yes, my lord," she answered quickly as she raised her head. The breathless beauty of Sabiya threatened to make me miss my flight to England.

"My love, we will bear children. It is just a matter of patience. You will do well to let others assist you while I'm away."

"Of course, sir."

"Very good." I leaned forward and kissed my wife. "I'll see you soon."

"Saint Victory, I wish you fulfilment in your protection of triumph."

A gentle warmth embraced my heart. "Because you have wished it, I will make it so."

...❀...

"Henry." I nodded as the Duke of Malta stood in the large foyer of his home. Henry Caille of Malta, and Chivalry, the King of England were tied very closely to one another so meeting with him was like meeting with King Chivalry.

Henry was the bastard child of Chivalry, but he rose to power and took claim over Malta during the recession and into the famine. With the countries coming under the ruling of the King of England, especially small lands like Malta, Chivalry was impressed that Henry refused his leadership. But it didn't cause an uprising, people actually hated Henry for a while for his resistance until King Chivalry adopted him back into the family—but that was only to get Malta under his ruling. So, technically speaking, Henry is a prince of England, but because of his royal impurity, he only holds the title of Duke for now.

"Victory, it's not very often that I'm visited by a saint," Henry said kindly.

"I can make more visits if that's what you're asking."

He chuckled, a half-smile crossing his face. "You seem to be a different man outside of your castle."

"I have built my home on old foundations, but the entire world doesn't work in such ways, so I'm forced to be a chameleon."

"Very well, then I can trust this is still the same man from Syria."

I nodded. "Yes, of course."

He frowned. "Then you have wasted your time coming here. I am not interested in a saint, nor victory. I am interested in peace."

"Me too." I jutted a hand forward in desperation to stop him from leaving.

The duke looked down at my hand, his sizzling blue eyes reaching back to mine.

"Your Grace, I am not such a man wrapped up in only victory. That is simply what my people call me," I said.

"You earned that name. There is a reason and story behind it. A battle." He lifted his chin. "And you have never disowned the title."

"Because I will not break the only hope my people have." I tried hard to keep my tone leveled, but this man was testing my patience.

Henry's bunched shoulders seemed to relax as he looked at me. "Tell me more," he said as he turned away.

I followed the duke down a long hall with walls filled with pictures of bored people. They were all frowning though they wore jewels and diamonds. I slowed as I stood in front of one portrait. It was a woman sitting in a chair alone in a diamond beaded dress, and a large crown on a red background. Empty green eyes, and dark hair tied away from her face left me with a plain visage to look at.

"This painting, does it speak to you?" Henry asked beside me when he noticed I'd stopped walking.

"No, sadly. It doesn't say a thing. None of them do. I want to see an image of someone that comes alive when you look at it. A portrait that captures the person so well, they're nearly speaking to you through the frame."

"That would be one powerful painting."

"It would, wouldn't it?"

Henry stepped back, a hand in his crisp blue pants pocket. "I know a fine painter, someone who's been looking for a challenge. I can give him a call."

"This man, he'd paint my portrait?"

"Of course."

I looked back at the paintings ahead of me. "I'd like that."

"Very good, then I'll give him a call tonight. So long as you tell me what you're really here for."

"Oh." I nodded, finally pulling my eyes away from the paintings. "Your Grace, I came today to ask for a favor. I need to make a ceasefire with the United States on China's behalf, but China is not cooperating."

He folded his arms, a scowl quickly taking over. "What kind of dirt did you bring to my home?"

"The kind you can plant in," I said curtly. "Duke Caille, if we don't stop China, they will keep beating down everyone's door until they rule the world. I'm not asking for your support; I'm asking for your help. I'm asking for you to stand by my side and help me stop China."

"How?"

"By helping America."

"What are you talking about?"

"Henry, Europe was one of America's closest allies. Helping them right now would change the game."

He backed away, shaking his head. "You dare bring this madness to my country." He looked around quickly before taking one big step towards me and whispering darkly, "You dare bring this into my own private property? How *dare* you?"

"You think China's going to stay loyal to you?" I challenged. "You think after they get what they want from the US, and become the most powerful and unstoppable nation in the world, they're going to care about you?"

Caille went to snap back a response, but I continued, cutting him off. "We've got to look out for ourselves. All of us will become nothing if China seizes Taiwan, America, and part of Israel through Russia. Come on, Henry, you know I'm right."

He closed his eyes, gripping his arm across his chest. "How does sending supplies help us stop China?"

"It helps the US fight back for a little longer. The fall of the US is inevitable now, but when and who catches the fallout is the question."

"Prolong it for what? Until when?"

"Until we can get Russia to sign a peace treaty with Israel. We do that, we become important to Israel, which means resources. We help Israel, they'll help us. We'll be strong enough to pull the world out of this spiraling fear of China. All I'm asking is for you to give the world hope again."

"Hope," he scoffed.

I nodded as he stood there, blinking aimlessly down the hall. It was a lot to ask for, but with the help of Europe, America would be secure a little longer and they'll be more open to talking about a ceasefire. China and America were both prideful. However, all I needed was to convince one of those countries that the other was willing to stop fighting at least for a little while.

Creating a hoax ceasefire would still benefit China and bringing in Europe would benefit the US. Overall, bringing in Europe turns one more country against China, seating them at my council table.

A ceasefire will give China time to retreat and regroup, while the US will have the same. Of course, they'll try to thicken their forces, but with China never really leaving or agreeing to the ceasefire, China will still be able to relaunch a stronger attack on the US. But we need this time to convince Russia into a peace treaty with Israel. If Russia and Israel can make this treaty work, then I'll have Israel in sights. All I've got to do is walk through their doors as their savior, and nothing more will matter. The world by then will be sitting at my feet.

"What's the end goal here?" Henry finally asked after being lost in thought.

"The end goal is to put you—and me—on top where we belong. We're the only two trying to change this world, trying to rise from the ashes of that famine. We do this, you and I, we'll have the world as our stage." I paused and patted his shoulder. "Henry, if we do this, we have the potential to save the world, and that's beyond hope for a better day. That's *guaranteeing* a better day. People won't need hope anymore. They'll only need you and me."

He swallowed. "This would more than likely qualify me to take my seat as a prince."

"It would, and you know what? A prince is only the beginning. You stick with me, and I can make you a king."

Deep within, Henry was just a sad kid who didn't get to grow up on the right side of the tracks. But he watched everyone else do it. Henry wanted to prove to the world that he deserved to be royalty, and I could help him do that.

"Henry, listen to me," I said calmly. "You do this, you're done proving yourself. You're no longer the crown's bastard, you are the crown itself. No one for the next lifetime will surpass the great turn around you did for the world, not just England."

He ran a hand through his blonde hair. "It's bigger than us."

"Much bigger."

There was a moment of hesitancy lingering between us, but I had to snuff it out. "Answer me this... Has China ever made a plan to make you king?"

"No," he said sheepishly.

"Then you need to reconsider your loyalty."

"I'll do it," he said quickly, "I'll help."

Taking a cooling breath, I extended a hand to him. "Do this, and I will give you the kingdoms of this world."

26

Patron Saint of Victory

"Ceasefire in the talks between the US and China," Volkov
read through his tight circular glasses. "Wow, I never would've
seen this coming."

"Because it isn't!" Jun snapped. "Victory is getting ahead
of himself. We made no decision or movement towards this!
We didn't want this."

"You needed this," I said matter-of-factly. "China was
spreading itself—"

"You are not a god!" Jun screamed at me. "You cannot
save the world! You're a true American, though you call
yourself different. You're not," he hissed. "You are nothing
but a fraud! You're trying to fix everything that isn't your
concern. That's why the US is an easy target. They rush to help
everyone but themselves. And you just inserted yourself into
something you have no business in!"

The room was still, but I felt like I was spinning. Heat
raged over me, taking over from the inside out. I'd gone ahead,

after Duke Callier agreed to send America aid, to spread the word that China wanted a ceasefire. It was a trickle down from a few guys I knew before it reached China. But England helped even more, making a display of helping the US by sending ships of food, water, and hidden weapons. Henry wanted to fight against China, and this was his chance, so he milked it.

I expected fallout. Going into a situation like this could only call for fallout. But this... this was unacceptable.

I am the savior.

I am the savior.

I! Am! The! Savior!

"Sir," Bastion's voice cut in, and I realized I was panting. My eyes moved, taking in my hand. I was gripping the armrest of the stone chair so hard my hand was cramping. There was stained blood on the armrest, evidence of the stress I've been under. Prying my fingers from the armrest, I began to massage one of my hands as I tried to contain myself.

The room was full of people, and I was losing my grip right in front of them. If I had been a different man, I would pray at this moment. But I refused to do it. I refused to ask God for a way out when He never gave me one before.

I will not pray... I will be the one they kneel before and pray to.

"You have nothing to say for yourself?" Jun asked darkly.

It took a moment to even lift my eyes. Pathetically, I looked around the table. Volkov wouldn't look at me, and Henry was sympathetic. The Twin Princes of Egypt had no reaction, they just watched in silence. A co-leader of the Taliban only folded his arms, he was interested in seeing what

I'd do. There were empty seats beside Hamas from the Taliban. They belonged to the Indian leaders, but over the past few months, India no longer needed representatives as they were completely under Chinese leadership now.

Then there was Jun. Such a proud man. I underestimated him and China. I thought they would go down easily, but they are ready to fight, so I must be too. I've come too far to let China fight and push back this hard. I must win.

I am the Patron Saint of Victory.

Even I don't always believe that... but Sabiya does. She believes in me. The thought of Sabiya made my heart stir, and the darkness clouding my mind began to float away.

"I have nothing to say for myself," I started, "but I do have something to say to you, and I want you to return this back to China. We will not sit by and let you try to take the world from beneath our feet. You don't get to have India, America, Taiwan, and parts of Israel. All while connected to England, the Middle East and Russia." I stood, my eyes burning through a wide-eyed Jun. "You don't get to underhandedly take over everything. You are not our ruler, we do not submit to your rulings, nor will we wait for them."

Jun scoffed, his white beard fidgeting with the movement. "*We?* Who is *we?*" He glanced around the table at the leaders.

I clenched my first, ready to spew a nasty remark when Volkov stood. "My men are dwindling by the day. I don't want to take orders from you any longer."

I was shocked, but Volkov gave me a slight nod before scowling back at Jun.

"Well then you're going to be—"

"I stand with Victory," Duke Henry Cailler stood from his seat. The chair screeched along the floor as he did so.

Jun looked taken aback but said nothing. He raised his chin as he stood slowly from his seat, but the new council was forming right before my eyes.

Hamas spoke directly to me from down the table before Jun could say anything. "China has power, what does this," he waved a hand around, "*saint* have?"

"I have nothing. But you have access to almost all the oil in the world right now. I can get you more if you let me." I glanced over Jun who was a bright pink color now. "And you'll have full control over your oil. I've read about the big shipments you send to China, sometimes paying double the tax because the import is so big. But China sends you meager rations and very little else in return. All they have are promises."

"Well, you just said you have nothing."

"I don't need anything to give you full control over your own imports."

Hamas pouted for a second as he thought it over. He shrugged his shoulder, his white head covering folding with the motion. "What can you offer me?" he asked Jun.

"If you have to ask," Jun replied through clenched teeth, "then you have never believed in the Red Dragon to begin with."

"Or maybe everyone's tired of fighting for your wings and getting nothing in return. Just dictatorship and conquering,"

Jabari said across the table.

I was surprised when Prince Jabari spoke up, but his twin brother quickly elbowed him and hissed, "This is not our fight."

"But it will be," I warned. "Africa is the home of staple foods. You made deals long ago with China that they never cashed in on until the famine. They used the land they brought from you, taking all your crops, and mining your fields for minerals and water. Many places were almost laid bare during the hardest time of our lives. You think you're safe?"

Prince Tafeef only tsked me, crossing his arms. "All of Africa is not so foolish as we once were."

"Then where you stand should be clear."

Neither of the twin princes said anything more. But they didn't need to. Jun, in his flowing robes and royal bun, had moved for the door. "You are all fools if you believe one man can save this world."

"We have been foolish for a while," Volkov admitted. "Believing one country could rule the world fairly. If one man cannot do it, then we'll do it together."

My eyes shot to Volkov who had been watching me closely. Nodding at him once again, I said to Jun, "A brotherhood can be formed, a council to change the world. Each of us has one part of what we need to get on our feet again. We can make a difference, and everyone who rallies with me will be the difference the world needs."

27

Chemistry

"It's getting cold," Cloud said as he sat beside me. The deer meat lasted us for a while, but we also had fresh squirrels since my traps worked out. Tomorrow we were planning to get more supplies; we needed more cans, more of everything to make traps. We also needed to get moving. The barn had been a good spot, but it got colder every day, and Lyla wouldn't make it if we stayed in the barn.

"I know," I said. "Do you think we waited too long to move?"

"The cold was going to catch us regardless," Cloud shrugged. "We just need to focus on moving forward now."

"Where do we go?"

"Somewhere to hold out against the winter. We need a house—something we can board up and shut ourselves in."

"What about food and water?"

"We'll still have to hunt, but in this area, there aren't many animals around during the winter. So, we need to find stores, cans—anything—and bring that back. But first, we need to find shelter. Once we've got a place to stay, the rest can be figured out."

"And heat? We won't survive the winter without it."

"We just need a wood burning stove, or a gas stove. But we'll need to keep the windows cracked if we're going to run a gas stove, so we won't burn out all the oxygen in the house."

I thought for a moment. "What about a kerosene heater?"

"That's good too. We'll need kerosine though, and I'm not sure where we can find that."

"Well, maybe we can drive somewhere."

He squinted. "Drive?"

"I saw a car, it's far away, but if we can get to it, we might be able to drive as far as the gasoline will take us."

Slowly, he nodded. "That's a good idea. We find that car, we save ourselves some time. Good thinking, Chem."

"Thanks."

"Alright, I'm going into the barn, don't forget to—"

"Stamp the fire out. I know."

Cloud gave me a soft smile before he said goodnight and limped for the barn.

Looking out at the sky, I wondered if Coco was looking at the same sky, the same stars. Or perhaps she'd gone on and she was looking at the sun while I saw the stars. Maybe she was inside and didn't look out tonight. But I knew she was still alive, and I knew we'd find her. Somehow, we would. It was just that Coco slipped further and further from our minds every day. Survival was the only thing any of us were thinking about now, and with Lyla being so delicate, survival wasn't just about the next meal, it was about the next breath.

For a long time, I hated my father for leaving me with my sisters. We needed time to get to know each other and to grow on each other. It wasn't easy. However, when I looked up at the stars tonight, all I felt was gratitude.

Somehow, all that hard work had prepared me for today. Prepared me to be strong enough to keep caring for my sisters. For my family. They're all I have now, along with Claudius. He's set his own thoughts and desires aside for finding his fiancée just to help us find Coco, but mostly just to survive.

We all want a lot of things; Cloud to reunite with Keoni, and my sisters and I to find Coco, but right now, who knows if we'll ever find Coco and catch up with Keoni? For now, it was better just to focus on one day at a time.

The next morning, we packed up and left the barn. It was warmer than the previous day, which was good for Lyla. She walked on her own for a while, hand in hand with King. The two were starting to mirror each other, though King was the color of honey and Lyla the color of chocolate. But their eyes and nose, cheeks and curly hair both looked so similar. I used to think Acoye and Lyla were a splitting image of one another, but now I think Lyla's a chameleon who looks like whoever she's with.

Brisk air whirled all around us as we walked. It was a far walk, but it didn't take all day. The road was quiet, only the sound of us trudging along made noise. We stayed quiet unless enemies or wrongs were lurking, and we stayed close, no one lagging behind. King and Ly walked together while Claudius took the lead. I gave him vague directions for where the car was, and he said it was enough. He wanted me in back to make sure no one attacked from our six. He stayed in front to set the pace. Since his leg had gotten a little better, Claudius could move a little faster and a little freer. Soon, the hunting would be easier with us going together.

We slowed when we came upon a black car. It was the one I'd spotted a while back. Thankfully, we'd made it there safely, and Lyla walked almost the whole way by herself. After a while, Kingsley began to carry her on her back, but the walk wasn't too long after that.

"This is good," Claudius said as he crawled out the car. He'd gotten inside to see if the car was working. He'd managed to get it running, revving the engine, and letting it run for a few minutes since it'd been sitting for so long.

"How much gas is in it?" I asked.

"A little over half a tank. That'll get us pretty far before we'll need to find more gas or get back on foot."

I was relieved. "Do you think we'll find any gas?"

"Maybe a gas station, maybe a shed or a store. We'll find something. And even if we don't," he shrugged, "we'll find shelter. We're heading in no particular direction, just looking for safety and to see what's beyond this deserted city."

"You think they've invaded the entire country?" Kingsley asked as she leaned against the car. Lyla was sitting on the trunk playing with the buttons on her jacket.

"I'm not sure," Cloud said. He looked off, like he knew the real answer but couldn't bring himself to say it. I couldn't either. America was the home of the brave and the free. Through the years, however, we became less brave, but freer at a cost we didn't know we'd accrued.

Nothing is truly free in this world; everything has a price. We thought we wanted more freedom. Freedom to be and do whatever we wanted, but the cost was not our bravery, it was our unity.

America was so strong because we all stood for something, believed in the same things and upheld the same standards. But what would you expect as the world's melting pot? We stopped being a melting pot and became a murky cesspool. Nothing but swirling defeat because we couldn't unite on anything. Not on religion, or on politics. Not on being *American* but instead on ourselves as individuals—as black, white, Latino, Asian, and African American. We thought we were having free speech, but truly we were just trying to silence each other, each group just wanted to be the loudest. Now, someone else has come in and silenced us… possibly for good.

In the overwhelming silence, there was a fear slowly festering in each of our chests. But that slow festering stopped and turned into sheer panic when a cry ripped loose behind us. I don't know if a *cry* was the right word.

A yell? A scream? It sounded human, like a very sad and broken person yelling for help. Yet something more sinister remained in the voice, heaving out a noise along with the cry that pierced you with fear.

"What… is… that?" Claudius whispered as a man stood no more than thirty feet away. His head hung to the side, his body stiff and fluid at the same time. He—or it—was blinking. Twisting its neck to listen. One step… then another. The creature ambled towards us, and fear had us glued to the pavement.

"Get in the car!" Claudius finally ordered, and the wrong in front of us bellowed out. His sagging flesh jostled as he raced right towards us, covering thirty feet in what seemed like an instant.

Kingsley snatched a crying Lyla from the trunk and raced around the car to get in while Claudius and I moved for the car doors. I got into the driver's seat while King, Lyla, and Claudius all scrambled into the back.

"Come on!" I screamed as King pulled the door shut.

Claudius was banging on my seat, yelling for me to hit the wrong, while Kingsley yelled for me to just *do* something as she clutched Lyla who was still crying. The only thing I could do was hit it, and in the fraction of a second I had to decide, I ripped the car into drive and slammed on the gas.

We lunged forward, ramming right into the screaming wrong. It flipped into the air, and in my rearview mirror, the body crashed back onto the ground with a splat. Hitting the brakes, the whole car rocked, and everyone screamed.

"Why are you stopping!?" Kingsley cried.

I didn't even answer, I just panted as I stared at the steering wheel.

"What was that!?" Claudius screamed in the back of the car.

"Stop yelling!" King screamed back.

"What are you saying!? Did you see that!?"

The two began to argue. I'd forgotten Claudius had never seen a wrong. He was freaking out and it was making Kingsley freak out even more. I didn't care either way, I just needed a second to breathe.

Lyla began to gag in the backseat from fear. Kingsley ripped open the door and hung her over the edge to vomit as Claudius screamed, "Close the door!"

"She's vomiting!"

"Let her vomit on the floor! Close the door before another one of those things—"

It was like the wrong heard him. Suddenly, the wrong we hit screeched, and I sat up. Looking into the rearview mirror, I saw the wrong snap its head up. Blood dripped down its face as it worked its mouth to lick up its own blood. I didn't know a thing about the wrongs, except that they ate people.

"Get her inside!" I hollered as I put the car in reverse.

"What are you doing!?" King yelled as she closed the door. Lyla was leaning into her lap, panting as tears rolled down her cheeks.

With a hand on the passenger seat, I watched over my shoulder as the wrong tried to stand. Despite King's protests, and Claudius' incoherent babbling, I slammed the gas and backed the car up, crashing right into the wrong again. Then I switched gears, and took off, driving forward to crush the body once more before zipping down the road.

Kingsley whimpered in the back of the car as we got further away. Claudius had stopped babbling and was just silently looking out the window. Eventually, Lyla fell asleep in King's lap.

I just drove, trying to focus on anything except what had just happened. We needed to find safety, shelter, food. Now we knew what we were up against.

Even if there were no people to fight, there were still wrongs, and they could not be overlooked. They were a threat to humanity, another threat to fight against for survival. Things just got crazier, and there was no telling what we were driving into as we headed down the road.

This changed things for me—probably for all of us. We were just planning to survive, to make it somehow. Now, we had to plan for something more than just surviving, more than just making it. We had to plan to live.

28

Keoni

Zion and I finally decided to leave the gas station. We figured out how to get into the work computers out front with one of the worker's IDs left behind, and we took as much gasoline as we could in containers. He wanted to take all the containers, but I wouldn't let him. Someone else may come along and need gas or supplies, it was only fair to leave a little behind. Besides, there was more gasoline than we could take anyway. We couldn't weigh down the van we'd found with gasoline or be trapped in there with that strong smell for too long. Too many containers with all the gasoline were dangerous anyways.

The van we found outback had the keys left in the ignition. It wasn't running, it just looked like someone got out in a rush. That wasn't a surprise since most places looked that way now.

We loaded the van with gas cans, anything that looked important for a car from the gas station, along with canned goods, dry food, and water. We even poured out soda bottles and refilled those with water from the bathroom sink. Getting to Washington wouldn't be so hard now, so long as we kept the car in good condition.

I tossed my wrench into the tool bag as I came around the van. One of the tires was flat, so we took one from one of the cars along the road.

"I didn't know you knew how to change a flat." Zion seemed impressed.

I shrugged. "Had to help change the tire on a Humvee before, so I've been changing tires ever since."

He nodded, though I knew he was a little embarrassed that he had no idea how to change a tire. When the tire was flat, Zion said our car plans were ruined unless we could get a car down the street to work. They were lined up near the gas station, like it'd been a busy day for the place when the Rapture happened. The funny thing was that there were no bodies left behind. The deeper into the city we came, the less damage was around. When we first entered this city, there was catastrophe, but over here there was nothing. No blood, nothing indicating that an invasion happened, wrongs came through, or the Rapture. It just looked like everyone ran, but from what?

Cars were still intact; keys were left in some ignitions. The only thing I could think of was that there had been a hostile situation here. Chinese forces could've set up perimeters and took all this captive or took this city as a base of their own and forced everyone else out. I just don't know why there was no blood. Not that I wanted any spilled, but it was odd in a ruined city to not have a single dead body be here when we passed so many of them along the way. For a city's outskirts to have felt the wave of destruction, but nothing further.

Shrugging back to reality, I grabbed duct tape from the little stool that held everything I needed to change the tire. The duct tape was for anything that may have been loose, like a bumper. However, the van was perfectly fine, just a flat tire, but I was keeping the tape anyway.

"We'll take the car jack, and wheel chocks. Along with the lug wrench, of course. And then—"

"What's a wheel chock or a lug wrench?"

I paused, suppressing a chuckle. "Those are wheel chocks." I pointed to the blocks beneath the tires. "They help keep the car sturdy. And that," I pointed to a long metal tool, "that's the lug wrench. It loosens and tightens the bolts."

Zion nodded. "Got it."

"Do you... never mind," I said before snickering.

"Yeah, it's so funny that I don't know how to change a tire." He crossed his arms as he leaned against the van.

"Come on, Z, I'm just kidding." I slapped his arm. "There are tons of things you know that I don't, and things I know that you don't."

"Yeah, but it doesn't matter as much for you as it does for me."

I raised a brow. "Why not?"

"Because," his shoulders bunched as he frowned at the ground, "you're not a man."

I rolled my eyes and grabbed the tool bag. "You think it's sexy that I've got one eye and can change a tire?"

He leaned forward, his anger sinking into contagious

laughter. He was trying not to laugh too hard, but I wasn't offended. Ollie was the only man alive who'd want to marry someone like me. Someone who was a soldier more than a woman and let her one eye be a badge of honor. I always thought men liked soft women, like Abbey. She was so beautiful, kind and sweet. She survived out here because she had to, but compared to me, Abbey and I were opposites.

"I'm used to your patch." Zion shrugged after laughing so hard. "I don't even notice it anymore."

"Yeah well, most men do. They notice my patch, and then they notice that their fragile masculinity hangs in question around me whenever I lift something heavier than them. Or change a tire when they can't." I waved a hand. "Or whatever."

"I don't think you realize how uncool it is that I had no idea what we were doing when we got that extra tire off the van down the street instead of using the spare under this one. I didn't know spare tires were just for getting you back home, they're not really for driving long distances."

"I don't think that's a man problem, I think that's all you, Z," I said as I poked his chest. He grunted, his firm frame now beneath my hand as I rested it on him.

Zion and I had gotten closer. We were like partners now. He hasn't opened up much about leaving Abbey and his daughter behind, and I can't help but feel like it's my fault. I've wanted to ask about it, but he was really torn up about it when we first got to the gas station. He's mellowed out, but when I mentioned Flower last night, that she looked just like him, the conversation ended abruptly, and we parted ways for bed. The topic is still too sensitive, but he's always better by the morning.

"Key, you alright?" he asked into my thoughts.

"Sorry…" I hadn't realized I was just standing there, a hand to his chest as I wondered about what condition he was really in.

"Keoni," he leaned down as he placed his hands on my arms, "is something going on?"

That wasn't fair. Before I realized that Zion was attractive, I realized he had a heart. He had emotions and voiced what made him upset. He apologized, talked to me, and asked me how he made me upset, how he could make it better.

Zion was a ball of concern, a guy you read about in stories. Considerate and gentle, yet he was tough and was not a bad soldier at all. Strong—spiritually, physically, and mentally. And his touch, it was always so warm and gentle, like if he could wrap his affection up and use it as a blanket for you, he would.

I did eventually notice that Zion was attractive, *very* attractive. He was muscular and strong, tan with beautiful eyes that held all of his emotion. They looked like burning flames that would consume you if you let them. Creamy skin that gripped every one of his muscles.

I'd caught him changing his shirt two days ago. I'd say that Zion and I were getting along well. He wasn't thin, he wasn't bony, he was still taut with muscle, all over, especially since we were still doing our pushups, planks, and now sit-ups. His back, his abdomen, his arms; it was a sight for tired, deprived, sore eyes.

300

However, Claudius still lingered in the back of my mind. Every day I missed him a little less, but I don't think I could ever truly forget him. I wasn't sure if I was missing Ollie less because Zion was always with me now, or because the distance had forced me to harden my heart again.

Jensen had managed to crack the shell off it when Ollie and I first separated. But now, I felt like my heart wanted to create another shell, but there's this haunting desire to find Ollie and at least know he's okay. And that's buried beneath this tugging in my chest every time Zion laughs or comforts me. Every time he tries to quote his favorite Scriptures correctly. He's this sponge, soaking up all the darkness that should be consuming me. And when he smiles, it's breathtaking... and I hate it. I hate him.

This is not the time for love or affection. The guy just left his daughter and future wife behind for his country. I should marry the guy. He's as dedicated as I've ever been, but it isn't right. His heart is still so set on his past, even though he keeps running for the future. My own feelings are just shadows dancing on the walls because a little light flickered on.

Lightbulbs die out, fires burn out, the sun sets. I won't feel this way for him forever. Eventually the light will flicker out and I'll be okay. The only light that ever stays on is Christ, and I don't think Jesus would be proud of me if I tried to move in on this guy right now. Besides, Zion and I have way too many other things to worry about, and Claudius is still out there. I still want to find him, and I know that when I do, he'll sweep me off my feet and make me forget everything and everyone like he always has.

"We should go." I nodded, raising my eye to Zion's.

Zion had emotional orbs that convicted you or rooted for you. The way they could downturn the instant he was sad or brighten the moment he laughed. Looking into them was a swirling defeat, but you didn't mind losing to him.

"You sure?" he asked. "We can stay a little while longer if you're not ready."

"I am."

He nodded, rubbing my arms like I was cold. "Okay. I'll get the van started."

Stepping away, I took a final breath, like a real one. Claudius had been the only person to make breathing difficult for me. Jensen had been the only one to make being emotional something I welcomed. Now, Zion did both. He made it hard to breathe, and he made me feel like I could be vulnerable with him. It's almost like Zion *wanted* me to be vulnerable, he wanted to protect me the way Ollie did, and support me the way Jensen always did. Zion was seemingly the perfect combination between Ollie and Jensen.

As we drove along, we discussed our winter plans, and possibly hunkering down if we couldn't make it to Washington before it got any colder. We should make it in time with our van, but the roads typically have cars along them. More than likely, there are multiple highways crowded with cars left over from people running mad. There was no way to tell unless we kept driving. If the roads were blocked, we'd get out and walk, which we prepared for.

302

Going back on foot would require us to leave most of the supplies. We wouldn't need gasoline anymore since we wouldn't have a car. But in the case that we found another and clear roads, we planned on carrying one canister of gasoline and our backpacks. We split our supplies evenly, so if we got separated or attacked and lost a bag, we wouldn't be out of food or water.

Bandages, medical supplies, that was all stuffed into our backpacks. We were careful not to overpack, so that nothing was too heavy and there was enough room to put anything else in there along the way. But the winter was a threat neither of us wanted to face. If we couldn't get to Washington soon, we'd end up finding a building or a house to hold out in.

"Key? You alright?" Zion asked drowsily. We'd swapped five hours back and he'd fallen asleep in the passenger seat beside me.

"Yeah, I'm good," I replied.

"You've been driving for a while."

"I'm actually a little surprised we haven't run into any blocked roads."

"Me too," he said through a heavy exhale.

I glanced over at him as he adjusted beside me, raking a hand through his hair.

"What were you dreaming about?"

Silence.

"I was dreaming about Flower. She was lying in a pond, perfectly fine. And then all this water started rushing in, and she began to drown. Abbey couldn't get to her, and I just wasn't there… no one could save her."

"Zion, that nightmare—"

"Is my own fear."

There wasn't much else to be said, at least, not from me. If Zion wanted to talk, I'd listen, but I wouldn't force him.

"Sometimes," he started after about twenty minutes of silence, "I wonder if I made the right decision. Abbey rejected me just one time and I leapt at the chance to leave. I thought… I thought I loved her; you know? But then, I got away from her, and I started loving this. I was worth something."

"I think I can understand you. Your worth, your *value*, was determined by how useful you were, how much you gave to the rest of the lives that yours is intertwined with." Tightening my grip on the steering wheel, I watched the night fade into day. "I was the same way. The military determined my value. Set me at a pretty high price which made me feel like I was worth something more than the ghetto I'd grown up in and left behind. And now, it feels like the only people who can see my value are my comrades."

He hesitated before he whispered, "Yeah."

"Just because you're away from her doesn't mean she didn't mean anything or that you didn't love her."

"That's the thing, Key…"

I glanced over, to find him leaning against the window, watching the trees pass by. "I don't think I ever loved Abbey. She came stumbling back into my life, and I felt obligated to her and was too afraid to tell my parents she was pregnant. We bonded, but it felt real. It felt like love."

"Maybe it was," I suggested. "Just because you walked away today, doesn't mean you'll have the strength to walk tomorrow if you're given another chance."

"Did you walk away?"

I took a short breath. "I walked away from Ollie after he gave me a promotion a while back. We parted ways in the hopes of moving on. And after a year, when we were reunited, we were inseparable."

"Funny. Abbey and I have a similar story. We separated, and when we came back together again, I couldn't unglue myself from her."

I snorted. "Really?"

"Yeah."

"We're way too similar."

He chuckled. "I agree."

"So that means you did at least like her if you couldn't unglue."

"I liked her." He nodded then sighed. "I just... I can't figure it out. Why walk away so easily?"

This conversation was a painful one for me and for Zion, obviously. But for Zion's sake, I pushed my feelings to the back of my heart and said, "Was it really that easy? You left in the middle of the night so you wouldn't have to face her."

He sighed, burying his face in his palms.

"All I'm saying is that maybe it wasn't as easy as—"

A sitting tank raged off the side of the road suddenly, ramming into the van and sending us spiraling. We spun across the highway, and I tried to hold control of the steering wheel, but it was no use. Spinning out of control was the least of our worries. We tipped over the edge of the highway, rolling down a path until our van crashed into a tree.

I panted heavily, trying to get my bearings. There was gasoline everywhere, and I wasn't sure if we'd explode in the next five seconds if I didn't move.

"Zion! Zion!" I screamed as he lay slumped against the window. The tank had hit us on his side, leaving him pressed between the airbag and his seat. I grunted as I worked my seat buckle loose. It clicked off, freeing me to fall against my own airbag.

"Okay, Zion, work with me," I whispered as I cut off his seatbelt. He was limp as he moved a little further into the airbag.

I grabbed my door handle, grunting as I ignored the pain rioting through my entire body. My head ached, my chest heaved, and there was definitely something wrong with one of my legs. But we needed to get to safety before whoever rammed us *caught* us.

Cranking open the door, I realized it was too late... we'd been found. In fact, I think we were being watched. The moment my door opened, bullets sprayed it down and I yanked it shut.

"God!" I screamed. "Help us!"

When the firing ended, I was laying over Zion, trying to protect him. My mind was racing now but I forced the panic mode in my head to shut off. I couldn't freak out, not now. I'd been through too much to get crazy, besides, I was a soldier, and this was just combat.

Leaning over, I pulled on Zion's door handle, it creaked, alerting everyone and bringing more bullet spray but, as I thought, they were only coming from the highway on my side of the car, not the forested area nearby.

Shoving his door open, I pushed Zion's body out and crawled over the center to get out through his door. I moved for the back door, yanking on it until it freed, riding its rack until the door opened all the way. Supplies fell out at us. Gasoline, water bottles and canned goods we didn't get into our bags. I dug through the supplies as pain continued to rile within me, and shots went off every few minutes until I grabbed one of our bags. Slipping it over my shoulders, I put my hands beneath Zion and dragged him deeper into the forest.

I stopped at the first big tree I could find, panting as I fell to the ground. No one had followed me, but that didn't mean I was safe. So I made quick work of getting Zion's shirt up. I felt along his frame, feeling for anything broken or weird.

"One of his ribs," I whispered as I felt along, "it's broken I think." There were scratches along his frame, and blood running down his head where he'd hit it against the window.

"Come on, Z," I whispered as I ripped open the backpack. I grabbed that duct tape I'd decided to keep and a wad of gauze. Folding the gauze, I pressed it to his head as I bit and ripped the duct tape to hold it down. I was working quickly, sweat pouring all over me when the sound of rustling grass echoed through the frightful silence.

I didn't stop to analyze it. Instead, I kept working on Zion and called out, "You can take me, just let me finish this."

"I have to say, I'm surprised to see you again, Lieutenant Colonel Banks."

My hands stopped. I was bandaging Zion's arm when that voice spoke. Slowly, I turned to find that I was surrounded by Chinese soldiers in US Army uniforms with one man standing in the middle of them.

"Admiral Zhao," I whispered.

The corner of his mouth ticked up the slightest bit, and he shrugged. "You've made it pretty far from Springville. You going somewhere?"

I wanted to explode, to scream and attack him for doing this to Ollie and me. To Zion, Abbey, and little Flower. To all of America. Zhao was responsible, but I would not get my revenge today, probably never, knowing that I was trading my freedom for Zion's.

We were taught as soldiers to preserve the life of the one who could carry on the legacy. Zion could do it, I believed in him, and I wouldn't let my comrade get taken in my place. He'd see this through, make it to Washington and be a hero without me. Then maybe he'll find Abbey, and things will be alright for them.

"Please," I whispered as I turned away. Everyone moved at once, shoving their guns at me, but I ignored them. I grabbed another piece of gauze, rolling it to press against the wound on Zion's arm. "Let me patch him up, then I'll go with you, admiral."

"Very well," he replied over my shoulder. "For old times' sake, I will give you a minute to treat him. Return her to the tank when she's finished," he said to his men as he left.

I could hear the group retreating. From the looks of it, the admiral had no use for a private or someone he didn't recognize. Zion was in civilian clothing, so he probably didn't know he was a soldier. But Zhao probably figured Zion was as good as dead anyway. No point in bringing back a body bag.

I wouldn't believe it though. Zion wasn't dead. He was just passed out... he had to be. His chest was rising and falling slowly, like at any moment it would stop. Until that moment came, I would do everything I could to extend his life.

"Hurry up," the angsty voice hissed behind me. He was the only soldier who'd stayed behind to guard me, a true demonstration of just how messed up this situation was. Zhao didn't feel the need to leave a bunch of soldiers to watch me because he was certain there was no chance of me getting away.

He's young... I realized, glancing at the soldier.

"Zion," I whispered after using all the gauze I could to treat his wounds. I leaned over him, pressing my forehead to his. "Wake up, okay? Go to Washington and then find Abbey like we planned."

"Washington?" the voice behind me snickered. "If this guy comes to Washington, he's going to be a prisoner, just like you."

I kept my forehead pressed to Zion's before leaning down and kissing him. His lips were soft, like he'd been wearing lip balm all this time. Plump and warm, his lips were pressed against mine until I pulled away.

"You're taking me to Washington?" I asked. "To be a prisoner at the capital of my own country?"

He bellowed out a wicked laugh. "Yes! I am taking you to be a prisoner at your country's headquarters. You'll never see the light of day."

"So, America's been conquered?" I asked as I looked Zion over, dark lashes covered his closed eyes. He looked peaceful as he lay there. I wished once more to see his fiery eyes, to see his smile. I wished for a chance for things to be different, but they weren't.

"Can't say," the soldier replied. "But that shouldn't concern you. You're about to be dressed up and shipped out to infiltrate Europe. We're taking the whole world, while you idiots fight for your measly country."

China was about to start another fire. They wanted to do another invasion, take over Europe, but they were too weak... That was why the cities were being emptied and no one had been harmed. *They need us alive...*

"You talk a lot," I said as I finally looked over my shoulder.

The thin man grunted, a smile cracking his face. "What can a prisoner and a dead man do?"

"I'm not a prisoner yet," I said as I stood. I glanced around, we were totally alone. Zhao would never let me go, there was probably another set of Chinese soldiers in the opposite direction if I tried to run. However, there was a reason Zhao left this young kid with me. He didn't want to take me in... or he would've already. He would prefer me dead. The

310

plan was to have a scuffle with this kid, either he kills me, or I try to run and get gunned down by soldiers hidden deeper in the forest.

Two dead Americans left to rot, that's what he wanted.

He'd get neither.

Lifting my fists, I took a fighting stance. All I had on me was my hunting knife. I could pull it quickly, but I'd need to dodge his first few shots before I could get close.

"Are you really trying this?" the young Chinese soldier raised his gun with a smirk.

"You thought I'd just walk with you? No fight?"

"I was hoping for a fight."

"Then be fair." I glanced down at his gun. "Fight me like a man."

He laughed. "You're afraid to die, so you want me to lower my weapon. Not happening."

I shrugged. "I'll just take it from you then. And when I do, I'm going to blow a hole in your leg."

"My leg?" He raised a brow.

"You're going to lead this boy back to your hideout after your leg heals. I don't want him trying to survive the winter alone. Your injured leg will force him inside."

"What are you talking—"

I ripped my knife from my waist and threw it. He hollered and fired. I dropped to the ground, moving swiftly back to my feet, and rushing him. We fell to the ground, shots firing off beside my ears. I ignored the ringing as I threw the hardest punch I could at him.

311

His head snapped left and right, before I jammed a fist into his chest. He heaved, eyes bulging, and I got hold of his wrist, ripping the gun free. In one fluid motion, I broke loose from our tussle and grabbed the gun. Moving around in the dirt, I hooked one arm around his neck. He squealed, patting my arm and flailing. I worked my hand into his mouth as I fired the gun, I shot him in the leg as I promised. He cringed, biting down on my hand. I screamed and he held on, releasing his own cries into my hand. I needed his cries muffled, so none of his soldiers would come looking for him.

He was whining now as tears raced down his cheeks.

"Get him to your hideout," I said in his ear.

Panting, I tossed the gun down, and pried my hand from his mouth. It was bleeding, but I had no time to focus on that. I found my knife nearby and pulled the strap on part of the backpack and bit it to cut it since I could only use one hand. Sloppily, I wrapped the strap around one of the soldier's hands.

"What are you doing?" he yelled.

"Making sure you don't get the gun." I shoved my knife through the strap and into the ground as a makeshift stake.

I looked back at Zion—one last look before turning away and limping to the Chinese forces.

Zhao was waiting outside the tank. Just him, and when he saw me, he grinned.

"You never cease to amaze me. You're as good as they always said."

"Is that why you're sending me to Europe?"

"You? No." He shook his head. "You're too valuable.

312

Besides, you'd somehow allude my men and make it back to America and kill me if I gave you that much freedom." He laughed. "You're going to be my prisoner and help me get these plans together for our European invasion."

"I'll *never* help you," I seethed.

Zhao pressed his thin lips together. "I would kill you, but you're so patriotic, you'd be happy. So, I've got a lineup of people who'll die every time you refuse one of my orders. Including women and children. The kids are hungry mouths to feed. We don't need them anyway. But the women—" he smiled wickedly, "they stand no chance. My men are hungry for a little loving."

Making only one fist, I fought the burning tears as I raised my chin and said nothing, silently accepting my defeat.

"Good girl," Zhao teased as he moved from the tank. "Now let's go."

29

Abigail

Diaz didn't speak to anyone for days. He came out of the room he was given, retrieved food, and went back. He'd come all this way to escort me and ended up getting stuck with me and this underground group. It would've been fine if Evelyn didn't have his own group he'd been traveling with. Now his group had moved on, and he was still here. I felt responsible, but I wasn't sure how to approach him. I tried to stay away, to give him space, but I wanted to at least apologize for getting him stuck here.

He could leave, I told myself. But Diaz had nowhere else to go, and we all knew the coast was dangerous. Even *we* couldn't leave. We'd be here another three to six months because of winter preventing us from traveling by boat, and the communication between underground shelters went radio silent in the winter.

A ship wouldn't be here to get us until early spring, probably when the waters finally warmed. But there was also the threat of Chinese forces and everyone else to watch out for, especially getting a boat back to Israel where there's an invasion happening too. For now, all we could do was stay inside and try not to kill each other. That began with apologizing to Evelyn.

"I don't know why you're so stressed about it," Eve said as he sat on my bed. There were only twenty of us down here in the underground fallout shelter, and we all got our own rooms since the shelter was big enough for fifty people. Some of the folks who were here came wandering inside, others were doom's day preppers and came to this specific location, like Whisper. She and her Israeli buddies set up this system long ago for whenever the world fell apart. They knew the final days were coming and wanted anyone who didn't make the Rapture to be prepared for the Tribulation.

"Because," I said as I laid Flower in the crib beside my bed, "we have to live with this guy. And he did all that work to get me here."

Everette rolled his eyes, snatching a pillow from the opposite end of my bed and stuffing it behind his head.

"What are you doing? You have to watch Flower."

"She's already asleep."

I rolled my eyes. "I'm just going to get Coco."

"Yeah, get Coco. Maybe instead of babysitting, we can do some baby making."

"Eve!" I snapped.

He snorted, tucking his hands behind his head on the pillow. Eve was cute, but he was only eighteen. Coco, who's sixteen or seventeen, was only suitable for Eve in *age*. She's lightyears ahead in maturity.

"I'm *not* calling her in here," I said, setting my fists on my hips, feeling very much like a mother. Eve did that to me sometimes, even though I was only three years older than him. He was smack in the middle of Coco and me, and sometimes he liked to blur the wobbly line we'd drawn around our friendship. Sometimes he was my little brother. Sometimes he was this flirty, uncontrollable kid who looked more and more like a man each day.

He smirked at me now, hands behind his head, shadows casting over his face, so the line of his jaw caught in the light. "Why?" He bunched his shoulders. "I'm just kidding. We're not going to do any baby making. Besides, Coco isn't like that." His smile faded. He wasn't angry, just thinking, I guess. He and Coco had spent a lot of time together. They'd been getting close.

She even convinced him to take communion with the group the other day. Eve is changing and I think it's because of Coco. I was hoping to do something amazing like that with Evelyn. He was cold, but I think that after some time, maybe he'll warm up to us the way Eve's warming up to our faith. In the long run, hopefully Evelyn will warm up to the faith too if he doesn't already believe. It's hard to know since he doesn't talk much.

"Well," I started after a pause, "maybe on my way back, I'll grab her so we can all hang out."

He shrugged.

"Thanks for watching Flower." I leaned over him and kissed his forehead. He kept his eyes closed as he nodded.

Outside the room, I pulled the door shut quietly so Flower (and Eve) wouldn't be disturbed. The fallout shelter was surprisingly spacious, it was just that the white walls and grey carpeting everywhere threatened to drive me mad. No splash of color anywhere, not even in the kitchen. White floors and stainless-steel appliances to provide us with the grey we lacked on the floor.

The bedrooms had wooden frames, and everyone was issued a set of white sheets and a comforter, and grey sheets and a comforter. If the people who built this weren't Christian, I'd swear they were building internment camps to drive us all crazy. Even the clothes... grey and white issued shirts, pants, shorts, underwear!

At least the food had color to it, and there was running water, good heating, and everything was clean. The shelter ran on its own power generated from the workout room and solar panels on the building. There are also two battery powered generators used on and off to preserve them.

Heading down the hall, I nodded to Jacinda. She was an older woman who was part of the doom's day preppers and was the best at making squash soup. I was heading to the kitchen to find a penance gift for Diaz when I bumped right into him. He was standing in the kitchen opening a water bottle.

"Hi," I said quickly.

He nodded, cracking open his bottle.

"Are you busy right now?"

Diaz didn't respond. He closed his bottle before taking a sip, and brushed by me to head to his room, the only place he ever goes. So I followed him. Walking quickly behind him until we reached his room. He didn't bother looking back. He opened the door and went inside. I slipped a foot in the door as he went to close it, but for whatever reason he was *slamming* it shut instead of just gently closing it, and he slammed it on my foot.

I yelped, trying to get my foot out the door. Evelyn whirled around, his face riddled with anger. "What is your problem!?" he shouted so loud the curls in my hair flew back.

"I was just trying to talk!" I yelled back, cradling my foot.

"Everything alright?" Whisper asked, she'd stepped into the hall from the living room.

"Yeah," Evelyn said flatly.

Whisper glanced over at me, and I nodded, though I was in a lot of pain. When she left us, Evelyn sighed and squatted in front of me.

"Let me see it." He flicked his hand, asking for my foot.

"No," I pouted.

"Fine." He stood, and I lunged for his arm.

"Wait a second!"

Grunting, he snapped, "Do you want me to look at it or not?"

"Yes."

Diaz hiked his sweats up and got down in front of me again to lift my foot. Supporting my calf, he looked over it in silence. He had long lashes, like Zion's, and that same honey wheat skin tone as him. His brown hair had gold streaks in it, and his handsome face told that he was mature, yet young.

I caught another glimpse of his tattoos. Dark lines swirled around each finger as if someone had begun a custom glove around each hand. The winding black markings were interesting. I felt like there was something to them, something much darker. His eyes lifted suddenly, and I almost gasped as I looked away.

"I think it'll bruise, but you'll be fine otherwise. Maybe a little swelling."

"Why were you closing the door so hard?"

"I was slamming it."

"Why?"

"Because you were annoying me."

Holding in a scoff, I settled for a sigh. I wanted to be angry and snap at him, but then I'd waste another day and another moment to apologize.

"I'm sorry."

"For what?" His brows came together on his forehead, something like a frown.

"This whole thing is my fault. You were supposed to be gone, back with your group, but you're stuck here."

He sighed, finally lowering my leg. "It's my own fault. I had a feeling something like this would happen. I'd get stuck or couldn't return in enough time. I just thought I could beat that feeling."

"If I hadn't left my own daughter, you wouldn't have needed to help me get here."

"Well, I'm here now." He stood, extending a hand to me. I took it, and he helped me stand up. "Get some ice on your foot."

"You're not going to help me to my room?"

His ever stoic and bored expression shifted for a second, his brow raised. Now he looked more intimidating than before.

"You don't have to," I tried to joke. "I was just teasing."

Evelyn rolled his eyes, and grabbed me, lifting me right off my feet. I gasped as I clung to him in confusion.

"It's faster this way, rather than holding you up to hobble." That was his explanation before carrying me through the shelter to my bedroom like an injured bride. He didn't knock, not that he needed to. He opened the door, and Eve sat up out the bed.

"What is this?"

"Get out the way, kid," Evelyn said. Mercifully, Eve moved, because if he didn't, I was certain Evelyn was going to put me down right on top of him.

As he sat me in the bed, I unclasped my hands from around his neck. "Thank you," I said softly.

Once more, his expression was a little different. His eyes lifted with a little brightness in them as he nodded. He turned to Eve on his way out and said, "Get some ice for her foot."

And just like that, Evelyn Diaz was gone again. He returned to being the mysterious man he'd been since I met

320

him. Maybe there was a way into his mysteriousness. Maybe in these next few months, Evelyn will let me in.

30

Zion

My lips felt warm and tingly for a second. I didn't want the feeling to end. Soft and lush, like I was kissing someone… or maybe someone was kissing me.

My eyes shot open, and I sat up, looking around. The sun was out, and there was a cool wind blowing through the leaves. Trees reached high, and thick bushes stretched wide across the grassy earth. And I was aching … a lot. I didn't notice it when I first sat up, but now my ribs screamed at me to give them a break.

"Where…" I grabbed my head as it throbbed. Pain ripped through my mind as I squinted at the world around me. A bag lay beside me, trees were all around me. This wasn't what I remembered.

"I was in the car with Keoni." I stopped. "Keoni?"

"She's not here."

There was a guy lying down in the grass a little further away. A gun lay between us, and his hand was staked to the ground with… Keoni's hunting knife.

"That knife," I pointed, "where'd you get it?"

"That wretched woman!" he yelled, startling me. "She left me here with you! And they never even came for me. They didn't try to see if I was alive or dead. They left me…" The man began to whimper but I didn't pay his cries or sorrow any attention.

"Where is she? Where's Keoni?" I asked.

"If she's the woman you were traveling with then she's long gone. They took her and left me for dead!"

"They who?"

His tear-filled eyes slid to mine. "The Red Dragon."

It was like the words recalled all the memories. Keoni and I were driving. We'd covered a lot of ground and were making good progress to Washington when something crashed into us. That was the last thing I remembered. Then, in the darkness, there was warmth, but only on my lips. My hand went to them, feeling the place where someone had kissed me.

"This is all your fault!" the man hissed at me. "She wanted to save you and I got left behind for it."

"My fault?" I dropped my hand from my lips and fought to get to my feet. "This is *my* fault." I gasped, dropping back to one knee as the pain in my abdomen winded me. Clutching my side, I heaved for a second, trying to catch my breath. Digging my hands into the grass, I fought off the tears. They weren't for my physical pain, just my broken heart.

Abbey had given everything for us to be together, even before she was pregnant. She would come late at night, between classes. Abbey was a woman worth loving. But I gave her up, broke her heart and hoped she'd just be okay with it. I knew leaving her behind with my parents was wrong, but I was too selfish. I wanted to be clapped for and hailed a hero by running down to the armory that day.

I killed my best friend and forced Abbey and my daughter—my own flesh and blood—to survive the darkness that prowled. And when we were reunited, I was still selfish. Still only focused on being a hero. Why did that mean so much to me?

It feels like the only people who can see my value are my comrades.

Keoni said that to me when we were in the car. She explained that she too found her worth in the military, and everyone around her saw it too. That's why we wanted to be heroes; because our comrades knew we were, but no one else did.

Becoming a hero meant everyone would acknowledge you. But that was the sad part... Abbey did acknowledge me. My father, my mother, the congregation, everyone saw me and acknowledged me. But it wasn't enough.

Every day I required more from Abbey than the day before, and even when she gave it, it was nothing compared to the military. They forced you to believe in your worth, that you were worth the cost of the lives of others. I wanted everyone to recognize that... but for what? To stand here and be without a single soul? To stand in the forest, aching in pain and trapped with an enemy?

After losing my fiancée because of my own stupidity, my

daughter too, and now… Keoni was gone.

A fire burned in my chest because this was all my fault. I walked away from God, walked away from my parents, walked away from Abbey, but every single one of them accepted me back. They took me in again. Abbey loved me all over again, even after leaving her with my parents. And my parents never stopped loving me. Even though I did all kinds of wrong behind their back. The day I left Abigail with my mother, she nodded at me. Smiling and understanding without even a hint of disappointment or judgement. Then… there was God.

True to His Word, to never leave us nor forsake us. True to His being as a father. God welcomed me back to Him with the same open arms I told Keoni about. I told her that He was waiting for her because I had experienced the same love. I had experienced the welcoming hug of a father when his lost son returned. There was no better feeling… but now I'd lost everything. All I had to hold onto was a bit of faith hanging on a frayed string.

Hiccupping, I tried not to cry, but I failed. Rocking over in agony, I wept loudly on the ground, making mud of my broken tears. I wanted help. I wanted Abbey. I wanted Flower and my parents. I wanted God. And I wanted Keoni. I wanted her so badly. She was my last thread of hope, the last bit of sanity to keep me from breaking. Now she was gone because of me too.

"God! Why!? Why!?"

"He can't hear you!" the Chinese soldier snapped.

I screamed out in frustration, wrestling with myself to my

feet and in that fit of rage, I ignored the blaring pain all over. I snatched up the gun and shoved it into that soldier's face. He was screaming now, begging for mercy.

"You did this to us! You took everything from me, from Private Gabby! You made me walk away from my daughter and my fiancée! You took my parents, and you took Keoni!" I screamed into his face, spittle speckling his porcelain skin.

"Please!" He tried to shrink away, but I shoved the gun harder into his forehead. "I'm sorry!"

"You will be!" I yelled at him. "You will be…" I glared at him. "I have to save her. I have to do something right." Pulling the gun from his head, I backed up and sat down in the grass again, sniffling and wiping at my tears. "What's your name?" I finally asked.

"Why do you care?"

"Because we're about to go on a long journey together."

"I'm not going anywhere."

I looked up, not even bothered by his unruliness. "I'm Zion Reinhardt."

"I don't care who you are."

Nodding, I reached for the backpack and searched through it. There were supplies, but I knew there was more in the van. If I could get back there, I could figure out a way to get the rest of the supplies, or at least get more and head out to find Keoni. I walked away from Abigail, and I didn't know how or if I should go back.

Maybe once I save Keoni, I can go back and make things right… but maybe I won't. Maybe I *shouldn't.* I couldn't think about my regret right now. All I could focus on for now was saving Keoni. She didn't deserve this, and I wouldn't let someone else down. I wouldn't walk away again. Not this time.

As I rummaged through the bag, the man asked, "What are you doing?"

"Checking for supplies. Since you aren't going, you won't need anything." Tiredly, I pulled my backpack on with a grunt. Stuffing the gun into my waistband, I pulled the knife out of his hand which made him scream.

"Wait! You can't leave me here!"

"You don't want to go. And you'll slow me down."

"You don't know where you're even going!?" he called, sitting cross-legged in the grass and cradling his bleeding hand.

I turned back to him. Sweat had slicked his hair, and his moon shaped eyes looked full as they widened. "Why would I trust you, anyway? You'd never take me to the right—"

"Washington. That's where they're taking her. I swear, man. They're taking her to Washington to join the forces to fight the Europeans."

"What?"

"China wants the whole world, and we won't stop until we have it."

"Why Washington though? Why take her there?"

"They've got some kind of way to get people onto aircrafts over there. It's a safe landing place since people think it's Americans sending refugees and important people out of the country."

I ran a hand over my hair. "We've got to move now."

"Wait, your friend, Keoni. She said that she didn't want you searching for her in the winter. She wanted you to wait."

"I can't wait if she's going to be shipped out!"

"There's a chance she won't be."

I raised a brow. "Why now?"

"Because…" he struggled to sit up as he grasped at his leg. "Zhao knew her. I've seen him save his old comrades before. She may just get locked away."

Flopping back down into the dirt, I palmed the back of my neck. "I don't know what to do. What if I go and she's not there? What if I miss her?"

The Chinese soldier started talking again, pleading his case to go back to Washington to give the Chinese forces a piece of his mind, like they'd care. If they left him to die, they'd kill him just for not dying when they first left him. I wasn't interested in him or his case since I could get to Washington myself. Winter was coming, and the cold would be bitter. With my own injuries, I'll be slower than normal. There was no way on foot I'd make it to Washington with all the stopping I'd need before the first frost.

God, I know I've messed up. But I need You right now. Please spare Keoni for me. Keep her in Washington until I get there, no matter how long it takes. In Jesus' name, amen.

Hanging my head, and keeping my eyes closed, I listened. I hadn't exactly been out of tune with God, but I hadn't been listening for Him the way I should've either. Now was my chance, and I wouldn't give it up. I had to make a change, had to make things right. So I was starting right at that moment. I

328

wouldn't force the Spirit or let myself be overwhelmed with anxiety. Calmly, I sat and waited.

I focused on God and on everything He'd brought me through. The end of the world, the throngs of wrongs, the overwhelming Chinese forces, losing my fiancée and then finding her again. Then losing her again…

And my daughter. An innocent little girl who had no idea the world wasn't always this messed up. The people travelling with Abigail, hoping she would be safe even without me. Wondering if my parents were in heaven with God now.

Then my mind drifted to Keoni. The woman who'd given her freedom so that I could live. I had to make it to her. I had to save her. But I couldn't do that without God. I wouldn't be able to do *anything* without God. But instead of focusing on my impossible chances, I focused on the One who could make a way out of no way. The silence was almost overwhelming, but I waited anyway.

And then He spoke.

Zion, your prayers have reached Me.

Continue the series…

Ordained Catastrophe Book III: The One Who is Man and Beast
Coming August 2023

More books by A. Bean & TRC Publishing!

Christian Fantasy
Cross Academy series
The End of the World series
The Scribe

Christian Post-Apocalyptic Fiction
The Barren Fields

Christian Science Fiction

I AM MAN series

Christian Romance

The Living Water

Withered Rose Trilogy

Fractured Diamond

The Woof Pack Trilogy

Singlehood

Christian Children's Fiction

Too Young

ACKNOWLEDGEMENTS

Jesus is the Christ, Son of the Living God.

I am thankful to God for giving me the idea for this novel.
Thank you, the reader, who made it this far. You are awesome.
I hope you take the time to read some of my other work and
finish this series. It's been quite a journey already, hasn't it?
Let's go on another.

Follow me on Amazon to get updates on new releases, pre-
orders, and reduced prices on my books. Also, follow TRC on
TikTok! We love meeting readers and discussing new ideas. See
you there!

The Rebel Christian Publishing

We are an independent Christian publishing company focused on fantasy, science fiction, and romantic reads. Visit therebelchristian.com to check out our books or click the titles below!

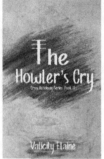

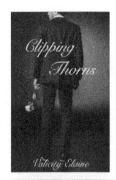

Clipping Thorns

Valicity Elaine

Valicity Elaine

Fractured Diamond

Valicity Elaine

PATCHES

Valicity Elaine

The I Word

Valicity Elaine

Made in the USA
Coppell, TX
05 June 2024

33132033R00204